HEARTLESS

A.S. TROTMAN

COPYRIGHT

Copyright © 2014 by A.S.TROTMAN

All rights reserved. No part of this publication may be reproduced, distributed, or transmitted in any form or by any means, including photocopying, recording, or other electronic or mechanical methods, without the prior written permission of the publisher, except in the case of brief quotations embodied in critical reviews and certain other non-commercial uses permitted by copyright law.

ISBN-10:**0692525513**
ISBN-13:**978-0692525517**

See all of our books at:
www.Moveoutpublishing.com

CONTENTS

CHAPTER ONE 1
Mother Knows Best

CHAPTER TWO 18
Knee Deep In The Game

CHAPTER THREE 24
The Beginning

CHAPTER FOUR 39
Clock Work

CHAPTER FIVE 55
The Meeting

CHAPTER SIX 78
Back To Business

CHAPTER SEVEN 98
Oh Boy

CHAPTER EIGHT 120
Is That Cho Chick

CHAPTER NINE 143
No Nuts No Glory

CHAPTER TEN 162
It All Falls Down

CHAPTER ELEVEN 195
The Truth

CHAPTER TWELVE 219
We Made It

ACKNOWLEDGEMENTS 227

CHAPTER ONE MOTHER KNOWS BEST HEARTLESS

"Momma. Moomm'ma!" Lil Chris screamed for his mother as he ran as fast as he could. He had run all the way from Ruffner Middle School across the street from the front of Tidewater Park to his tiny project apartment in the back of the Park on Holt Street. The long sprint took only four minutes as the young pre-teen kept his speed in top gear, leaving his attackers more than a block away. He made it to his Park house, opened the door, slammed it shut, and took a seat behind it. Completely out of breath he stood up wiping the sweat that was pouring from his forehead and walked towards the kitchen.

"Christopher Cameron, what the hell is wrong wit' choo?" A short, full sized, dark skinned woman asked in a demanding tone.

Chris ran over to his mother and gave her a hug. "Momma. Lonzo, Mike, Tommy, and Sam chased me home from school, but I'm way faster than them so they couldn't catch me. I smoked all fo' of 'em." He said with a big smile on his face.

"Who chased you home from school and what the hell are you smilin' for?"

"Bee'cuz! I got away. They chase me almost ev'ree day and they nev'ah catch me." He answered still smiling.

"Boy take that stupid lookin' smile off yo' face." She said as she opened the door to see Lonzo, Mike, Tommy, and Sam standing on the corner of Holt Street harassing everyone that passed by. "JUNE! You, Mike, Tommy, and Sam get cha'll lil asses over here and stop messin' wit' dem people." The four kids immediately respected Chris's mother's commands. They had all heard stories of the woman from their parents and knew that she was nothing to play with.

June knew of her wrath first hand because he and his mother were neighbors to the woman and she allowed her to discipline him anytime he misbehaved or was disrespectful. Dorothy Cameron or "Ms. Dot" as she was referred to by everyone younger than her. Although she hated being called Ms., they continued to do so out of respect and fear. Ms. Dot was born in Tidewater Park. The largest, most grimiest Project in the city. She was the youngest of seven, five brothers and one twin sister. Ms. Dot was so vicious that she hardly ever fought females calling them too easy to beat. The boys turned out to be just

as easy for her and her twin sister Regina who never allowed her to fight alone. They both had flawless records growing up and that was hard to do coming up with Lil Charles, Black John, Redd, Fast James, and his brother Ed.

"Which one of ya'll got a problem wit' my son?" She asked in a scary tone of voice. The four teenagers stood on the sidewalk looking dumbfounded.

June emerged from the crowd with his chest poked out. "I do." He said.

"Well ya'll two fight it out and get it over wit' and none of ya'll bet' not jump in."

Chris grabbed his mother by the arm. "Momma I don't wanna fight him. He older than me and bigger." He whined.

"Boy get 'cho soft ass over der and fight. I ain't bring you in dis world to be no ho. You don't have a pussy so stop actin' like one. I could'ah had a girl for dat." The four boys laughed at Ms. Dot chastising her son. She shoved Chris off of the porch and onto the sidewalk.

The porches out The Parks didn't have steps but she pushed him so hard that it caused him to stumble and nearly fall. Chris caught his balance and was now standing face to face with June. He looked the heavy set, knotty head brown skinned kid in the face. "Lonzo I don't wanna fight 'choo. I thought we were friends." Chris continued to whine.

"Boy I didn't send you out der to talk. Now ya'll bett'ah fight now so ya'll can go back to bein' friends."

"Ooooh!" The crowd sang in chorus as June punched Chris in the eye. Chris instantly began crying uncontrollably as he grabbed his eye in pain. "Ooooh!" June swung again this time connecting a powerful upper cut to the gut, knocking the wind out of Lil Chris. Chris's cousin Turquoise made her way through the crowd to see what was going on. She made it to the front of the group of bystanders where she saw June standing over Chris who was balled up in a fetal position.

"Alonzo, why 'on't you fight somebody who gone fight back?" Turquoise asked.

June laughed. "I 'on't hit gir......." Before he could finish his sentence Turquoise punched him in the mouth.

"Ooooh!" The crowd sang again

."Well she hit 'choo so you my-as-well fight back." Ms. Dot said knowing that her niece could probably take her neighbor. June contemplated both what Ms. Dot said and the fact that he too believed that Turquoise could whip him. "You got that shorty. Come on ya'll let's go." He said. Mike, Tommy, and Sam all walked off behind June. Turquoise helped Chris to his feet. Ms. Dot shook her head and walked back into the house.

"Turk I hate my mom." Chris said still in pain from the blow to the stomach.

"Why? For trynna make you tougher. Chris you ain't got no reason to run from nobody. You gotta learn to fight. Only two things can happen. Either you can win or you can loose. But you can't get no respect runnin' and trynna be friends wit' everybody." She said as her and Chris walked into the house.

"Chris get 'cho black ass up here." Ms. Dot yelled from upstairs. Chris walked upstairs and entered his mother's room. "SMACK!" You could hear the sound of Ms. Dot's hand connecting with her son's face throughout the entire house. He grabbed his face and began crying all over again. "Shut up all that gotdamn cryin'." She demanded and grabbed Chris by his throat. "From this day forward. September the nineth, Nineteen Eighty five if I catch you or hear about you running from anybody and I mean ANYBODY or crying for any reason so help me God I'mma kill you. Do you understand me?" She said through closed teeth stressing every syllable in every word to ensure that she was fully understood.

"Yes ma'am." He answered coughing and gasping for breath as his mother released his throat so that he could answer her. He took a seat on the bed.

"Son I love you and there is no way that you can make it out here in the Park bein' soft. You are growin' up around some of the grimey'est most untrustworthy people known to mankind. The Park won't shit when I was growin' up and these niggas are gettin' worse. Your girl cousin got more heart than you and that's a gotdamn shame. Any time a girl has to fight for a boy." Ms. Dot said as she thought back to the numerous occasions that she and Gina had to fight for the youngest of their brothers because the older four wanted to teach the younger three how to fend for themselves. Dot and Gina caught on quick. "Chris listen. It hurts me to see other kids pick on you. Your black ass daddy ain't shit. All he wants to do is get drunk and high all fuckin' day and hang out all night. I work too hard for you to let other kids take shit from you or for you to give it away trynna make friends wit' the whole damn neighborhood. Respect is not somethin' you buy it's somethin' you earn. That's all you need Chris is respect. Fuck ah friend. Who needs 'em. Earn your respect son and you'll feel like you got all the friends in the world." Ms. Dot walked over to her dresser and removed the middle drawer completely. In the empty spot rested a small .32 caliber revolver. She pulled the pistol out and held it in her oversized hands. "If anyone ever threatens your life, or more than one person jumps on you at the same time this is where you can find this." She held the gun up with one hand and pointed to the hole where the middle drawer used to be with the other. She walked over to the bed and took a seat. She motioned for Chris to take a seat on her lap. He did and she held his small hand inside hers. She removed all six bullets from the chamber then gripped her son's hand around the trigger. Chris pulled the trigger repeatedly. "Pow, Pow, Pow." He made the noise with his mouth as he continued to squeeze the trigger.

"Chris this gun stay's loaded. Never pull it out unless you are going to use it. Never let a motha fucka take anything from you or Turquoise or bring harm to ya'll. I'll much rather see you in jail than put you in the ground." Ms. Dot reloaded the gun and placed it back in it's hiding spot. Just as she closed the drawer her boyfriend of fifteen years walked into the room. "Otis where the hell you been? It's six o' clock in the evenin' and I haven't seen you since seven o' clock yesterday morning."

"I was out lookin' for work." Otis lied, with cheap liquor leaking from his pores causing the entire room to smell.

"Lookin' for work my ass. You was out gettin' drunk while yo' punk ass son was gettin' chased home from school AND he got his ass kicked." Chris hung his head in embarrassment. He held back the tears as he thought of his mother's promise to kill him the next time he cried.

"Chris what is your mother talkin' 'bout?" Otis asked half drunk, slurring each word, while reaching out to grab his son.

"Don't put 'cho fuckin' hands on him. I'm the one who has to teach him how to be a man so I'mma be the one who disciplines him." Dot said pushing Otis away. He raised his hand like he wanted to hit her. "I know you done lost yo' mind." She said as she popped Otis upside his head. "Chris go do your homework, take a bath, and get ready to eat." Chris left his mother's room and went downstairs where Turquoise was sitting on the floor solving a math problem.
"Turk you know Lonzo gone get me tomorrow because you hit him wit' yo' stupid ass."
"Forget Alonzo. I'll fight him, Tommy, Mike, Sam, Dee-Dee, Grimey, and whoever else that think they can rumble out here. Now shut up before I hit you." Turquoise said, balling up her fist in her cousin's face.

The next morning Chris walked into his mother's room before heading to school. He opened up the middle drawer and removed the .32 from the dresser and placed it in his book bag. He quietly put the drawer back in place, walked over to his mother and kissed her on the cheek like he did every morning. Ms. Dot smiled. "Remember my promise." She said half asleep. Chris walked out of the room and down the stairs. He headed out of the house locking the door behind him. He slid the key through the mailbox which was actually a slot in the door. He walked to Turquoise's house to get her so they could walk to school together.

Turquoise lived with her mother Gina around the corner from Chris on Charlotte Street in the front of the Park. She stepped out wearing all black. Nothing she or her cousin wore was name brand except for their shoes.
"What's all the black for? You goin' to a funeral?"
"Maybe! If a nigga fuck wit' you today. Plus I got some'm to handle after school."

"Don't worry about me. I wish a nigga would fuck wit' me today." Chris said boldly.

You ain't gone do shit but run like a little bicth. She thought. The two cousins continued to walk to school. As they reached the front door of the school, Turquoise turned to her cousin to give him the instructions for the day. "Don't leave here with out me and if anybody fuck wit' you come get me out of class."

"Whatever." Chris said and they went their separate ways. Chris sat nervously in the back of his English class. Every five to ten minutes he would open his book bag to see if the gun was still inside. School was about to end for the day and there was a big fight scheduled immediately after between Tidewater Park and Calvert Park or "Carrot" Park as it was often pronounced. The two projects sat side by side and often stayed in confrontation. Carrot Park was only half the size of Tidewater Park but it was home of the City's most dangerous teen. The school bell rang alerting the students that it was time to go home. Tidewater Park grouped up on the basketball court behind the school where the fight was supposed to take place while Carrot Park teamed up in the front of the school.

Boys, girls, middle school students, high school students and dropouts all gathered with their respective Park in preparation for the "Back to School Rumble." A group of at least twenty five male and females walked passed the basketball court towards the railroad tracks that led to Brambleton.

"Man them niggas deep. They look like they about to fuck some shit up." A very tall light skinned slim kid said.

"Ain't nobody but them soft ass Tidewater Park niggas. Boo-Boo, Speed, Sherwood and them niggas from Carrot Park gone kill them niggas." Said a short stocky brown skin older kid with waves brushed to the side of his head.

"You just say that 'cause you, Speed, Boo-Boo, and Sherwood fam'lay Messy. Da-Da, Mike, June, and them niggas go hard. Don't get that fucked up."
"Well I tell you what Tim, I bet you ten dollars that Carrot Park whip them niggas today."
"Bet! Speed probably won't even come out here for that bullshit." Tim said.
"Believe this, if it's violence involved, Speed'll be there." Messy said with a guarantee as they both touched fist ensuring that the bet was official. "Dee-Dee the only nigga out Tidewater Park I fuck wit'." He finished.
Turquoise was on the court putting vaseline on her face when she noticed the Tommy Boys heading towards Brambleton. They exchanged grits with each other, as the Tommy Boys and girls disappeared across the tracks. "I can't stand them bitch ass Brambleton niggas." She said as she focused her attention on the herd of students that were coming from the front of the school. The clique from Carrot Park was deep but not half as deep as the crew that was standing on the court. Turquoise turned to Chris. "A Chris go 'head home. You 'on't gotta stay if you don't want to."
"Yeah Shorty go home. This shit ain't fo' you. We can handle it." A well built light skinned fellow said.
"Dee-Dee I got ya'll back." Chris said excitedly. "Trust me!" He said adding assurance as if he grew a heart over night.
"Okay but this shit ain't gone be pretty. Niggas gone get fucked up." Dee-Dee warned. The clique from Carrot Park grew close. "Damn we should've bought Speed, Tony, Boo-Boo and them wit' us. They got niggas from the T (Booker T. Washington High School), and grown ass men wit' them." One of the youngens said out loud, as the Parks were now standing face to face with each other. Before words were exchanged the rumble was on. The fight was pretty evenly matched until Chris reached in his book bag and pulled out

his mother's .32. He nervously fired the first shot into the leg of a young boy who was being easily handled by June. The shot caught the attention of each and everyone of the fights participants as they searched to see where the shot came from. The next shot he fired was into the arm of a female who was searching the ground for her hair weave that Turquoise had pulled out.

"Them niggas got gunz!" Sherwood said angrily while stomping a kid from Tidewater Park more aggressively now that he knew his opponents were fighting dirty. Chris continued to fire shots. By the third shot he was no longer nervous and began shooting with confidence. The clique from Carrot Park started to retreat back towards their Park. Chris fired two shots at the backs of the fleeing bunch of teens.

Once the members of Carrot Park were all gone some of the people from
Tidewater Park headed home, while the rest stood around Chris with mixed emotions. Some were excited about his sudden show of bravery while the rest found his act cowardly.

"Yo' Shorty if you didn't wanna rumble you should've cared yo' little ass home. What the fuck you have to pull that pistol for. Now them niggas gone come out the way shootin' and all of us don't got guns." June said.

"So I do and if them niggas come out Da Park lookin' for trouble I'll bust at dem niggas again."

"Shorty you gotta have heart ta' fuck wit' them niggas. For real, for real you gotta be heartless because when it comes ta' violence some of them dudes don't give a fuck. What 'choo about ten, eleven." June said as they all headed for the back of the Park.

"Twelve!" Chris answered.

"Well twelve thirteen it don't matt'ah them niggas'll body yo' lil ass. One of them Carrot Park niggas pushed they own mother in front of a movin' TRT bus(Tidewater Regional Transit), so you know he won't think twice ta' body a nigga he don't know. June mentioned now standing on his mother's porch.
They talked for a little while longer then Turquoise and Chris headed inside the house. When they entered the house they walked into a wonderful smell.
Ms. Dot was in the kitchen frying chicken, with collard greens and cabbage. The two cousins walked into the kitchen. "Chris where the hell have you been and Turquoise why you look like you comin' from Norfolk Zoo fightin' wit' the animals."
"We had a fight wit' Carrot Park momma." Chris answered. Turquoise looked at him like she wanted to slap him in the mouth.
"You talk too much." Turquoise said. Chris walked towards her with his fist balled up.
"Okay that's enough." Ms. Dot said jumping between the two. "Chris get somewhere before this girl kick yo' little ass."
"She can't beat me." He said knowing damn well she could.
"I said knock it off. Now if ya'll were in a fight wit' Carrot Park how come you don't look like you been fightin' at all." She asked Chris. "I know yo' black ass bet' not had run."
"He didn't Aunt Dot. He fought." Turquoise quickly added before Chris said something to get his self in trouble.
"That's my boy. Now let me see the gun!" Ms. Dot caught the two cousins off guard.
They looked at each other as if to say how did she know and then both shrugged their shoulders to say I don't know.
"Chris where is my gun? I saw you take it this mornin', now give it here." Chris reached in his book bag and handed his mother her gun. She spun the revolver open and checked to

see if any bullets were fired. Dropping all of the shells into the palm of her hand she realized that all but one shell was empty. Ms. Dot's eyes lit up. "Did you hit anybody?" She asked with a smile on her face while reaching out to hug her son. Confused by the question neither of the two answered. "Turk did he hit anybody and you better not lie."
"I guess I 'on't know I was too busy fightin'."
"Oh you know you lyin' heifer. Chris did you shoot anybody wit' this gun?"
"Yes Ma'am." He answered with his head down. He looked up just in time to see his mother's smile widen. She handed Chris the gun back.
"You gone need this more than I do. Besides I got two more where that came from." Ms. Dot said. "Now ya'll go do your homework and get ready to eat. Chris I'll talk to you later." Chris and Turquoise did as Ms. Dot requested. The family sat down to eat and Turquoise left shortly after. Chris took a bath and went to get in the bed. Moments later Ms. Dot walked into the room and sat on the edge of her son's bed.
"I suppose you think you ah man now? If not you better, because those kids out Carrot Park got guns too and believe me they plan on usin' them now, so you better beware. I'm not tellin' you to go out and start trouble or run around shootin' people for nothin' but if it comes to you deal wit' it before it deals wit' you. When you play wit' guns it's always shoot first. And remember if anybody ever take anything from you, you have my permission to shoot 'em. ANYBODY!"
"Momma, what's being heartless? June said that I gotta be heartless."
"Go get the dictionary and look the word up." Chris went to retrieve the dictionary and
located the word. "What it say?"

"Heartless. Without sympathy or compassion; pitiless; cruel:" He read the definition that was given in his American Heritage Student's Dictionary.

"You read good son." Chris smiled. He had been an "A" "B" honor roll student since the first grade. He was a very intelligent young man. "What that means in street terms is to be cruel and the definition of that is...." Ms. Dot took the dictionary from Chris and looked the word up. "Cruel. Liking to cause pain or suffering; unkind; merciless. Which simply means not givin' a fuck. Willing to sacrifice anything or anybody to protect one's self. Always put your self first. These are the only things that I ask of you. Always stand up for yourself. Get 'cho own money so that you don't have to depend on nobody for shit. Don't even depend on me because I won't always be here. Never fuck a man. I ain't raisin' no homo. And never tell. Turquoise was right when she said you talk too much. Always remember that loose lips sink ships and snitches get stitches and end up buried in ditches. With that said you go ahead and get some sleep." Ms. Dot kissed Chris on his lips and headed back down stairs. She stopped in her tracks and headed back towards Chris's room. "I almost forgot. Don't trust nobody. And I love you son." She closed the door and walked down the steps. Ms. Dot reached into her right front pocket and removed two bags of heroin. As she placed the first bag to her right nostril and inhaled deeply a barrage of gun fire broke out a block away from Holt Street on the basketball court. Chris jumped up as the rapid gun fire jolted him out of his sleep. Ms. Dot shrugged it off as normal as the effects of the first pill began to kick in. Things got quiet and she placed the second pill up to her left nostril and inhaled deeply. As Ms. Dot rose from the couch to get something to drink the gunshots started again. This time they sounded closer. "Blaka, Blaka, Pow, Boom, Pow, Boom, Blaka, Pow, Blaka, Blaka" were the sounds of the 12-gauge, .45, and .38. "Crassshhh!" was the sound that the window made as bullets crashed through the plane of glass. Bullets traveled through the house and ricocheted off the walls. Two bullets found their way into Ms. Dot's back causing her to cough up blood and fall face first to the floor. She crawled for the phone just to be reminded by the silence that Otis had taken the money for the bill and done God knows what causing the phone to be disconnected earlier that day. *If I make it I gotta leave this dope alone. It's fuckin' wit' my train of thought.* She thought to her self. She tried to yell for Chris but couldn't.

Chris was already on his way downstairs where he found his mother bleeding to death. He ran over to her and leaned over top of her body with tears forming in his eyes. "Run next door and call an ambulance." She whispered. "And if one of them tears drop down yo' face, I SWEAR TO GOD!" Chris jumped up and ran next door to use the phone.

He called the ambulance. "Nine-one-one. My mother has been shot please hurry up. I live on Holt Street, Ten fifty six. Pleeasse hurry up." Chris hung up the phone and raced back to his mother's side. The woman was losing consciousness. Her eyes were shut and she was fading with every minute that passed. "Please momma hold on." Twenty minutes passed and the ambulance showed up. They rushed Ms. Dot inside and hurried her to the hospital. Norfolk General was just a short drive away and they got her there in time and rushed her into emergency surgery.

Chris ran all the way to his Aunt Gina's house and repeatedly banged on the door until Turquoise answered.

"Boy what the hell is your problem and why are you out of breath?" She questioned.

"My momma got shot. Tell Aunt Gina. We gotta get to the hospital." Chris took off running up the stairs and barged into his Aunt Gina's room.

"Boy what the hell is wrong wit' you? Have you lost yo' damn mind?" Gina was in bed with some man. They were both naked and you could smell the sex in the air.

"My momma got shot. We have to get to the hospital." Chris explained. Gina pushed the heavy set man off of her and jumped into her clothes that were lying on the floor at the foot of the bed.

"Gi'mme yo' keys." She said while reaching into the young man's pocket without waiting for a response. She grabbed the keys and headed for the front door with Chris on her heels. "Come on Turk, let's go." She said. The three of them rushed outside and into the old 75' Buick. It took all of five minutes to start before they were on their way.

They arrived at the Emergency Room and Gina was out of the car before she had the chance to park it good. "We lookin' for Dorothy Cameron." She said.

The nurse that rushed Ms. Dot into surgery stood there in awe at how much the identical twins looked alike. "She's in surgery." She said still amazed. "Are you two twins?" The blue eyed blonde hair nurse asked. Ms. Dot and Gina looked too much alike. They were always called the other. No one could tell them apart.

"What the fuck does it look like stupid?" Gina responded with attitude.

The nurse snapped on her way back into surgery. "Well I never."

"And you prob'lee nev'ah will." Gina said to the lady's back. Gina sat impatiently with her daughter and nephew for four hours. She ran back and forth to the desk to ask for an update on her sister's condition. On the fourth hour the doctor came out with a clip board in his hand.

Dr. Andrews was a handsome black man in his mid thirties. "I'm looking for the family of Ms. Dorothy Cameron." He said scanning the crowded waiting room. Gina stood to her feet

and rushed over to the doctor. Under normal circumstances she would have tried to holla but since it wasn't she got straight to the point.
"How is she?"
"Well she just came out of surgery. We lost her on two separate occasions but she's a fighter. She lost a lot of blood. The good thing is that neither of the two bullets did any damage. One traveled straight through and we were able to remove the other before it struck any vital organs or a major artery. She's on a lot of medication right now and needs her rest. She's gonna be fine. You all can come back in the morning to visit. We have to run a few more test and keep her on the IV's for the night but trust me she'll be fine.
"Thank you doctor. Thank you so much." She said while shaking hands with the doctor. I'll be back for you tomorrow as well. She thought with her mind back in the gutter now that she was sure that her sister was fine. "Come on ya'll let's go home." I gotta dick in bed waitin' on me. She thought as they made their way to the exit.
After more car trouble the hooptie finally started and they drove back out the Park. Gina rode past her sister's house so that Chris could gather up some clothes.
Ms. Dot stayed in the hospital for only three days before she demanded to be released. Doctor Andrews considered her to be in good enough shape so he released her.
Ms. Dot walked into the house happy to be home. She scanned the house and noticed that the NHRA (Norfolk Housing Redevelopment Association) people had come to fix the window and repaired the wall. That was fast. She thought. "They probably wish that I was dead so they could rent the place to some one else." She mumbled out loud. She walked upstairs where she found Otis asleep in the bed. Nigga here ain't shit! She thought as she shook him to wake up. "Otis get 'cho no good ass up." She said shaking him

violently. "Ahh what the hell." She said as Otis was out like a lamp. Tired from her bus ride home she went to lay in Chris's bed.

Ms. Dot slept for hours. When she woke up it was pitch black outside. She yelled for Chris. When he didn't answer she realized that he was still probably over her sister's house. She walked downstairs and opened the door. She looked down the block for someone she could send to get her son. She knocked on the door next to hers to use the phone.

"June, go over Turk's house and tell Chris that I'm out of the hospital." She said as she spotted him through his mother's screen door.

June jumped up happy to see his neighbor. He ran to the door and gave Ms. Dot a hug. "We gone straighten them dudes that did this to you."

Ms. Dot smiled. "Boy just go do what I told you." June took off walking down the block. Moments later he returned with Chris and Turquoise in tow.

"Momma." Chris said flatly looking the woman over. The incident with his mother made him bitter. He blamed her for her being shot because she should've never given him the weapon in the first place. He remembered every word she said that night and the night before.

"Christopher." She placed her hands on her son's shoulders, holding him at arms distance. She studied the cold look on the young boy's face. "You becomin' heartless already."

"But you made me like this momma. You did this to me. Did this to the world." Killah Cam mumbled in his sleep. Killah dreamed of his mother often. It had been fifteen years since Ms. Dot overdosed on heroin leaving young Chris alone to deal with the evil ways of the world. He jumped up out of his sleep and looked over at his wife who was sleeping

peacefully beside him. "Oh shit I forgot to call and check on Turk!" He
whispered to his self before picking up the phone.

Lil Chris grew up to be extremely Big Chris. He stood six foot six inches tall and weighed three hundred fifteen pounds of muscle. He kept his head shaved bald and was jet black. He earned the nick name Killah at the age of thirteen after he killed his father on June 20, 1986 for allegedly stealing sixty dollars from him. Ms. Dot lied to detectives, telling them that Otis was abusive and that the shooting was accidental, but the State of Virginia still found Killah guilty of involuntary manslaughter and sentenced him to eighteen months in a juvenile facility.

Not once during his entire incarceration did his mother return any of his letters, answer his phone calls, send him any money or visit him and on December 18, 1987, less than a week before Killah was scheduled to come home Ms. Dot died from a heroin overdose leaving him to answer a question that he still didn't have an answer for. "Why?"

CHAPTER TWO Knee Deep In The Game Heartless

"That's it baby. Right der, Ssss, Oooh, right der, right der." Turk sang in ecstasy as the young man's tongue found it's way into her rectum. The sound of her phone ringing momentarily woke her out of her daze. She sat up to locate her phone, glanced at the clock and realized that it was 12:56 am. "What's up Blackey?" She said as she answered her phone knowing that it was Killah after reading the caller I.D.
"Where you at?" He questioned.
"On my way out Da Park." She lied. Turk motioned for the young man in bed with her to stop while she searched for her clothes. The light in the hotel room as well as the television were still on so they were relatively easy to find.
"It's one ah' clock in the mornin' and you ain't been out the Park yet? What the fuck you been doin' all night? And who the fuck is that trynna whisper in the back ground?"
"Nobody! Just this boat boy ass nigga I met at Garry's last week. He said he wanted to lick my ass so I stopped by the Marriott down Waterside to see what stick man was talkin' 'bout. I talked to Drea and she been pass all the spots, I just gotta meet her out Da Park. I got dis cuz. Just meet me out Pinewood in ah half an hour". Turk hung up her cell phone.
"Well Boo, I gotta make ah run. What 'choo gone do? You gone wait for me ta get back or you wanna catch a cab home?" Before the young man had a chance to respond Turk grabbed him by the penis and began stroking it gently with her soft manicured hands. "I'd wait if I was you. It'll be more than worth your while. If you decide to leave....Here's fifty dollars so you can catch a cab." She said as she reached inside of her Prada bag and removed a $50 bill. The young

man smiled as he envisioned Turk's big soft ass bouncing up and down on him.
"How long you gone be?"
"A couple of hours. Maybe. I 'on't know for real. If I take too long just leave and call me tomorrow."
Turk wasn't the best looking woman in the world. In fact she wasn't pretty at all but she had a dime body. Nice firm breast, slim waist and a big ole' ass. Her appearance and the way that she carried herself attracted many of men. She had a walk and an attitude that spoke "I'm the shit!" and from the back that's exactly what they thought. Couple that with the fact that she was worth millions and it showed and you had enough to cover up her funny looking facial features and extremely dark skin. She kept her hair and nails done weekly and never wore and outfit or pair of shoes twice.

Turk rushed out of the hotel room and took the elevator to the lobby. She slowly walked to her 2003 Ferrari 360 Spider and climbed in the car. She checked herself in the mirror then pulled off.
Waterside was located in the middle of Downtown Norfolk less than two blocks away from Tidewater Park. A tourist site where people went to party, eat at a nice restaurant, stay at a nice hotel and over look the Ocean, ride the Spirit of Norfolk or catch the Ferry across the water to Downtown Portsmouth.
Turk made the short drive out The Park and pulled up in front of the house on Holt St. that Ms. Dot once lived in. She pulled out her phone and dialed a number. "I'm outside." She said to the voice that picked up. Moments later a short, well built, caramel complexion female appeared with a book bag in her hand. Turk popped the trunk and the female placed the bag inside and closed it.
"It's ah hundred and twenty five in the bag." She said.

"Yo, my bad Drea. I got caught up wit' dis nigga and you know how that go. How long you been out here?"
"About two hours. Tasha two-wayed me about ten thirty and said they was ready. I got out here 'bout eleven thirty." Drea answered.
"Chris gone meet us out Pinewood. Follow me so we can get this shit and get it to Tasha and Lady early. This our last day on the grind so we gotta do it big."

Drea jumped in her 2002 Lexus SC 430 and followed Turk as they took the drive across town. Andrea A. K. A Drea was the head of Turk's operation.
She was responsible for supplying all of the spots with enough heroin for a day and collecting all of the money at the end of the night. Drea was drop dead gorgeous. She was a little on the chubby side but her face was beautiful and her light brown eyes were mesmerizing.
Killah and Turk were knee deep in the dope game. The two cousins combined brains and killer instincts to form one of Norfolk's only organized crime gangs. They both had three member crews. Turk's was all female, Drea, Tasha and Lady while Killah's was composed of two males and one female Fu, Blue and Shatika A.K.A. Tika Bell. Each crew rotated every ninety days, hustling six months each, every year. It was the end of December 2002. February 2003 marked the beginning of the crews fifth year as an organization.
Turk followed by Drea pulled into the apartment complex out Pinewood Gardens, a mixed middle class neighborhood consisting mostly of military families which is located off Little Creek road and Military Highway. The Gardens is in the Northern section of the city. Killah and Turk each owned an apartment in the neighborhood under false names. One apartment was used to hold the dope while the other was used to count money and relax.

Turk and Drea walked into the apartment. Killah was sitting on the couch playing NBA Live 2003 on his Sony Playstation II with Fu when the two ladies walked in.

"What's up Blackey, Big Head?" Turk spoke as she walked over to the kitchen table and sat the bag of money on it.

"What's up fellas?" Drea spoke and plopped down on the couch in between the two large men. Killah paused the game after he made a three pointer. "Come on Fu so we can count this money. We'll finish this later. You down a dub (Twenty points) anyway. You can't come back." Killah said as he stood from the couch.

"Yeah, I'm tired as a bitch anyway. Let's get this shit over wit' so we can bounce. But a dub ain't shit. I could come back if I wanted to. I 'on't know what the fuck you talkin' 'bout." Fu responded.

Fu was the head of Killah's operation, who was like a mentor to young Fu being six years his senior. He hailed from Carrot Park and even though he was young and the only member out the crew that wasn't from Tidewater Park, Killah still labeled him Captain over Blue, someone he knew his entire life and Tika Bell his best friend. Fu stood six foot one and weighed two hundred and eighty five pounds. He was light skin with long curly black hair that he kept braided, a chubby face and baby brown eyes. He was a quiet, shy fellow who only resulted to violence when absolutely necessary.

Killah, Fu and Drea joined Turk at the table and they all took a portion of the money to count. They counted the money by hand then used the money machines to recount it. Each time they came up with $125,000. Killah and Turk both took out their thirty percent of the income giving them $37,500 for the day. That left $50,000 to be split six ways. Drea took sixty percent of the $50,000 which equaled $30,000 to divide with her crew. She put $15,000 aside for her and $7,500 a piece for Tasha and Lady. Fu took the other forty percent which totaled $20,000 pocketed $10,000 and $5,000 a piece for Blue and Shatika.

The crew that didn't hustle during the quarter always took in forty percent of the break down money with the Captain making half. The four of them tucked their money away, Killah turned off the TV. and they headed for the door.

"How much you need for today." Turk asked Drea as they headed towards the next apartment complex to pick up the heroin.

"I 'on't know. Dudes gone be tryin' to get right for the first. Just give me seven fifty." (grams) she responded.

The crew only sold bundles and grams and whatever amount the Captain requested was all that was put out on the street for that day. Never did they re-up (return to the stash house to get more) during the day. Once it was gone they were through unless mid-night came first. Twelve o'clock was the cut off point no matter how much dope they had left and they sold out almost everyday.

Killah unlocked the door and turned on the light. He walked to the closet and removed a freshly wrapped kilo (1,008 grams) of heroin while Turk went into the kitchen and removed four blenders, four shifters, some Banita and Quinine from the cabinet to cut the heroin. Killah took out a Triple Beam scale and weighed it until he measured out 750 grams. He returned the other 258 grams to the closet and he and Fu joined Turk and Drea in the kitchen to work their magic. The heroin was pure and uncut from Afghanistan. It could take better than a ten but they would never put more than a seven and a half on it.

Killah pulled out two decks of playing cards and four plates and placed them on top of the table. Each one of them took 28 grams of heroin and grinded it up in the blender, they each took a spoon to beat the loose rocks off the top back down into the blender. They ran the dope through the shifters, cut it up with the playing cards then placed it back into the blenders with some banita that they had sitting in quinine for two days. They bagged each ounce up separately then repeated the cycle until each gram was complete. Turk was the fastest and best at cutting dope in the crew. For every two ounces that the rest of the crew would cut she would cut three.

A little more than an hour later they were complete and the God father was once again brought to life. They cleaned up their mess and prepared to leave. Fu picked up his cell phone and called Tika Bell while Drea used hers to call Tasha to inform them that it was time to bag up and prepare for the day.

"Tasha call Lady and tell her we ready."

"Tika Bell. Hit Blue and tell 'em we ready."

The four of them grabbed their belongings and headed for their cars.

"We need to have a meeting tomorrow before we go on vacation." Killah said.

Everyone nodded in agreement.

"Drea call me when you get home." Turk said.

"Don't I always?" The two females exchanged smiles and both went their separate ways.

Turk jumped in her car and took the ten minute drive back downtown to Waterside. She parked inside the parking garage and slowly walked to her room. She placed the card key into the hotel door. She smiled as she noticed that her little boy toy was lying in the bed sleeping like a baby. Turk placed her gun on the night stand closest to her side of the bed, removed her clothes and climbed into the bed.

CHAPTER THREE   The Beginning Heartless

Killah had a connect from Afghanistan that he met while he was doing time in the juvenile system. The young boy Ali Hussein was a United State citizen at birth. His father was heavy into politics and came to the Country on a business trip in the late Sixties. During his brief stay he was responsible for getting Ali's mother (An African American teenager) pregnant. He made sure that Ali and his mother were well taken care of but he never once returned to the United States. Not even to visit. Ali was doing time for possession of heroin when he met Killah in 1986. They were both housed at the Tidewater Detention Home in Norfolk before they were shipped to Hanover (A Correctional facility for juveniles) less than three weeks apart. The two became more like brothers than friends for the thirteen months that they were together.
Ali was three years older than Killah, tall, slim, with a golden bronze complexion and green eyes. He was released five months earlier and stayed in touch with his friend through Turk.
Turk fell in love with Ali's way of living the very first time he came through Tidewater Park in his black, with gold trim and sliver bottom 1988 Mercedes 300 CE Coupe to drop off five hundred dollars and some pictures for Killah. He also gave her his phone number for him to call. Turk took the money and pictures over to her Aunt Dot's house to mail.
"Aunt Dot one of Chris's friends dropped off some money and some pictures to send to him."
"How much money?"
"Five hundred dollars."

"What friend he know that got that kind of money?"
"Ali. The boy he was locked up wit'. He came through here in a new Benz and everything, and told me to give Chris his numbers."
"Well make sure you send him the pictures and numbers but don't send him any money. I want my son to learn to survive on his own. Save the money for when he comes home."
Turk walked past the Post Office on her way home to mail a brief letter along with the pictures and phone numbers. When she got home she decided to call Ali herself to inquire information about how he was able to ride so clean. They talked for hours and he explained everything to her and taught her a little bit about the dope game.
The next day he dropped off three bundles for her to sell and told her to bring him back ninety dollars and keep the other two hundred and ten. She sold three bundles a day for a little more than a month. Next he showed her how to cut the dope and started fronting her eight balls (3.5 grams or an eighth of an ounce) for three hundred and fifteen dollars. Young Turk stayed on her grind making seven to eight bundles off every gram. She was able to sell three to four eight balls a week. She decided to save her money so that Killah would have something to come home to. She did get the urge to go on large shopping sprees but opted to spend lightly, never spending more than five hundred dollars a month. With the money that she made from selling heroin and the five hundred dollars that Ali would drop off every two weeks for Killah, she managed to save up more than fifty five thousand dollars during the last five months of his bid. She gave the money to Ali to lock up in her own safe at one of his stash spots.

A week before Killah was scheduled to be released, Ali planned a shopping spree for him and Turk in preparation for his friend's return to the outside world. He pulled up to Ms. Dot's house and blew the horn.

"Aunt Dot. Come get the door, my ride here." Turk yelled up the stairs.

"TURQUOISE!" Ms. Dot walked downstairs looking ill. "How long you gone be?"

"I don't know. A few hours. We going shopping for Chris."

"Look. Give me a couple of bags till you get back and I'll pay you later."

"A couple bags of what?"

"Girl don't act stupid. I know what you into. I been livin' out this park for thirty four years. I know everything."

"Aunt Dot I can't sell you no dope."

"Why the fuck not? I'mma get it from some one. So if you give it to me or I get it from some where else ain't gone change the fact that I get high. Now if you got it give it to me 'cause I'm sick."

Ali blew the horn again. Turk opened the door and ran outside to the car. Ali rolled down the window and handed her a small bag. "Here go a quarter. Put it up and hurry up so we can go."

"Okay. I'll be right back." She ran back inside and went upstairs to Chris's old room to lock the heroin up. She broke off a piece before she locked the door. She ran back downstairs and handed her Aunt the dope on her way out of the door. Turk climbed in the passenger seat and Ali drove off.

"What's wrong?" Ali asked. He noticed the confused look on her face and grew concerned.

"Nothing! Why?"

"Cause of the way you lookin', but if you say it's nothin' then it's nothin'." He turned the music up as he drove less then two blocks away to Granby Mall on Granby Street.

Granby Mall was an outdoor Mall equipped with shoe stores, clothing stores, jewelry stores, places to eat and a movie theatre. They stopped in Zig Zag's a shoe store and Super Star's a jewelry store.
Next they drove to Military Circle. Ali bought more shoes, jewelry, clothes and underwear. They walked into Wilson's Leather store and Turks eyes lit up as she laid them on a beautiful three quarter length tan leather jacket with fur around the hood. She walked over to the coat and tried it on. It fit perfectly. She walked the coat to the cash register and placed it on the counter. She reached into her pocket book to pay the cashier.
"Shorty what you doin'?" Ali asked.
"Buying this jacket. I like this shit!" She said excitedly.
"Man put your money up. It ain't no good when you with me. Go find a black one for Chris."
Ali shook his head then turned and smiled at the cashier. Turk went over to find a black coat for her cousin. She returned with one just like hers. Ali gave the young lady behind the cash register sixteen hundred dollars cash and forty seven cents. He grabbed the bags and headed for the door. "You ready?"
Turk nodded her head up and down in agreement, and they headed for the exit.
"You know I find that shit very disrespectful."
"What?"
"You pullin' out your money around me."
"Why? I got money. You don't have to buy everything."
Ali laughed. "Money." He laughed again. "You ain't got no motha fuckin' money. What you got fifty, sixty thousand? And you gone give Killah half of that. That ain't shit. Buy a house, a car or worse catch a Fed case and see how far that shit take you. Listen shorty. I'm not trying to dis' you, I'm just givin' you game. Let your money stack. You'll know

when you can afford ah' eight hundred dollar jacket." He opened the trunk and placed all of the bags inside.
He put his arms around her and kissed her lips. It was her first kiss so she tensed up at first. "Relax. Just follow my lead. The same way I guided you through the dope game, I'll guide you through this." He hugged her tightly then unlocked her door. They both boarded the car and he drove towards Chesapeake. "Let's go past Greenbrier Mall."
"Okay." Turk smiled. She was beginning to feel like a woman. Riding shot gun in a Benz, with a man who has plenty of money, showed her the way to get her own and still spends his on her. *This gotta be love*. She thought. The two shopped at Greenbrier Mall then drove to Lynnhaven Mall in Virginia Beach where they ate at Chick Filet in the food court and did a little more shopping.
"You tired?"
"No not really. What's up?"
"Just ride." He took highway 64 back to Downtown Norfolk. He got off on the Downtown exit and drove down Waterside. He pulled up to the Marriott and checked into a luxury suite. He got the key from the man at the front desk and returned to the car.
Turk was sitting, staring out the window thinking. She had never had sex before and was sure that that's what Ali wanted. Besides she just watched him spend over eighteen thousand dollars in less than thirteen hours. *Tasha and Lady both fucking and I'm older than them.* "I'm sixteen going on seventeen. I can do this." She said in a whisper as she took a deep breath.
Ali tapped on the window and she let it down. "We staying here tonight." He said. She removed the keys from the ignition and locked the doors. He grabbed her by the hand and led her to the room.

Turk stood in awe as she admired how beautiful the room was. Wall to wall carpet, tan sofa and love seat, dining room table, refrigerator, stove, oven and a king sized bed in the bedroom. Ali removed his shirt and walked towards the bathroom. "I'm going to take a shower. Turn on the T. V. and chill. Unless you want to join me." He smiled. She contemplated for a moment. "I was just joking relax." Turk breathed a huge sigh of relief. She liked Ali and didn't want to do anything to upset him. She took off her shoes and stretched out across the bed. She picked up the phone and dialed Drea's number.
"Hello." A young female voice answered.
"May I speak to Drea?"
"Hold on".....A Drea! Pick UP THE Phone."...She comin'."
Turk waited impatiently for approximately two minutes.
"Hello."
"What the fuck took you so long?"
"I was outside talkin' to Lady. Where the fuck you at?"
Turk giggled. "I'm at the Marriott down Waterside."
"WHATTT? Wit who girl?"
"Ali. We been out shopping all day and now I'm in a room almost bigger than my house."
"You fucked'em?"
"No, but I will if he want to."
"Bitch you ain't shit. Call me wit' all the details.
"Okay. I'mma come past there when I leave here in the morning. I'mma call my mom and tell her that I'm staying with you so if she call tell her I'm sleep."
"Okay." Drea said and they both hung up. Turk called her mother and told her that she was staying with Drea.
"Have you talked to your Aunt Dot? I been calling her all day and she won't answer. I need to get my lazy ass up and go 'round there. I'll do it tomorrow." Gina said. They exchanged a few more words then hung up.

Ali stepped out of the bathroom wearing nothing but a towel. He looked almost as if he was glowing in the light of the television. He removed the towel and began to dry himself off. Turk stared in amazement at the size of his penis. Ali stood in the mirror and admired his physique as he applied lotion all over his body. He caught Turk sneaking glances at him through the mirror and smiled. "Youn't gotta peek." He said as he stepped into his boxers then walked over to the bed and got in. He pulled her close to him and kissed her softly on her lips. "Shorty I like you. You know that?" Turk nodded in agreement. "You down as shit, on the corner and shit hustling so that Killah can have something to come home to, you ain't selfish, you go hard and you jive young. I could mold you into the perfect woman, all you gotta do is stay by my side." He kissed her again and this time their tongues met. He began to unbutton her pants. Turk helped him get them off then she removed her panties. Ali fingered her clit until she was moist. He pulled his boxers off and tried to enter her wetness.

"Sssss!" Was the sound she made as she jumped back. "What's wrong? You ah 'ight?" He asked in his sweet and innocent voice.

"Can I ask you a question? What the fuck do you plan to do with all that dick? I never done it before and that shit might hurt."

Ali smiled. "You can't be the same thoroughbred that hustle dope and don't take no shit from nobody. Scared of a little pain." He raised up and looked at her as if he was staring. "Naw it can't be you. Besides I would never do anything to hurt you. You're my most prized possession. Wit' cho' scared ass." He said laughing.

"Shut up." She responded with a huge grin of her own.

"Look, we don't have to do it if you're not ready. I'm not going anywhere, we gone be together for a while."

"I'm ready." She said and took a deep breath. "And I am thorough and I'm down for whatever." She poked her chest out and pulled him back on top of her.
"You sure?"
"Mmm Hmm!"
"Well relax. It might hurt at first but once it's in I'll do it slow and easy." By the time he finished speaking he was already inside of her, stroking soft and easy.
Turk clawed at his back as she began to enjoy herself. Although he was taking it easy, she could feel every stroke in her throbbing vagina due to his large manhood. After ten minutes of slow, long stroking sex he ejaculated all of him inside of her. Turk was so far gone that she never realized she had an orgasm. Not that she knew the feeling anyway. She also didn't know that she was bleeding. She didn't want to let go of the moment or Ali for that matter so she just laid there holding him tightly while he played in her hair.
A few moments later they were back at it. This time the strokes were a lot harder and it lasted a lot longer. Tears flowed down Turk's cheeks as she held on tightly for the ride. She never knew that pain could feel so good. Once again he drained every drop of sperm inside of her as she continued to hold him tight. Ali got up and led Turk into the bathroom. He ran a tub full of water and they both got in. He cleaned her body from head to toe then washed his. They finished their bath, he changed the linen on the bed and they fell asleep in each other's arms.

The next morning he treated her to breakfast at Shoney's, then drove her to Ms. Dot's house and dropped her off. He kissed her on the lips after placing all of the shopping bags on the front porch. "Listen, I got some things I gotta take care of. I may get lost for a few days but I'll call you when I'm finish so don't call me. I'll call you!"

Turk looked at him with a confused look on her face but instead of asking questions she said; "Okay" and walked into the house.

The house was completely still. Not a sound could be heard. Turk began calling and searching for her aunt at the same time. She walked into the kitchen and became startled. She ran over and kneeled down on the floor.

Ms. Dot was laid out in the middle of the floor, with a leather strap wrapped tightly around her arm and a needle hanging out of it. She had never shot heroin before but after one sniff, she considered the drug that her niece gave her too strong to snort.

Turk screamed to the top of her lungs then ran next door to get June. She banged on the door until he answered. "June I need help. I think Aunt Dot O-deed. She ain't movin'. She ain't movin' June. Why ain't she movin' June?" She said while crying uncontrollably.

June called 9-1-1 then hurried next door to check on Ms. Dot. He ran into the kitchen and confirmed that Turk's intuition was in fact true. Ms. Dot had overdosed on heroin. "Yo Turk she dead."

Turk continued to cry. I knew I shouldn't've gave her that shit." She mumbled while breathing snot back into her nostrils.

"What? Shorty pull yo'self together. You got anything in here because I called 9-1-1."

Turk remembered the drugs that she had stashed in Chris's old room and ran upstairs. She gathered the rest of the quarter ounce and ran it next door to June's house. She decided to call Ali while she was next door. The phone rung but no one answered. She dialed the number again and got the same result. She decided to try again later and ran back next door to assist June and wait for the ambulance.

"Damn. That nigga Chris gone be fucked up when he come home. First he killed his pop then his mom O-deed." June said. Turk remained quiet and a few moments later the ambulance pulled up. They pronounced Ms. Dot dead on the scene and drove her body to the morgue.
Turk walked home to deliver the bad news to her mother. She crashed through the front door with tears in her eyes. "Mom Aunt Dot, She she dead mom! I think she overdosed." Ms. Gina jumped up from the sofa where she was sitting watching television. She grabbed her daughter by the shoulders and began shaking her uncontrollably. "What did you say Turk? Where's my sister? Where is she?"
"She dead mom. The ambulance just took her." Turk sighed. Ms. Gina broke down. Her knees buckled and she fell back onto the couch. "Mama! Mama!" She shook her mother in attempt to break her out of her daze. "You gotta call the people to get in touch with Chris so they can tell him about Aunt Dot." The sound of Chris's name brought Ms. Gina back to life. She realized that he would suffer enough and had to be strong for her nephew.

Killah was on the rec. yard playing basketball when they paged him over the intercom to report back to his unit. When he arrived he was told to report to the Chaplain's office.
"Christopher, we have some very bad news." She began. He stared the plus sized, middle aged, white woman in her blue eyes, without blinking as she continued. "Your mother was pronounced dead early this morning. Your Aunt Regina called. She left her number and wants you to call her. Are you okay?" She asked as she handed him the phone.
Killah showed no emotion at all. "If it's okay with you I would rather call her later. Can I go now?"
The Chaplain was startled. "Well I guess so."

He stood to his feet and headed back to his dorm. He gathered his thoughts for a minute then picked up the phone to call his Aunt. After the operator informed her that it was a collect call and gave all of her instructions Ms. Gina pressed the "0" to accept.
"Chris baby what took so long for you to call?"
"I had to take care of a few things. You called up here looking for me?"
Ms. Gina took a deep breath. "Baby your mother is dead."
"What happened? And I'm not a baby so could you please stop calling me that." He snapped.
"Boy who the fuck do you think you talkin' to? Did you not here me say that my sister is dead?"
"Yeah I heard you. Did you not hear me ask what happened?"
"She overdosed on heroin this morning."
"She should've left that shit alone like she said. She killed herself." He said as he shook his head.
"Chris this is your mother you're talking about. You better respect that woman. She gave you life you ungrateful mother fucker." She snapped showing her anger.
"And that's all she gave me. She the reason I'm locked up now. Gave me that gun and told me to kill anybody who stole from me. Then she never wrote me or sent me shit. Now she had the nerve to die on me. I loved my mother and I believed that she loved me but did she love herself?" The phone went silent for a moment. "You can't answer that can you? I didn't think so. Aunt Gina I love you. I just got a lot of shit on my mind, don't take it personal I'll talk to you later." He hung up the phone and went to take a shower, to prepare for bed. He laid in his bunk with his mind wondering all night. He watched his entire life up until this point play out in the matter of hours.

Killah respected his mother for making him tougher, although he didn't necessarily agree with her methods. He never understood how such a strong woman could fall victim to drugs. He smiled when he thought about going home soon to be with Turk and Ali. Without them two he probably would not have made it through his incarceration. He thought about how he and Ali use to run a store out of their lockers together. They would sell candy and sodas for a fifty cent profit off every dollar, as well as cigarettes for items off the canteen. When Ali left he handed everything over to Killah and he ran the business by himself for the past five months. His smile disappeared when he thought about the responsibilities that he had to face as a fifteen year old boy. A newborn baby girl, both parents dead, a criminal history and a beef with Carrot Park that he felt obligated to finish now that his mother was dead. He quickly jumped off of his bunk startling the other boys in the room. He opened his locker and retrieved a letter from Turk. He opened the envelope and the letter read.

Chris,
What's up cuz. Before I start Dee-Dee, June, Tika Bell, Drea and Lady all said what's up, and they can't wait for you to come home. Enough of them your friend Ali stopped by and dropped off $500 and these pictures for you but your mother told me not to send you the money. She do be tripping sometimes but I guess your mother knows best. Nothing really is new out here. We still beefing with Carrot Park all the time and Brambleton sometime. They still looking for the people that shot Aunt Dot. My sister said that she was going to write you but she be so busy with your baby that she don't have time to do nothing. That bitch ain't shit. Anyway I'm about to go. Drea is talking my head off while I try to write. Love you Turk

P. S. Your friend Ali is cute and he got a brand new Benz. That's gone be us one day. Smile. He said for you to call him at 545-9370.

Killah looked at the envelope for the post date. "July." He said. It was now December and he just received this letter three weeks ago. He jumped back in his bed, closed his eyes and went to sleep.
The next morning they called him into the office and arranged his paper work so that he could go home a few days early to prepare for his mother's funeral.

Killah took the Greyhound back to Norfolk. He exited the bus at the station on Granby Street and Brambleton Avenue, and walked to Tidewater Park. When he arrived at his Aunt Gina's house he found the door unlocked.
Turk was sitting on the couch and was surprised to see her cousin standing in the doorway. He was at least five inches taller and twenty pounds heavier. "What's up cuz. I thought you got out next week." She said still staring. "You got big as shit."
Killah smiled. "They let me out three days early for the funeral."
She got up and gave her cousin a hug. "I got something for you. It's put up at one of Ali's stash spots." She still had not gotten in touch with Ali and it had been four days. She called again and this time he picked up. "Hello."
"Ali what's up. This Turk where the hell you been?"
"Didn't I tell you that I had some things to handle? Didn't I tell you not to call me and that I would call you? So why the fuck is you calling me?" He screamed.
Turk couldn't believe that he would talk to her that way. To say that she was hurt would have been an understatement. "First of all I'm calling you to tell you that Chris mom O-deed

on that dope and that they let him out early so I was calling for him, so you don't have to talk to me like that you punk ass nigga." She shouted back and threw Killah the phone.
"Yo my bad shorty."
"This ain't Turk."
"Oh what's up my nigga. Welcome home. Sorry to hear about your mother. Did you get your clothes?"
"Naw."
"Well get'em from Turk and throw something on I'll be through in a minute."
Ali drove up about and hour later. He walked to the door with two bags full of clothes and shoes for Turk. "We gotta take a ride to pick up your money. Where Turk?"
"Upstairs. Good lookin' on all this family." Killah said sporting a black and white Adidas sweat suit, some black and white shell toes, a white Kangol with the black Kangaroo and two huge gold rope chains. "You, Turk, my Aunt Gina and my daughter is all the family I got." He finished saying and gave Ali a hug. "A Turk, Ali here."
Turk walked downstairs with attitude. "Let's go get my fuckin' money."
"Shorty let me talk to you for a minute outside." The two of them walked out front. "Listen baby! When you called I was a little upset because you called after I told you not to. I thought that you were acting childish and was just calling because I had not called in three days."
"Four." She corrected.
"Well four days. Anyway, when you're out here hustlin' in the streets it's gonna be days when you won't hear from me. I told you I would call you because my father sent me a package and I had to pick it up and drop some weight off out of state. When I make runs like that it's dangerous and you never know when I might get jammed and them folks might get my phone so I don't want you calling me until I let you

know that everything is okay. You understand? Here these are for you." He handed her the bags and reached out to hug her.
"I guess so. Thank you." She smiled and he kissed her on the lips.
"That's my girl. Now get Chris so we can get this money." They drove from the park out to a stash spot that Ali had out Pinewood Gardens. "So what's up KIllah. You know me and Turk out here gettin' this paper. You ready?"
"Naw. I'mma fall back and chill until I at least finish school. I got enough to deal with right now."
Turk turned to see the expression on her cousin's face. "Well whenever you're ready we'll be here." They went inside and Ali removed a picture from the living room wall that concealed a safe. He opened the safe and removed five rubber band stacks of bills before closing it and placing the picture back on the wall.
"Yo, this ah good ass stash spot because with all of these military families out here coming and going no one ever notice you." He handed the stacks of money to Killah.
"Shorty this fifty grand. Don't spend it all in one place. Part'na." Ali said with a smile.
Killah held the money while looking over at his cousin and friend. Ali had his arm around Turk and they were both smiling. "This might be the beginning of a beautiful friendship. Part'na." He said with a smile as he hugged them both.

CHAPTER FOUR   Clock Work Heartless

Drea and Fu dropped the packages off to Tasha, Lady, Tika Bell and Blue around three o'clock in the morning. The four of them capped bundles, bagged grams and by a quarter to six the dope was on the street.
Tasha made her drops on the South Side of the City and Downtown. She started in Berkley and ended out Olde Huntersville. Lady ran the North Side and West End starting in Ocean View and ending out Park Place. After they both completed their drops they met up out Tidewater Park as they were accustom to doing.
"Lady what the fuck took you so long?" Tasha asked as Lady drove up in her black on black Suburban. Tasha was top of the line mean. Five foot eleven maybe six feet tall, beautiful brown skin, pretty brown eyes, long legs and a slim waist. She had short black hair that she kept braided in a different style weekly.
Her only flaw was her vicious attitude that she never hesitated to show. Lady stared at her friend from inside the truck while her twenty-three inch Spreewell's kept spinning. Lady was average looking at best. She was a rather big woman, not fat but Big! She stood around six foot two and a half inches tall and weighed two hundred and twenty pounds. She carried most of her weight in her hips, legs and breast. Her stomach was just as flat as Tasha's. Her skin was a dark brown and she wore a variety of different colored contact lenses so it was almost impossible identifying the true color of her eyes. She too had short black hair that she kept braided weekly and her attitude was just as bad as Tasha's. The two stayed at odds with each other, partly because in many ways they were one of a kind. "I was out

Park Place Trying!, to get some shit straight. If You Must Know." She answered sarcastically.
"Look bitch I don't have time for your bullshit today. Let's ride down the mall so I can get something to wear tonight, and I got us both appointments at Kapital Kuts to get our heads done."
"Okay hoe. I gotta drive myself 'cause I gotta meet Fat Shawn from Portsmouth around twelve so he can get these ten grams."
"Why youn't tell him to meet choo before twelve?"
"Because he said he gone meet me at twelve. What the fuck is up wit' choo and all these questions bitch? Just hop in that lil' ass BMW and follow me." Lady said and drove off. asha hopped in her white with peanut butter leather interior X5 and followed her partner.
"Oooh!" A young boy shouted excitedly as he witnessed the Lamborghini doors open up on the platinum colored 2000 Mercedes Benz CLK GTR. "That's my car! That's my car!"
"Man yo' mama or yo' daddy ain't got no car. That's my man car stupid." His friend ridiculed.
Killah stepped out of the Unique Super Sport model machine that he paid almost three quarter million dollars for wearing a plain white Coogi sweater, some blue Coogi jeans, and a fresh pair of white Gucci sneakers. He approached the two young children. "What's up lil' D? Go get Blue for me." He said as he slapped lil' D five. He got up from the porch and ran inside the house to get Blue.
"Man! What kind of car is dat?'
"Ah Benz. That's all I drive is Benzes." He answered with a smile on his face. Killah fell in love with Mercedes when Ali gave him his 300 coupe for his sixteenth birthday. "What's your name shorty?"
"Chris."

"Yeeah?" That's my name too, but all my friends call me Killah but you can call me Chris. How old are you Chris?"
"Five. You sell drugs don't choo? 'Cause dat's a drug dealer car."
"Man what do you know about drug dealers?" He asked with a giggle.
"Blue! He ah drug dealer and he tell me and Darius that we don't have to go to school because he didn't gadge-uate and he rich."
"Well I graduated and you do need to go to school." Blue walked out of the front door. "Don't listen to Blue, he just be joking."
"Blue be jokin' about what?" He asked. Blue was six foot three, high yellow with bluish
green eyes and a slim muscular build. On one hand he was a ladies man and the comedian of the crew. On the other he was a threat to anybody who stood in his way.
"About these youngens not having to go to school."
"Shiiit! They don't. Look at me." He said with his arms open wide exposing his platinum chain, fully equipped with a diamond and platinum TWP charm. He then rolled he sleeve up on his Ice Burg sweater to reveal his Audemars Piguet Royal Oak platinum paved diamond watch with baguette-cut pastel blue sapphires. "Why the fuck would you go to school when you can drop out and live like this? Naw I'm just shittin' shorty." He laughed. "What's up Killah?" He greeted his partner then turned his lip up at little Chris, shook his head from side to side and whispered; "Youn't gotta go to school shorty", behind Killah's back then turned to face him. "So what's on your mind?"
"We got a meeting tonight at Shadows around twelve thirty? I got the VIP rented out so we can chill and have a good time and still have some room to talk.

"That's what's up homey. Any specific reason for the meetin'?"

"Yeah but I'll let ya'll know in due time."

"Okay fam' I'll see you then. I might be able to scoop me a couple of jump offs before the night is over." Blue said with a grin showing his two platinum teeth.

"I'm sure you will player. We bringing the trucks out tonight too."

They gave each other a pound. Killah walked to his car jumped in and drove off. He cruised the entire City of Norfolk checking his traps. Like clockwork he would wake up around five thirty every morning and be out of the house by six. He would drive pass all of the spots without stopping just to make sure that everyone was out doing what they were supposed to be doing.

People came from all over Virginia and parts of North Carolina to cop bundles and grams of the God Father. Killah named the dope the God Father after Ali since it was his connect and he was Lil' Dot's God Father.

He continued to patrol the city until he ended up at Tika Bell's house in Middle Town Arc. (An upper-class predominantly black neighborhood located behind the campus of Norfolk State University). He opened the door and walked inside.

White Natuzzi leather sofa and love seat, glass marble tables and a sixty-one inch television stood out as he passed through the living room en route to the kitchen. "Tika!" He shouted in search of her location.

Tika Bell walked down the back staircase that led into the kitchen wearing a pair of blue tight fitting DKNY jeans, a black DKNY shirt, black DKNY sneakers and a pair of DKNY sunglasses. Everything about her screamed sex appeal, from her flawless dark chocolate skin, to her five foot six inch frame, slim waist, huge ass, toned stomach, legs and mouth

sized breast. Her long black hair and two gold teeth added points making her a complete dime. She was considered by many as the best looking female in the C. O. C. (Cameron Organized Crime family) because she had a better attitude and personality than Tasha. "What's up Chris? To what do I owe this surprise visit at nine forty five in the morning." She asked then hugged and kissed him on his cheek.
"Just stopped by to tell you that we have a meeting tonight when shop closes at Shadows."
"Well I was on my way out the door. You can stay here if you want or you can ride with me."
"Where are you going?"
"To the mall. Tasha just called and told me about the surprise meeting and asked me to meet her at McArthur Mall. So what's up?"
"I'll ride with you. I don't have shit else to do. And it's about seventy degrees outside so we can pull out the six." He said with a smile.
Tika Bell shook her head and smiled at her friends infatuation with Benzes as she hit the alarm to her five car garage. They hopped in her black with red leather interior Brabus edition SL 600, dropped the top and cruised to the mall.

Turk woke up around 10.00 AM. She brushed her teeth, showered and was dressed by 10:30 AM. She called her boy toy a cab, woke him up so that he could get his self together then dialed Tasha's number on her cell phone. "What's up Tasha? What's the situation?"

"Everything is in order. Me and Lady at the mall.
"What mall?"
"McArthur. Too many niggas shop at Military Circle. That shit ghetto."

"Bitch you ghetto."
"My point exactly. I might ride up there when I leave here. Don't too many hoodlums be out this time of day."
"Well I'll be up there in a minute. Where ya'll gone be at?"
"I 'on't know. I'mma walk in Dillards for a minute. Just call when you get here."
"Okay." Turk said and hung up. She dialed Drea's number and she answered on the first ring. "Hey hon. Where you at?"
"Down Lynnhaven Mall. What's good?"
"What the fuck is everybody doing in the mall this morning?"
"I'm looking for something to wear tonight. You know I don't go out."
"Well look, I'm about to ride up McArthur to meet Tasha and Lady. I'll call you when I leave them so we can hook up.
"Okay." They hung up. Turk and her little boy toy exited the hotel. She hopped in her Spider and headed to the mall.
"Tasha that bitch fat as a mother fucka ain't she?" Lady asked without taking her eyes off the young lady's rear end.
"Lady, you know I ain't the least bit on that gay shit." Tasha responded disgusted.
"Youn't gotta be gay to see that bitch fat. I'mma holla at shawty." She said as she approached. "Hey beautiful. You wearin' them jeans."
"Excuse me?" The young lady asked with a confused look on her face.
"And you fine as a mother fucka. Listen I'm 'ma be straight up and down wit' cha. I'm not trynna turn you out but I am trynna get in them jeans. Just name yo' price." She said pulling out a wad of money. The young lady contemplated for a moment as she eyed the money in Lady's hand along with the diamonds in her ears, around her neck, on her hands, and wrist. "Look just take my number and here, buy

yourself something nice." She said as she wrote down her numbers, peeled back fifteen, one hundred dollar bills and handed them to her. *If she take it I got her.* She thought. The young lady took the money and placed it along with the numbers in her pocketbook. "Thank You!"
"Lady. And you are?"
"Toinette." She said with a smile.
The two women chopped it up for a minute while Tasha was at the cash register paying for an outfit, when a large dark skin male walked up behind her. "Shorty hurry the fuck up. You been standin' there forever."
"Nigga wait cho' mutha fuckin' turn." She said heatedly as she turned around to finish reading the rude individual in line behind her. "You know what? You play too mutha fuckin' much. I started to pull this ratchet out and smack the shit out of you."
Killah continued to laugh. "Shorty you gotta do something about that attitude."
"Shit I'm ah'ight! I can handle myself. What the fuck you doin' in the mall anyway?"
"Riding with Tika Bell."
"Where she at?"
"Next door in Kid's Footlocker. You know shorty foot small as a mother fucker."
"What's up Tasha? You ah'ight?" Lady asked standing behind Killah as if to say what's up?
"Yeah I'm cool. Ain't nobody but Killah crazy ass startin' shit."
"I heard you makin' all that noise, I thought we had drama. What's up Killah?"
"You know that bitch crazy as a mother fucker." He said. Tasha paid for her clothes and they left to join up with Tika Bell. As they entered Kid's Footlocker her phone rung.
"Where ya'll at?"

"In Kid's Footlocker."
"I'm in front of K and B. I'll be there in a second." Turk said and hung up.
"Fu what's up baby?"
Ain't shit Blueburry. What's the deal?"
"Just left my girl crib."
"Which one? You got so many."
"Ha Ha. Very funny nigga. You now who I'm talkin' 'bout."
"So what's up fam'lay?"
"Ain't shit for real. I'll be through in a minute. I gotta holla at cha'."
"I'll be here."
"Okay bet." Blue said as he headed towards Fu's house out Burbage Grant in Suffolk. He dialed Fu back as he pulled up to the lovely five bedroom three and a half bathroom home.
"Yo fam' I'm outside."
Fu stepped out front wearing a wife beater tank top and some Nike basketball shorts. He removed the chains from his two full sized Rotwilders allowing them to run loose while he and Blue stood out front and talked.
"What's up baby boy?" Blue asked with a hug.
"You know me. Laid back. What's happenin'?"
"What's the deal wit' Killah and this meetin'?"
"I 'on't know fam. Last night after we cut up he said we needed to have a meeting before we go on vacation."
"Yeeaah? I wonder what the fuck this nigga wanna talk about."
"Beats me. Can't be about no money and I know niggas ain't got NO problems.
Financial or otherwise. So he got me. We'll just see when we get there."
"True indeed. Let me bust yo' ass in Madden real quick before I bounce."

"Shiitt nigga lets go. You know got damn well you can't beat me." Fu responded as he gathered his two dogs and headed inside. The two friends sat in front of the Tv. and cranked up the Play Station II.

"Yo ain't that them C.O.C. niggas?" An older looking black male asked his partner as Killah, Turk, Tika Bell, Tasha and Lady headed for the exit. "Yeah that's them." He said answering his own question.
"Youn't usually catch them niggas out in the day time. Especially not together. That's over ah hundred million dollars you lookin' at. Some'n must be poppin' tonight." The partner said as the crew grew further out of their eye sight.
"Shorty if we could rob them
niggas there, we'll be set for life."
"No bullshit. Nigga we need to get on that."
"We can't rush into no shit like that 'cause anyone of them'll body you quick. I 'on't expect them to just lay down. We gotta lay them down, or get up under one of them bitches."
"I 'on't give ah fuck what we gotta do to get that paper. We just gotta get it." The older looking guy said as they closed the gap enough to witness the crew loading into their vehicles.
"Look at that shit. Two hundred thousand dollar Benzes, X Fives, Suburbans and what the fuck is that, ah Porch or a Ferrari? Man them niggas got money and I need it." The partner said as they watched the crew converse from a distance.
"Yo Tasha you still ridin' up Military Circle?" Turk asked.
"Me and Lady gotta get our heads braided first. We can ride up there after that if you want to."
"Well look I'mma call Drea and tell her to meet me there, then we gone go to Apple Bees so hit me when you finish gettin' your head done. Killah what cha'll 'bout to get into?"

"I'm going to Tika's house to get my car, then I gotta take care of some things. I'll catch up with ya'll later on tonight and don't forget to bring the truck out tonight."
"Ah'ight" Turk said and drove off followed by Tika Bell, Tasha and Lady. She dialed Drea's number and told her to meet her at Military Circle. Tasha and Lady rode to Kapital Kuts by Norfolk State while Tika Bell drove home.

Fu and Blue sat in front of the television for hours betting $1000 a game. After five games Blue was down $5000 and ready to leave. He looked down at his watch. "Damn nigga it's almost five ah clock. I been here since eleven. It's time for me to slide." He said and stood up to stretch.
"Yeah I'll say that too if I got beat five hot." Fu said laughing.
"Nigga that ain't shit. You ain't won nothin' but five grand. I'll see you again." Blue
said as he walked out of the door.

Turk and Drea walked around Military Circle for a while before Tasha showed up. The three women continued to browse through the mall before they headed to Apple Bees to eat. Lady and Tika Bell both decided to show up at the restaurant simultaneously. The five women sat at a table in the back of the restaurant and talked for a few hours while entertaining what few men who built up enough nerve to approach the group. "Ya'll ready?" Turk asked.

"Yeah we can go now. Me and Lady gotta make some moves anyway." Tasha said and rose from her seat.
"What the fuck you mean you and Lady? Bitch speak for yourself and keep my name out yo' mouth." Lady said.
"What the fuck evah."
"Do ya'll two hoes do this every day?" Turk asked.

"Basically." Drea said and shook her head. "Come on ya'll so we can handle our business."
As the crew prepared to leave a tall light skinned cat approached. "Ya'll leavin'?"
"Ummm? Is that a question you can answer yourself? I think so." Tasha said with attitude.
"What's your problem?"
"Don't mind her. She's always like that, but yes we are about to leave. Sorry!" Turk said as politely as she could.
"Nigga we been in here three hours and you been in here at least two and now you wanna hold us up with that weak ass game." Ya'll leavin'?" Get the fuck outta here, you clown ass niggas make me sick. Come on ya'll let's go." Tasha barked and brushed pass the guy bumping him on her way out of the door.
"Shorty got ah fucked up attitude. Out of respect for ya'll I didn't slap the shit out of her for bumpin' me." He said heatedly.
"I think that was out of respect for yourself." Lady said revealing the butt of her Desert Eagle .44." You'll never live to see tomorrow." She added with a smile staring the man eye to eye.
"What choo think you the only one with a mutha fuckin' gun?" He said far beyond his boiling point, but before he had a chance to reach for his gun Turk cuffed him by the arm. "Suck that one up. You can't win, just walk away." She said with the barrel of her .40 caliber pointed at his rib cage. The guy decided to take her advise and return to his table. The four remaining ladies headed for the exit. "Lady you know we gotta kill that nigga now don't choo?" Turk asked.
"And you say that to say what?" Lady questioned as if she already knew.
"Just makin' sure you know what you started. Now get this nigga license plate number and call Uzi or Tank (The crew's

two most notorious hit-men.) to handle that and get this money off the street so you can make it to The Meeting."
"That's ah small thing to a giant." She said with a smile. "I can handle this nigga myself."
"Be careful. We out." Turk said. "Drea call me when you ready." She said and jumped in her car. Drea and Tika Bell did the same and drove off.
Lady hopped in her Suburban, reclined the chair and waited for the light skinned cat to leave. Less than two minutes later the guy and his cousin stormed out of the restaurant, jumped into a pearl white big body Acura with chrome rims and drove off.
"Yo I can't believe them bitches drew heat on me." He said with his head down, eyes focused on a blunt he was rolling.
"You gettin' soft nigga." His cousin said laughing.
"Well I'll tell you this, let me catch them bitches again. I'mma merk every last one of them hoes." He said as he lit fire to the Purple Haze. His cousin continued to laugh and tease. "Yo nigga I know what the fuck you tryin' to do. That shit ain't funny neither nigga."
"Don't get mad at me. I ain't pull no toast out on you." He said still laughing.
"Okay! Now when I kill one of those bitches what the fuck you gone say?"
Shiitt! You just killed one of them bitches. What the fuck do I care? I don't know them hoes nigga we fam'lay." The two cousins continued to argue as the shots of Cognac from Apple Bees and the Purple Haze began to get the best of them.
Lady tailed the two men so closely that if they were paying attention her cover would have been blown.
"What the fuck you think I'm soft nigga?"
"What the fuck is you talkin' about?"
"Nigga you said I'm gettin' soft nigga."

"Man I was just jokin' but if you feel some kind of way." His cousin said and the car fell quiet for a brief second. "Shiitt, I ain't one of them bitches nigga. If I pull ah ratchet out on you, our fam'lay gone walk wit' cha'. Believe that! We fam'lay and I love you but I'll blast yo' bitch ass if you get to actin' stupid."

"Who the fuck is you callin' ah bitch? What the fuck is you trynna say cuz?" The light skinned cat asked and pulled out his gun. His cousin made a left on Lake Edward Drive out Lake Edwards and parked the car on the side of the street. Lady killed her head lights and pulled up right behind them. "Man I said what the fuck I had to say. You know why them hoes pulled them guns out on you? 'Cause you ah pussy and ah bitch could smell ah pussy ah mile away. You'd be ah cold bitch if youn't pull that trigger." His cousin said and opened his door. The light skinned cat hopped out of the car, gun in hand and ran around to the driver's side.

Lady clutched her pistol in preparation for a shoot out. She was completely ignorant as to what was taking place in front of her.

As the light skinned cat approached, his cousin quickly removed his gun from the small of his back and fired a single shot to his face killing him instantly. "Nigga what the fuck wrong wit' choo? You know how I go nigga. Pull ah pistol out on me and don't use it." The cousin said over the lifeless body. He looked around to see if he spotted any witnesses before he could flee the scene when he noticed a black SUV behind him that he didn't remember being there when he drove up.

Lady sat still thinking of her next move. She was all for letting the driver get away with his crime. As far as she was concerned he did her a favor.

She witnessed him approaching as she reclined in her seat. He walked to the driver's side to see if any one was inside.

Lady raised the seat and her .44 in one motion and fired three shots. "Boom Boom Boom!" The driver fell to the ground as Lady made a U-turn and got the hell out of Dodge. Once she was clearly out of sight she dialed Tasha's number on her cell phone. "Where you at?"
"Out Da Park. What's up?"
"Shit. I'mma ride to the crib and get ready for The Meeting before I pick this money up. Plus I gotta switch trucks."
"You ah'ight?"
"Yeah I'm good. I'll meet choo out Da Park in about two hours."
"Shiitt I'm 'bout to come home and get ready my got damn self. I'll just meet choo at the crib."
"That's what's up." Lady said and they both hung up.
Tasha and Lady shared a six bedroom four bathroom house out Berkshire Estates in Chesapeake. Since neither one of them planned on settling down anytime soon they decided to live together even though they stayed in disagreement. Lady was inside getting dressed when Tasha drove up. She walked up the stairs and headed straight towards Lady's room. "What's up?"
"Hey girl. You'll never believe what happened tonight."
"What?"
"You know that light skin nigga that you cursed out in Apple Bees?"
"Yeah."
"You know after you left that nigga had the nerve to say somethin' slick like if it wasn't for us he would have smacked the shit out of you.
"Smacked the shit out of who? That nigga wouln't've done a got damn thing to me." She said aggressively.
"Anyway! I laughed at the nigga and told him he would never live to see tomorrow then showed him the dess'ee.".
"So what's up? You wanna get this nigga?"

"Check this shit out. I sat in my truck and waited for him to leave Apple Bees. Then I followed him and his man out Lake Edwards. I 'on't know what type of shit those niggas was on but when we got out Lake Edwards he jumped out the car and ran up on his man and got his dumb ass killed."
"Who killed him?"
"His man. So I'm leaned back waitin' for this nigga to jump back in his car and drive off so I could get the fuck out of there. But guess what that stupid mother fucker did?"
"What the fuck he do, kill his self?"
"Hell naw. That nigga walks up on my truck and tries to peep inside the window. Girl I lifted the seat up and hit that nigga three times in the head."
"Yeeah?"
"You got damn right. All the nigga had to do was leave but that nigga wanna be nosey."
"Well his dumb ass got what he deserved."
"Got damn show'll did."
"So we good then?"
"Ooh shit yeah"
"Well I'mma get ready so I can get this money up early. Everybody done hit me on my end and said they ready."
"Yeah? Everybody ready on my end too except Freeze and his fat ass. As quick as diseal move out Park Place I always gotta wait on that fat ma'fucka." Lady said as she threw on her jewels and her black mink coat putting the finishing touches on her out fit. They both finished getting dressed and took to the streets. Tasha hopped back in her X5 and Lady jumped in her all black Hummer. By 10:15 all of the money was collected and Tasha two wayed Drea so that she could come and pick the money up from out The Park. Drea showed up less than ten minutes later. The three women counted the money then Drea called Turk. "I'm ready." She said and hung up.

Turk was already out The Park so she got there in no time. She pulled out her phone and dialed a number. "I'm outside." She said.

Moments later Drea appeared with a book bag in her hand. Turk popped the trunk and Drea placed the bag inside and closed it. "It's ah hundred and eighty seven in the bag."

"Well come on and follow me so we can divide this money up and get to Shadows. Killah and Fu already at the spot." She blew the horn at Tasha and Lady who were both standing on the porch. Drea jumped in her 2003 4.6 Range Rover and followed Turk. Once it appeared that Turk and Drea made it out of The Park safely, Tasha and Lady both hopped in their vehicles and headed for the club.

Turk and Drea walked into the apartment. Killah and Fu were sitting on the couch in front of the Play Station II as usual. Killah jumped up and cut the game off as soon as he heard the key in the door.

"That's some dirty shit. Won't but thirty seconds left in the game." Fu said upset with his friend.

"Man we gotta hurry up and count this money so we can get out of here."

"We could'ah finished the game. That's ah'ight I'm up a game."

"You wasn't up but six points. Two threes and the game tied. We don't have time to play no overtime. But if you want it like that you got it. I owe you a grand."

"Oh I know. Now let's count this money."

CHAPTER FIVE   The Meeting
Heartless

Killah pulled his Mercedes Benz G-500 up in front of Shadows shortly after Twelve followed by Turk in her Porsche Cayenne, Fu in his Cadillac Escalade on twenty three's and Drea in her Range Rover. They parked directly in front of the club next to Tasha's X5, Lady's Hummer, Blues customized Ford Excursion also sitting on twenty three's and Tika Bell's Mercedes Benz ML 320.

Shadows was the most happening adult night club on Thursday night in all of Hampton Roads and this particular Thursday was no exception. The four heads of the C. O. C. approached the Virginia Beach night spot like they owned the place walking directly to the front of the line.

"Oh hell naw!"

"Who the fuck they think they are?" Were the words from the crowd of people who were waiting in the cold line for hours.

"Hold up! Hold up! Where ya'll think ya'll goin' wit' them tennis shoes on?" The baby face bouncer asked looking down at Killah, Turk, Fu and Drea's feet.

"Yo shorty you must be new. Where Ty at?" Killah asked. Ty was part owner of the club and a very good friend of Killah's.

"He inside." The bouncer answered and tapped the glass window that was connected to the front entrance.

A short dark skinned bouncer walked outside to see what was going on. "Yo what's up fam." He spoke as he greeted Fu with a hug and Killah with a pound. "Blue and them already inside. Yo they good homey." He said to the other

bouncer as he let the crew inside. Killah gave him four $100 bills and headed towards the V.I.P.
The music was pumping and the atmosphere was live. The crowd sang along to a "2000" hit by Ruff Ryders and Cash Money. The D J would play one verse then cut the music allowing the crowd to sing the following verse. *"Do ya'll niggas bust yo' guns?"*
"Hell yeah we bust our guns."
"Do you fuck 'em 'till they cum?"
"Damn right we make 'em cum."
"I'm screamin' NORTH!"
"HEY!"
"*SOUTH!*"
"HEY!"
"*EAST!*"
"HEY!"
"*WEST!*"
"HEY!"
"Ruff Ryders gonna show ya'll niggas who ride the best." The music continued to echo throughout the club. The crew made their way through the crowd. Mostly everyone that they passed on their way to the V.I.P booth showed them love.
Killah stopped at the bar. "Let me get those two bottles of Remy X. O. Excellence that I had Ty order and double shots for everybody in the club. Tell the Dee-Jay that the drinks are from Killah Cam and the C.O.C and tell him to put on some of that G-Unit shit; Oh and get Ty for me." He said and gave the bartender three hundred $100 bills. He grabbed the two $6,000 bottles of Cognac, stuffed two more $100 bills inside of the pretty, young bartender's tip jar and went to join his friends.
Everyone stood as Killah entered the room. He took a seat, followed by Turk, Fu, Drea, Blue, Tasha, Tika Bell then Lady

in order of rank. "I called this meeting to discuss our future as an organization." He started. "Sunday we will be leaving for Casa Tres Lobos and staying for a week then it's Back To Business. Drea your crew did a great job this quarter. Ali's father was more than satisfied and shows his appreciation. He sent me nine key's for ya'll to split three ways free of charge. A hundred and fifty-seven thousand was the average daily income for the quarter. That's a thirty four thousand dollar increase from your previous quarter."

"You said something about our future as an Organization. What about our future?" Turk questioned.

Killah looked down at his 18 karat Yellow Gold Piaget Polo watch. "It's twelve twenty. Meet me back here at one forty five. That'll give us all a chance to have a good time before we get into all that. Chill cuz, relax, enjoy yourself. We're rich. Filthy!" He said with a grin and stood from the table. Everyone followed in order. Turk, Fu, Blue, Tasha and Lady all exited the booth. "What's up with you two.?" He asked Drea and Tika Bell. "Enjoy yourselves."

"I got a husband at home and I really don't feel like being bothered with no lame ass niggas. I got enough of that earlier." Drea said.

"What about you?"

"I'm chillen. I'll go out there in a few. You know how hard it is to have a good time with Blueburry thinking that he's everybody daddy." Tika Bell added.

"He ain't that bad is he?" He questioned with a smile.

"You know he is." She said and gave him a funny look. He started laughing and the whole room of three burst into laughter.

"Well I'll stick my head out in a minute to chaperone. I'm waiting for Ty, we have some business to discuss. Just avoid Blue." He said still smiling.

"Umm Hmm!" She sounded off with her lip turned up like he just put her on an impossible mission. She stood up and walked out of the door.

"So Drea what's up? How's the family?"

"Everybody's good. Me and my husband still have our moments. He still disagrees with my life style and really hates that I'm worth so much money. I mean he used to hustle but he never saw the type of money we see. He acts like it's my fault he was a petty ass nickel and dime hustler." She sighed.

"What about all of the businesses you set up for him. He's not satisfied. I know that I would love to have a strong beautiful black woman with both street and book sense with as much ambition as you have. And you're responsible and treat that nigga with much respect."

"I guess he appreciates it and he never disrespects me. I don't know Chris. Do you ever feel like..." Before she could finish a tall brown skinned man with long permed hair knocked on the booth's door.

"Excuse me for a minute Drea." Killah said as he stood to greet his friend at the door.

"Drea we gotta finish this conversation later." He said. She nodded in agreement then left the booth. "Ty Boogie! What's the deal Player?" He questioned as the two men embraced.

Ty was dressed in a white Giorgio Armani suit with a matching blue shirt and a pair of blue Donald J. Pliner shoes. Killah poured two drinks and they both took a seat.

"Chris Cameron. How's it going? I can't believe it's been three months already. You look good Play'ah so what's new?"

"Same shit different toilet. You know that this is my crew's fifth year as an organization. June told me that all I needed

was a five year run in the dope game. To be honest with you I got more than enough already in four."
"Speakin' of June, that cat called me last night. He called so late I didn't know who the fuck he was until half way through the conversation. He say he in a camp down Carolina somewhere. He say it's on an Air Force Base surrounded by the projects. Them cats got cell phones and everything down there. He gave me his number and told me to tell you to call him. If he don't answer leave a message."
"No need for that. I'll see him when he get out. Just make sure that his account stay's full and if he need to get something in there make sure it gets to him. Other than that we have no business contacting each other. He'll understand later. How's the club doing?"
"I can't complain. But what's this talk about you got more than enough already and June saying that all you need is a five year run I know you of all people not thinking about calling it quits." Ty questioned with a puzzled look on his face.
"Honestly Homey I am."
"Not you Hustlah. You love that shit too much." Ty smiled. "For real some times I think that's all you love."
Killah smiled. He mummed over his next words. His friend was right, that's really all he did love. The hustle, the power, the money, the respect but more than all of that, he loved the fear that came with the respect. He loved the way people would bitch up when he became angry. He remembered his mother's words; *Respect is not something' you buy it's somethin' you earn. That's all you need Chris is respect. Fuck ah friend. Who needs 'em? Earn your respect son and you'll feel like you got all the friends in the world.* And that's exactly what he had done, earned respect by any means, but he felt that he had milked

the game for all that it was worth. "Let me ask you a question Ace. What's the main reason most people hustle?"
"To get money."
"And I did that. We did that. You know the difference between me and a lot of these other so called hustlers? I made sure that my whole entire crew was full up, from the bottom to the top so I could never go broke. Plus I earned a lot of respect in these streets. I never played fifty with no one. I always kept it one hundred either I fucked with you or fucked over you no in between. I was hard but I was always fair."
"I feel you cuz."

"I know you heard the saying; When you're up there's only one way to go and that's down. It doesn't make sense to me to have hustled all these years, literally putting my life on the line everyday to die or get life in prison and never truly enjoy the fruits of my labor. I want to be able to sit back with my family that I have been neglecting since I had one. I wanna be able to relax without worrying when and if the FEDS are going to run up on me. Sort of like how you feel. You feel me? I got a real estate investment company, three laundry mats, my dealers license with a small car lot. I have a successful law firm plus Tehran got two hair salons and a massage parlor, not to mention my food trucks and eighteen wheelers. I was also thinking about buying the old Sports Authority building and turning it into a night club.
I got well over eight figures in my Swiss account plus I got close to ten million dollars worth of cars and those are just my personal ones. I'm set for life. I asked you the reason most people hustle and you said money. Well I'm not like most people because I have more than enough money. I hustle for the adrenalin rush. It's my way of getting high. I love beating the system. I love how the jealous ones envy.

How they can't stand me but act like they like me because they know that I'll touch them or have them touched. I love the respect these scared cats show. I love making people feel good. But don't none of that shit love me back and for real Ace I'm just getting tired. Tired of the senseless murders, the long hours, the constant headaches that come from having to keep all of the addicts that I deal with happy. This boy is a whole lot different than that girl. You can't deny a dope fiend his fix like you can a coke head because it ain't no telling what they might do when they sick."

"You make good sense homey and you've reached a point in your career where you can afford to call it quits. To be real with you, I'm happy for you. I love to see a young black cat get money and make it out of the game Scott free. What does the rest of the crew think?"

"I haven't talked to them yet. It really doesn't matter though. I'm out whether they agree or not. Turk can run the Organization, bump Fu up to my spot if he still wants to hustle and move on from there."

"What about Ali's father? You know that he will more than likely want you to buy your way out."

"I was thinking about offering him ten mill plus work but I'mma let him make an offer first."

"So you dead ass serious?"

"I'm for real Ace. This is it."

The room fell silent as the two friends studied one another. Moments later the entire club went into a frenzy as a sea of gunfire hailed throughout the club. Killah and Ty stood at the glass window of the V.I.P booth to get a look at the melee.

Bodies were trampled in what looked like a stampede. People were literally fighting for their lives in attempt to make it out of the front door. Turk, Blue, Tasha and Lady were all in the middle of the crowd firing rounds and carrying on like their normal selves while Fu, Drea and Tika Bell played the back ground with their guns drawn posing as a second line of defense. A few minutes later the shots ceased.

Drea swung open the door to the V.I.P. booth, "Come on let's go!" She said and grabbed Killah by the arm.

They made their way through the front entrance that led them back to the parking lot. "Yo meet me at Tika Bell house tomorrow morning around nine o' clock." Killah said and the entire crew jumped in their whips and peeled out.

Killah drove out to his twelve million dollar home that he, Turk, his wife and daughter shared out Bay Colony in Virginia Beach, located on what seemed like a small Island with captivating water views. The house was gorgeous. Twelve bedrooms, five bathrooms, two elevators, two pools, a tennis court, indoor and out door basketball courts, a movie theater and a boat dock.

Turk pulled up to the gated entry shortly after Killah walked inside. He checked the surveillance camera's monitor to make sure that it was her. She walked inside of the house and found her cousin in the living room.

"What's up cuz, you alright?" He questioned.

"I'm good." She answered as she removed her Prada sneakers and flopped on the couch as if she was exhausted.

"What was that all about?"

"Honestly I don't know. You would have to ask your stick man Blue since he always seems to be the center of confrontation."

"That figures. You staying here tonight, or are you going to your suite?"

"I'm home for the night. I'm tired."

"Well I'll get you up in the morning."

Killah pulled out his cell phone and called all of his people to see if they made it home safely. Turk called all of her people as well and everyone was secure in the comforts of their own homes. Everyone except Blue.

"What's the deal Ace? Where you at?" Killah asked voicing his concern.

"I-Hop."

"With who?"

"This broad I met at the club earlier."

"Nigga are you crazy.? Why the fuck are you not at home? Do you know the kind of trouble you might have created. And you out with somebody who was there? What the fuck is wrong with you?" He asked now voicing his anger.

"Ain't shit wrong wit' me and I am just a little crazy. Besides shorty was gone when that shit jumped off. She don't know shit, I bagged her early. And how the fuck you know I started it?" Blue questioned getting defensive.

"Because I know you. For real Ace that shit is irrelevant. I'm worried about your safety. That bitch you out with don't give a fuck about you."

"And I don't give a fuck about her."

"Listen Blue stop thinking with your dick long enough to use your brain."

"Listen Ace, I'm cool. I'm about to take shorty to my little spot out the Beach, knock 'er back loose and send her on her way. I'm not about to let some bullshit as drama wit' some pussy ass nigga stop me from doin' me. I had to merk them niggas homey. I'll explain everything to you in the morning. Trust me you'll understand."

"All I'm asking you to do is think. Think about the people who will die and kill for you."

"I'm thinking. Right now I'm thinking' about knockin' this bad ass red bitch off." He laughed.

"You just don't get it fam. I promise that these women will be the death of you. I'll talk to you in the morning. Be safe cousin." He said and hung up. He took the front lobby elevator to his room and joined his wife in bed.

Tehran was a complete beauty. A traffic stopper who caught the attention of every male and most females that she came in contact with. She was only five foot but had a face and a body like Halle Berry, with Stacy Dash eyes and Megan Good lips. "How was your meeting?" She asked still half asleep. "Something came up so I didn't get a chance to have it. I put it off until nine in the morning."

"What came up?"

"Nothing major. Go back to sleep. I'm tired." He said and kissed her on the forehead.

"Chris I'll be glad when this shit is over. You never have time for me. Your daughter will be seventeen and graduating from High School next year and you haven't spent any time with her since Turk came home five years ago. The two of you been runnin' the streets like ya'll trynna take over the world every since." She said dejectedly.

"Listen my only job as man of this house is to provide for and protect my family. You live in a twelve million dollar house, got a closet full of designer clothes and keep the most expensive foods in your mouth, seven days a week, twenty four hours a day, three hundred sixty five days a year and three hundred sixty six in a leap year. So what are you complaining about."

"Time Chris. When was the last time we been out together? When was the last time you took your daughter out? That's what the fuck I'm complaining about."

"Listen, I got twelve months left of this life then I'm out. If you decide to get your act together and stay with me then we can spend all the time in the world together. If you want to leave, get the fuck on. Carry your ass back out Carrot Park for all I care. Complaining about time. I barely have time for myself."

"That's how you feel?"
"Look Tee-Tee. Right now I can't be seen in public with you or Diamond. These cats would love to snatch either one of you and toss you in a trunk wrapped in duct tape and hold you for ransom. And I'm in a game where I can't afford to show no weakness, so I don't try to get attached to nothing or no one that I can't afford to lose."
"You know what Chris? That's the dumbest shit I've ever heard. Do you love your daughter?"
"If I didn't, you wouldn't be here. Twelve months then it's over alright. Now I'm tired, I got a lot of shit on my mind and I have to get up early in the morning." He said and placed another soft kiss on her forehead.
Tehran removed herself from the bed and walked to her daughter's room. Diamond was sitting on her bed conversing with her Aunt who posed more as a best friend than an authority figure. She was the splitting image of her mother, with her father's complexion and her Aunt Turk's body. Diamond and Turk were drinking Patron mixed with Remy Red while watching "Set It Off" on DVD when her mother walked in.
"Hey Turk. I didn't know you were here. What cha'll doin'?"
"Nothin', watching this old ass movie that your daughter seems to love while we drink the night away." Turk said and took a big gulp of her drink.
"Turk what I tell you about getting my child drunk."
"Don't come in here wit' that bullshit Tee-Tee. This girl got more ass than you. I'm grown and she's far from a child. You was doing a whole lot more than just gettin' drunk when you were sixteen, so miss me with that bullshit." She said and waved her hand in her sister's face as if to dismiss her.
"Just pass me the bottle so I can pour me a drink. You and yo' black ass cousin get on my fuckin' nerves." She said and mixed herself a drink.

"What my daddy do now?" Diamond questioned. She was once considered a daddy's girl but the lack of time that Killah spent with her forced her to out grow that role. Tehran sipped her drink to measure it's strength. "I'm just tired of him not spending any time with us."
Turk laughed. "You mean to tell me that you got a man that you've been with for seventeen years, who is a multi millionaire, doesn't cheat and never put his hands on you and you complainin' about time. If I was with a nigga that long I wouldn't give a fuck if he never came home. Just keep the doe comin' in." She laughed again causing her niece to laugh.
"Well we got more than enough money and I don't know if he's cheating or not."
"It really shouldn't matter. He ain't got no more kids and he ain't never gave yo' ass no disease. So what if he get a little pussy or head every now and then. You ain't paid a bill in your life and we all know that yo' little red ass done cheated."
Tehran caught every word that her sister spoke and agreed that she made a lot of sense. Most women would be satisfied and to an extent she was. She only began complaining about time after her secret lover mysteriously disappeared. "Well he claims that he's through hustlin' in twelve months. If not I'm leavin'. Just let me keep my cars, clothes, jewelry, and my shops, buy me a little house for my daughter and I'm good." She said and swallowed down the rest of her drink.
Turk gave Tehran a hateful look. She sat her drink down on the dresser, jumped off the bed, grabbed her sister by the neck and began choking her. "Bitch you trynna fuck up my business? You ungrateful bitch." She shouted.
While the three females carried on in Diamond's room, Killah was tossing and turning in his sleep.

"Momma somebody stole my money."
"What choo tellin' me for? I ain't take it."
" I know! Otis took it."
"Well if you know Otis took it, why did you say somebody stole your money?"
"I don't know."
"Look boy I gave you a gun and told ju how to use it and when to use it, so don't run to me. Go handle your business." Lil Chris looked up at his mother with fear written all over his face. Don't sit there with that scared ass look on yo' face. Go do what I told ju." She said and smacked him in the back of his head. She snorted the remaining contents of her bag of dope and leaned over on the couch.
Lil Chris hated when his mother was high. He went to retrieve his gun from his room. He walked up on Otis while he was asleep and shot him between the eyes. He rummaged through his father's pockets where he found $30 a bag of weed and two bags of herion. He placed the contents of his search in his pocket and walked out of the room. He kept the weed and flushed the two bags of heroin down the toilet. When he turned to exit the bathroom Ms. Dot was standing in the doorway. "What choo doin'? Get out of these clothes and take a shower so I can call the police and report the accident. And what did ju just flush down the toilet?"

Killah awoke from his dream once he heard the commotion. He jumped out of the bed and headed down one flight of stairs to his daughter's floor. He entered her room and found Turk on top of his wife and his daughter on her bed watching television. He grabbed Turk with one arm and flung her across the room. "What the fuck is wrong with ya'll? I'm trying to sleep and you two stupid ass bitches in here fighting in front of my daughter. Tehran get up and get your ass back in bed." He said pointing towards the door. Tehran picked herself up off the floor and headed back to her room. "Turk I'll see you in the morning."

"Naw you can see me now. What's this shit about choo leavin' the game in twelve months?" She asked as she approached her cousin.

"Turk I'll see you in the morning." He said and walked out of the room.

Later that morning he woke up around five thirty. He went upstairs to Turk's room to wake her. Surprisingly she wasn't there. He walked into the surveillance room to check the monitors. There were three surveillance rooms located in the mansion. One on the first floor, one on Killah's floor and another on Turk's floor. Each room as well as the front and rear gate had a camera. After a thorough investigation he realized that Turk was no where in sight. He noticed on the front gate's monitor that her black on black with suede leather interior and burr walnut wood trim Aston Martin Vanquish was missing. "Man where the fuck is this bitch at?" He questioned his self. He finished getting dressed and dialed her number on his way out of the door. No answer. He dialed the number to the Marriott at Waterside. "Suite Twelve please."

"Ms. Cameron didn't come in last night but I can forward your call any how if you want to be sure."

"No thank you." He said and hung up. He walked outside and climbed in his Midnight Blue Maybach and rode out. Killah drove out to a large house in Georgetown. A handsome black male in his early fifties was leaving as Killah walked to the front door. "Good morning Doctor Andrews, is my Aunt awake?"

"Yeah son. She's in the kitchen. How are you doing Chris?"

"I'm good Doc. I could be better but I could be a whole lot worse."

"Turquoise was here when I woke up. She must've left while I was getting dressed. Maybe five minutes ago."

"Oh yeah? I figured that this is where she would be. I was hoping I would catch her. I'll just see her later. I'mma run in and chat with my Aunt Gina for a few. You good?"

"Yeah I'm good son. On my way to work. Everyone can't be as successful and rich as you are." He responded with a smile.

"Well I'm about to retire. Maybe I can lay up with my family like you do."

"That'll be good son. Even though I never agreed with your method of living in the first place, you always been a very responsible and respectful young man. Quit while you're ahead son. Your Aunt loves you and thinks the world of you. Any how whatever you decide, you have our support. I gotta run so I'll catch you later." Doctor Andrews said as he walked away, jumped in his Lexus LS 430 and drove off. Aunt Gina was out of the kitchen and in the living room when her nephew walked in. "Now I know something is wrong. No wonder we've been having all this nice weather in the middle of Winter. First I wake up and find Turk sleep in the guest room now you show up. What's going on Christopher" She asked. Aunt Gina had aged considerably well. She even lost a few pounds and looked better at fifty than she did at thirty five.

"Nothing's up. I just stopped by to see you." He said as he gave his Aunt a hug and kissed her on the cheek. He took a seat on the couch. "Isaac Jr in school?" He asked looking around. The living room had a plain set up. Pictures of Turk's and Killah's prom and graduation along with plaques and medals from Turk's basket ball and track days aligned the wall. Turk won the state in the 100 and 200 meters and was an All State point guard for three years in a row.

"Yeah. Turquoise dropped him off." She answered joining Killah on the couch. "Now what's the real reason you stopped by. Turk seemed to be a little upset with you. Said that you were acting funny."

Killah rubbed his chin. He grabbed his Aunt by the hands and looked into her eyes. "Turk is upset because I'm through with selling drugs at the end of this year."

"And what made you come to this conclusion?"

"Just tired Aunt Gina. That's all. I feel like I've done enough. The only things my mother ever asked of me I accomplished. I remember like yesterday when I was twelve years old, she said the only things she ask of me is that I always stand up for myself, get my own money, never fuck a man and never snitch. That's crazy ain't it? She didn't say anything about graduating from high school or getting a college degree. I did both and I got my own money and I'll die before I fuck a man or snitch on somebody. Now it's time for me to enjoy myself. I never wanted to be this heartless mother fucker that kills people at the drop of a dime or pays someone to kill. I was cool just being little Chris but for some reason my mother seemed to have a better plan for my life."

"Your mother meant well Chris. The life's lessons that she taught were beneficial. She taught you how to survive and make it out of the Park the only way she knew how. A whole lot of mutha fuckas that graduated from college are still stuck out the Projects or living with their parents either strung out on drugs, broke as shit or both. But look at you. You're educated and rich. You may not have gotten there through your major but you got there and believe it or not your mother God Bless Her Soul, my sister had everything to do with your success. She wanted nothing but the best for you. I remember when Turk first started chasin' behind that friend of yours Ali. Dot was so happy to see her getting her own money, that she wrote you telling you everything. You remember?"

Killah stared at her like she was crazy. "My mother never wrote me."

"She did write you 'cause she gave the letter to that crazy ass wife of yours to mail to you. She told me because she called and asked a million and one questions about Turk after she wrote it." She said positive that her sister wrote the letter.

Killah rubbed his chin again. He searched his Aunt's eyes. From what he could see she was telling the truth. Killah stood up from the couch. "Aunt Gina I have a meeting to get to. I have to break the Good yet unfortunate news about my retirement to the rest of my family."

"Well son you do what choo gotta do. You don't owe your friends or Turquoise's black ass a damn thing. If they haven't saved enough money by now their useless and all they're gonna keep comin' up with is reasons why they don't have as much money as you do. I wish you could talk some sense into Turk." She said as she glanced at the pictures on the wall. "I remember when all I had to worry about was her getting suspended from school for beating up some body's child, now she has already done five years in prison for murder and that girl shows no signs of slowing down. She has a son that she hasn't seen since he was born and he lives right around the corner from here. I pray for her but she's always been like this. You know that's who Dot tried to mold you after?'

"Don't remind me. I'll see you later." He kissed Aunt Gina on her cheek and walked out of the door. He jumped back in his whip and drove around the corner. It was there that he spotted Turk's car parked in front of a large brick house. Killah walked to the front door and rung the bell.

Moments later a petite mahogany brown complexioned woman in her late forties answered the door.
"Hello Christopher." She said inviting him in.
"How are you doing Ms. Melissa?" He asked as he accepted her invitation to come inside. He observed the scene. As soon as he noticed Turk noticing him she removed herself from the couch and headed toward the front door.
"Excuse me Melissa but I have to make a run. Thanks for the information." She said and brushed pass Killah on her way out of the door.
"Don't forget about The Meeting." He said to an ignoring Turk. She continued to approach her vehicle, jumped in and sped off.
Killah turned his attention back towards the beautiful woman that was in front of him. "Ms. Melissa what did Turquoise want?"
"She stopped by and asked for Osamas' contacts. She said that she needed to get in touch with him about some important business."
"Did you give it to her?"
"Well I called him and asked him if it was okay. They talked for a few minutes and I believe that he eventually gave her the information that she was looking for."
"Damn." He responded dejectedly. "How's little Ali doing in school.? I haven't talked to him in a few weeks. I've been real busy." He asked changing the subject.
"He's still making straight A's. Is everything all right? She questioned sensing that something was wrong judging by the tone of Turk's conversation with Osama and the response Killah made after he learned that Turk had contacted him.
"Yeah I'm good. Here, give this to Ali, tell him I stopped by and said keep up the good work." He reached in his pocket,

handed Ms. Melissa a $100 bill, gave her a hug and headed out the door.
"I will. You be safe Christopher. It was nice seeing you again." Ms. Melissa stood outside long enough to watch him drive away in his luxury automobile then she walked back inside.
Killah looked at his watch and noticed that it was a quarter 'till nine. It would take him roughly all of that to make it to Tika Bell's house in time. He put his foot on the gas and raced down Campostella Road, across the Campostella Bridge and made a right. He cut through Chesterfield Heights and entered Middle Towne through the back way. He pulled up in front of Tika Bell's house with only two minutes to spare. He surveyed the driveway and noticed that everyone's vehicle was parked out front except for Turk's and Lady's. He suspected that Turk wouldn't show and figured that Lady more than likely rode with Tasha. He exited his vehicle, walked to the front door, inserted his key and walked inside of the house.
The entire committee was in order except for Turk at the kitchen table. They all rose as he took his seat. "Turk probably won't be joining us this morning. I'll collect her fine money the next time I see her." He instructed.
"She called already and told us that you planned The Meeting to inform us that this was our last year as a family." Drea said.
"I know that ain't the reason you got me up at nine 'ah clock in the A.M. on my day off." Blue said.
"Actually it is. And since it's already out in the open and ya'll had time to think about it, do we have any objections?"
"What about us? What the fuck we s'pose to do?" Tasha asked.
"If any of you want to continue doing business then I nominate Fu as my replacement. Fu you can pick your

Captain and invite someone into the family that can be trusted. Don't accept no one that has not went through a thorough background search and initiation. Drea your entire crew is still in order. Turk has all of the contacts to the connects so everything can continue to progress without skipping a beat. Now I feel like we all should have enough money to call it quits. I understand that this has been our entire lives for the last four years, so it will be hard to walk away from. I will have no ill feelings towards anyone who wants to stay or anyone who wants to join me in retirement. Now is the time to decide." He said eyeing everyone at the table.

Fu spoke first. "To tell you the truth Ace, I've been feeling the same way that you feel. I'm wit' choo. I'mma just stack extra hard this last year and call it quits myself."

"I'm with ya'll." Drea added.

"Me too." Said Tika Bell

"All ya'll trippin'. This is my life. I'mma hustle 'till they bury me." Tasha said.

"No bullshit." Blue chipped in.

"Lady what about you?" Killah asked.

"You know me. I'm rollin' wit' Turk." She said.

"Well it's settled. Blue you can have my position, select two people to replace Fu and Tika Bell and push on, or select either Tasha or Lady as Captain and let Turk handle the rest. With that said; What took place last night at the club?"

While the C.O.C were having their meeting, a meeting via telephone was also being conducted.

"Yo Homes what's up? You know Boo died too?"

"What?"

"Yeah cuz. They pronounced him dead at eight 'ah clock this morning'"

"Man I told that nigga to chill and not approach them C. O. C mu fuckas on no bullshit."

"He said you told him to get up under one of they hoes. He tried but I guess one of them bitches recognized him because I saw how they grouped up when he was talkin' to that bitch Tika Bell. That pussy ass nigga Blue walked up on Boo while he was talkin' to shorty. They exchanged words for a minute then Blue stole 'em so my brother walked up behind Blue and popped the shit out of that nigga, then that big bitch Lady shot my brother
in the back of the head. All them niggas had guns. Blue saw Boo creepin' through the crowd and that's when he hit 'em four times in the back."
"Damn my nigga. We gotta merk these niggas now. If we come up on some loot off 'em that's cool, if not oh well. I want them niggas dead."
"K.O. listen. Them niggas killed my brother. You know I want them niggas dead but we ain't cold blooded killah's like them. But if you ready to join Boo and my brother Gotti fuck it. Let's do it."
"So how you wanna handle this?"
"I was gone call the police." He answered like he was proud.
"Tae you out cho mu fuckin' mind?" K.O. asked.
"Hell naw but you are if you think I'm trynna go out like that."
"Nigga listen to yo' self. This some street shit and we gone handle it in the streets. As many niggas we done robbed we can't go to no police."
"So you think because we rob, the police don't want murderers off the street. Shiitt cuz we might got warrants and this shit might spare us."

"That ain't what I said. Listen I'll get back wit' choo but we definitely goin' at these niggas and not through no police niether." K.O. said and hung up.

Blue looked at Tika Bell, then at Tasha, then turned towards Killah. "You remember Boo?"
"Little cat from Ballentine that used to hang with Kurk?"
"Yeah him. Anyway word is him and his lil' weak ass crew came up wit' this brilliant idea to rob us."
"And where did you get this information?"
"The streets talk but it really don't matter. I saw him hollerin' at Tika Bell when Tasha pointed him out and said that she saw him grillin' ya'll down the mall earlier. So I stepped to the nigga and hollered at him." He said and flashed back to the episode that took place at the club....
"What's up broke ass Boo? Ain't found no body to rob lately?" Blue asked with a grin showing his two platinum teeth. The diamonds around his neck and wrist nearly blinded Boo.
"What choo talkin' 'bout Blue? I'm out chillen, I ain't on that bullshit." He said in his defense.
"Yeah well you can find somebody else to chill wit' cause she ain't interested." Blue said stepping in between the two.
"Shorty why the fuck you wanna ruin a good night. I ain't come here on no bull shit, so why you trippin'?"
"Cause word on the street is that you and that bitch ass nigga K.O. and Kurk plan on robbin' me and my fam. You know what they say; Once you tell one person your secret, it ain't a secret no more. Now get the fuck on."
Boo had guilt written all over his face like the cat who swallowed the canary. "Fuck you nigga." He said seconds before Blue punched him in the mouth. Boo stumbled to the ground and his partner Gotti stole Blue in the back of the neck. No soon as the punch landed Lady blew a baseball size

hole in the back of his head. Blue shook off the punch just in time to spot Boo scrambling for the exit. He charged behind him with his gun blazing. Turk and Tasha were also in hot pursuit. Boo took four shots to his upper torso and fell to the ground, as the scared party goers screamed and scrambled desperately to make it out of the club alive…..

"I ain't wanna kill the nigga in the club like that but he had to get it."

"You know everybody that roll with them clowns don't you?" Killah asked.

"Every last one." Blue responded.

"Well I'll call Uzi and Tank, put a hit on all of them. We'll stay on vacation until they're all dead. When the job is complete we will return Back To Business and continue getting this money. Like I told ya'll in the club, we will be leaving the day after tomorrow. I called Charter Auction to check on the Jet and everything is in order. Now all I gotta do is catch up with Turk and we good to go. With that said I'll see you all Sunday. Any questions?" No one said a word. They all just shook their heads from side to side to say no. "In that case this meeting is adjourned.

CHAPTER SIX   Back To Business Heartless

The C.O.C. spent the New Year the same way that they spent New Year's for the last four years, on vacation, together and out of the State of Virginia. Uzi contacted Killah after only two days to inform him that the job was complete but they still decided to stay an extra week in Casa Tres Lobos to allow the City of Norfolk to calm down. Even though Uzi and Tank were experienced contract killers who never left a mess Killah wanted to let the situation blow over, plus he had a situation back home to deal with that he needed some time to think over.

The entire crew returned to the City with money on their minds. Turk began to put a few things in motion in preparation for her career without Killah and Drea while her crew was off for three months. Killah was on another mission in itself. He had a couple of days before his return to the streets. That was just enough time to find what he was looking for. He stayed up all day and all night in search of this important piece of mail. Buried in a box underneath some old photos, he found what he was looking for. He opened the letter that was post dated December 10, 1987 and read intensely.

Christopher,

I'm writing to inform you that I received everyone of your letters. I'm very proud of the man that you're becoming. I'm also happy to know that you have been continuing your education and plan on going back to school when you get out and graduating on time. You are very wise for your age. Use the sense that God gave you and turn it into a profit.

Son I never wrote you or came to visit because I wanted you to experience your time in jail without any support from your family so that you can appreciate your life more when you come home. Now you know how it feels to be alone with no family support and it sounds like you are handling it well. With these valuable lessons learned I suspect that you will never return to prison for anything foolish. Make everything that you do from this day on be for a reason and money motivated.

Chris I know that I haven't been the type of mother that you can be proud of and I'm sure that you may not agree with some of the methods that I used to raise you, but I'm raising you to be a strong, independent black man. Understand that this world ain't gone give you shit and it's sad to say because they enslaved us for so long but the truth is the way I understand the truth is that the world don't owe you shit so don't look for no handouts. I've come to live with the fact that I'm a heroin addict. That's pretty much what my life has come to. Understand that not once did I allow my habit to keep me from feeding you, clothing you or keeping a roof over your head. I know if I don't kick soon that this dope will more that likely claim me. At least I'll die high and happy. I know it's not funny but it's reality. Maybe when you come home you'll make a lot of money and get your mother out of this Park finally.

Dee-Dee and June ask about you all the time and they can't wait for you to come home. You know that Tehran had a beautiful baby girl last July. She turned one a few months ago and she is truly adorable. Diamond Cash Cameron, I call her Lil Dot. She's chocolate just like you. When you come home you have to get money so that you can provide for your daughter. Don't turn out like the man you killed; Your father. Your friend Ali drops money off for you all the time. It'll be here when you get home. I don't

know what Turquoise is in to yet but I'll find out. All I know is that the girl is running around with new clothes and jewelry like she done hit the Virginia Lottery. Whatever it is you need to find out and get with her because she has heart and is determined not to let anything stand in her way of getting what she wants. You could learn a lot from her. I don't know what to say about her sister. This little bitch thinks that she is God's gift to the world. I don't see what you see in that pretty red bitch anyway. But she's your problem. Your only obligation is to provide for your daughter and look after Turk. You don't owe that bitch Tehran a pot to piss in or a window to throw it out of. But like I said that's your problem. I love you son and I'll see you when you get home. As you can see I've been reading the dictionary and working on my speech. It's not perfect but it's a whole lot better than it was when you were home. It's important that you learn how to talk and think like the white man because believe it or not they have a lot of power. I also have a few pointers that you can use to make money. I'll share them with you later.
Love always Your Mother- Dot.

Killah closed the letter and placed it in his pants pocket. He sat still for a moment allowing the words from his mother to sink in. He collected his thoughts then yelled for his wife. "T-E-E- T-E-E." He screamed knowing damn well that she couldn't hear him in that big ass mansion. He boarded the elevator adjacent to the basement and rode it to the third floor.

Tehran was in the Master Bedroom completely naked. She was preparing to get in the shower when Killah swung open the bedroom door like a raging bull. "What the fuck is this?" He asked holding the letter up to her face.

"I don't know. What's wrong with you?" She asked scared shitless. Killah held the letter back from her face far enough so that she could read the names on the envelope. She looked closely at the names on the front of the envelope, then searched her husband's eyes. Killah had the eyes of a deranged serial killer. The expression on his face frightened her more. She swallowed hard then spoke. "Where did you find that? I looked all over for it but couldn't find it." She said lying.

"It doesn't make a difference where I found it. You should've mailed it to me when you were supposed to." He said and mushed her in the face.

Tehran pushed his hand down. She stumbled a few steps back before gathering herself. "You know what Chris, I said that I misplaced the letter, I apologize. I don't know what the fuck was in the letter but I don't have time for you puttin' yo' hands on me. It's too late, so if you will excuse me I'm going to take a shower so I can get to bed."

"You got time for whatever the fuck I say you got time for and you ain't going no where until I say so. I spent the last sixteen years thinking that my mother died without once taking the time to write me when the whole time your lazy ass not only didn't mail the letter to me, you never even mentioned the fact that she wrote."

"Chris I was seventeen years old. I was into so much different shit when I was a teenager. I placed the letter in my pocket book and forgot about it. You know how hard it is being a teenage single moth…."

Killah cut her off mid sentence. "Yeah I bet you forgot about it, the same way you forgot about me while I was locked up and don't keep using Diamond as an excuse." He shook his head as he grew angrier. " I don't see what the fuck I saw in you either. My mother was right."

"What? Youn't see what the fuck you see in me? Baby you trippin' for real now but since you on the subject of your mother. When she was alive you acted like you couldn't stand her and hated her for overdosing on hair-ron. Then you go and take the same dope that killed your mother and sell it to the rest of the world and separate yourself from me and your daughter. I guess you wanna kill off the rest of the world huh?" She said getting in his face.

Killah balled up his fist and punched his wife in the mouth drawing blood. "Fuck the world. The world ain't never gave me shit. Everything I got or ever had I had to hustle for it. Most of this shit was to provide for my so called family when in all actuality Turk is the only family I've really had since I went to jail and if you wouldn't've never had Diamond I would have left your stupid ass long before I came home. And don't ever talk about my mother bitch. My mother died happy because she died doing what the fuck she wanted to do. I like what she said in the letter she wrote that took me sixteen years to get. I don't owe you shit and I don't owe the world shit either." He argued and stormed out of the room slamming the door behind him.

Tehran sat on the bed with her head down between her hands. "Man I'm so tired of this nigga!" She yelled out loud to an empty room.

Killah took the elevator downstairs to the garage. He walked outside to the drive way and hopped in his Maybach. He drove to Norfolk and rode around in circles out Tidewater Park where he once lived with his mother, until he finally decided to drive out to Tika Bell's house. He opened the door, walked over to the sofa, removed his Mauris and stretched out. He grabbed the remote control from off the table and turned on the television.

Tika Bell heard the sound from the Tv. And walked downstairs. She noticed her friend sprawled across the couch. "Hello Mister Chris. What did I tell you about poppin' up over here? One day I'mma have a man in here." She said with her beautiful smile exposed and her hands on her hips.

"Yeah one day after we retire. Until then you are not about to show no nigga where you lay your head at and you know it."

"I know that's right. So what brings you by this time of night or should I say early in the morning?" She asked as she plopped down on the couch in front of him.

"It's a long story. I'll tell you about it in the morning."

"You okay?"

"Yeah I'm good. I was born for adversity."

"Guess who I saw today."

"Who?"

"Ms. Debra."

"Ms. Debra? Oh Dee-Dee's mama. Oh yeah? How is she doing?"

"She's doing good. She not too long ago got married. She told me that Carl got knocked by the feds."

"I heard about that. He down the jail right?"

"I didn't ask all that. She gave me her number and said for you to call her sometime. She said that she hasn't seen you in nine years since you killed her son."

"She said it like that?"

"She know that it was an accident and she still loves you."

"I'll call her tomorrow. I'm tired right now. I gotta get with Fu early tomorrow so we can get ready for Sunday. It's time to get Back To Business."

"Well get some rest and I'll see you tomorrow but don't fall asleep on my couch, I got five guest rooms that you can sleep in."

"And what if I want to sleep in your room?"

"The door is always open. Good night!" She said with a smile and kissed him on the cheek.

Killah laid still for a moment thinking about his friend Dee-Dee. His mind wandered back nine years ago to the day he was killed...

"Yo Killah I told ju to get them niggas at the light. That was ah easy lick and you let them pussy ass niggas get away." Dee-Dee said from the passenger seat as Killah pulled his Benz up to the basketball court in the back of Tidewater Park. The two friends exited the vehicle. "Man them niggas just scored and you let them get out Da Park. The fuck wrong wit' choo man?" He questioned rubbing his nose.
The two young adults were high as a kite and drunk as a skunk. They spent the entire day together smoking weed, snorting heroin, drinking cheap bottles of Banana Red Mad Dogg 20/20, while searching for someone to rob. "We'll get them niggas Stick. Chill!" Killah said.
"Chill? Them niggas was probably loaded down with bread and you talkin' 'bout chill." Dee-Dee said now standing toe to toe with Killah.
June was leaning against the fence that surrounded the basketball court watching his two side kicks go at it when he interrupted. "What the fuck ya'll niggas arguing about now."
"This nigga Killah slippin'. We had them pussy ass niggas and he let 'em get away." He said and pushed Killah. Killah pushed him back causing Dee-Dee to fall down. June jumped between the two.
"Let who get away?" He asked.
"Madd Dog and them man. We had them niggas." Dee-Dee said and pulled out a .357. He started waving it while he talked. "All this nigga had to do was ride up on them niggas at the light and I would've done the rest, but this so called Killah always got ah better plan."
"Yo cuz chill with that mother fucking gun." Killah said knocking the gun down towards the ground but not out of Dee-Dee's possession. The two became tangled and started tussling.

"Ya'll niggas better chill before somebody get…." POW."
Before June could finish his sentence the gun went off and Dee-Dee fell to the ground clutching his stomach.
"Dee-Dee. Dee-Dee." Killah called as he kneeled down beside his friend." He turned to face June." We gotta get 'em to a hospital."

Killah remembered. He remained still on the sofa trapped in time. He remembered how Dee-Dee stayed on life support for twelve days before finally dying on Halloween. He remembered how he vowed to never get high off any type of drug again or condone any of the people close to him to abuse drugs. He thought about how Ms. Debra spared him from doing any jail time. How Dee-Dee begged from his death bed for his mother to prevent anything bad from happening to his little stick man behind this terrible accident. He shook his head from side to side bringing his attention back to the present. He turned off the television, put his shoes back on and headed upstairs to the bathroom. He splashed some cold water on his face and washed his hands. He left the restroom and went to join Tika Bell in the bed. He removed his shoes, pulled back the covers and climbed in. "Shorty you need to put some clothes on." He said looking at her naked body.
"Excuse me but I do believe that this is my room and my bed, and I sleep naked Boo. I live by myself so I don't feel the need to sleep with clothes on. If you don't like it you know what you can do. It ain't like you ain't never seen it before." She said poking her rear end out towards him. "When you came upstairs I started thinking about Dee-Dee and how he died."
"I was out there that night remember. You can't dwell on that. That's in the past. Pay your respects to him and his mother and move on." She said turning to face him. She put

her arms around him and pressed her vagina against his jeans. "You still be having night mares?" She questioned. Killah stared his best friend in her beautiful eyes. Tika Bell had eyes the color of honey. "Almost every night. Man I can't believe it's been nine years. I should've been gotten in touch with Ms. Debra."
"You wanna talk about it?"
"Not tonight, I'm tired. You know I'm going to tell you everything anyway." He said with a smile. Tika Bell and Turk were the only two people that he shared everything with.
"Well you can't sleep in here with all them clothes on."
"Why not?"
"My bed, my rules."
Killah laughed at his friend before removing his Polo jeans. "You happy now?" He questioned.
"No! Keep going." She said gesturing towards his Polo shirt and boxers.
"What you want me to strip?"
"That'll be nice." She smiled.
Killah removed the rest of his clothes and snuggled close to Tika Bell. "What about now?" He asked. He couldn't prevent his manhood from growing rock hard.
Tika Bell smiled a devilish grin then grabbed his penis." All this for me?"
"Girl I'm a married man."
"We best friends remember? I know everything about you." She said and leaned her head down towards his crotch. She placed his manhood in her mouth. She began sucking and slurping uncontrollably. Tika Bell was stroking with her left hand while her right hand played with his genitals. Killah controlled the back of her head causing her to take the muscle deeper and deeper into her mouth. The deeper he went inside of her mouth the more he became excited. She could sense his excitement and began working even harder

forcing him to ejaculate. The taste of his pre-cum excited her even more causing her to suck harder. She sucked harder and harder until she received all of the sperm out of the head and swallowed. Tika Bell stroked and grinded Killah until he became erect for the second time. She straddle him and began bucking like a wild horse. Even though he was enjoying the ride of his life, Killah preferred being in control so he turned her over on her back and delivered the hammer from the missionary position. He placed her legs on his shoulders and began driving with force.
"Oh Killah! Oh Killah! Kill this pussy! Kill this pussy Chris. Take it harder. Harder Killah!" She moaned as she threw it back. He continued to pound away like he was trying to drill a deeper hole. Tika Bell continued to throw it back and take it like a trooper. "Take it from the back Chris." She moaned. He watched her toned body as she rolled over onto her hands and knees and poked her ass out. Killah slid inside of her wet vagina from behind, and picked up right where he left off. He continued pounding her soft box with brute force. "Damn this shit good. Killah! Killah! Killah! Killah!!!" She moaned his name at least twelve times before she climaxed. Shortly after he ejaculated a second dose of sperm inside of her wetness. Tika Bell collapsed and rolled over. The sex was a whole lot better than it was when they were teenagers. Killah examined how beautiful her body was when soaked in sweat. How her six packed abs formed every time she exhaled. She kissed him on the cheek and dosed off clutching him tightly.

Killah rose from his sleep at his usual time. He showered, got dressed and headed out of the door to meet up with Fu. He dialed his number as soon as he entered his car. "What's up Ace? I'm on my way to the spot." He said and without a response from Fu they both hung up. Killah drove out to the spot in Pinewood and waited for Fu to arrive.

Fu drove up approximately twenty five minutes after Killah. He walked into the apartment where he found his friend sitting at the dining room table jotting down some numbers. "What's up Ace? What cha doing?" He asked slapping his partner five.

"Trying to get these figures together. I'mma call Osama to give him twelve months notice. See how much he is going to charge a nigga to retire."

"Shiitt. He shouldn't charge nothing. All the money we made him plus Turk gone keep it moving so it ain't like he about to take a loss. The only reason niggas should buy they way out the game is when they plan on cutting off that connects' life line. He still gone have the keys to the Seven Cities."

"You know what Ace? You make a good ass point. I'll still give the cat at least two mill'. Never know when we might need him again. Feel me?"

"I guess you right. Just let me know what's up."

"Okay bet. Let's ride out. I gotta stop pass Ali's mother's house to make this call." He said as he opened the door. "It's Back To Business tomorrow baby. Your first day back on the grind in almost four months. You know cats going to be thirsty too. I know it hasn't been shit but garbage on the street since we went on vacation." He said as they walked through the parking lot. "Let's take you car."

The two friends hopped in Fu's 2002 Cadillac Seville DTS. Fu wasn't big on buying expensive cars like his mentor and the majority of the crew, he had one Bentley that he hardly ever drove.

He cruised towards Georgetown while Killah reclined in the passenger seat. "Yo Killah I been meaning to ask you this for that longest time Ace. How do you speak so proper all the time?" Fu asked breaking the silence.

Killah laughed. "I guess because I practiced it so much. I always try to pronounce every syllable in every word in case I have to use it one day. I learned a lot in my Public Speaking class at State, (Norfolk State University) but practice makes perfect. I like to think of it as sounding professional."

"It's something I always wanted to work on. I really need to work on it now that I have to become corporate."

"It'll come to you little homey."

"Man I had a ball on vacation." Fu said changing the subject. "Did you see Tika Bell in that two piece? Shorty always had a body but she look like she been puttin' in some extra hours in the gym. If I didn't have a girl and we wasn't a family I'd wife shorty. Youn't never try'n hit that again?"

Killah gave Fu an awkward look. He just finished blowing her back out less than six hours ago and now all of a sudden his partner becomes inquisitive.

The question caught him completely off guard. *I know Tika didn't put our business out.* He thought. He took another second to respond. "Me and Tika are best friends. When I had sex with her I was sixteen and she was fourteen and we only did it once then. We've been tight every since plus I'm married."

"Bad as she is and the way she be clinging and catering to you, I 'on't know. Like Biggie said; "She gotta body make ah nigga wanna eat that I'm fuckin' wit' cha." He said with a laugh.

"Shiitt in that case Tasha bad as a mother fucker, Drea look good and Lady ain't bad looking."

"Yeah Tasha crazy as a mu fucka, Drea married and Lady gay as a bitch and don't none of them show you the kind of affection that Tika Bell show you so you can save that best friend shit for Tee-Tee 'cause I know if she throw that pussy at you you'll take it."

"I can't say."

"I said it for you."
"Yo Ace, what's all this talk about Tika Bell all of a sudden?" Kiliah asked agitated.
"Oh ain't shit homey. I was just sayin' that she's ah bad mu fucka."
"Like that's some new shit. All of the women in the C.O.C bad." He responded as Fu continued to drive.
Fu pulled up to Ms. Melissa's house and parked. They both went inside. Killah went in the back to call Osama while Fu sat in the living room playing Mortal Kombat with Lil Ali. "Hey Boss…….. I'm calling to announce my retirement on one years notice…. Turk will continue to run the operation along with half of the crew… No Sir. Things will continue to proceed as usual…. I want to know how much you are going to charge me to call it quits….. Thank you sir… I have twelve left. Send me two hundred and sixty three and I'll contact you when it's complete. I also want to send you an extra two million as a token of my appreciation…. I understand sir but I insist…. I will sir…. Thank you." Killah ended his conversation. The entire conversation was spoken in Arabic. Killah had Ali to teach him how to speak and write Arabic while he was still alive. Osama was very understanding of his retirement although in his Country they believe in hustling until the day you die the same way Ali did. He told him that he thought of him as a son and that he appreciates all of the money that he made him. He also said that he wouldn't charge him anything to retire as long as he still had a way to get rid of his normal supply in that area. He told him to tell Turk to call him and that he only would accept the two million dollars because Killah insisted.
Killah turned towards Ali's mother. "Thanks Ms. Melissa." He said then called for his nephew as he walked towards the front door. "Ali come here."

Lil' Ali came walking towards the front door. Shorty looked as if his father spit him out.

He didn't carry any of his mother's features. "Listen nephew, I gotta go on an important trip with my job and I may not see you again until this time next year. You be easy on your grandmother and when I come back I'mma come and get you; Okay?"

Lil' Ali nodded in agreement. He was almost thirteen years old and understood exactly what it was that his uncle Chris was in to. Killah gave him a pound and walked out of the door followed closely by Fu. As soon as they entered the car Killah's phone rang. "Yo." He answered.

"What time you want to get together tonight?"

"Around eight. What's up?" He questioned but the line went dead.

"Yo who was that?" Fu questioned.

"Turk but I guess that she's still mad. Oh well. She'll get over it and if not fuck it." Killah said as Fu continued to drive back towards Norfolk.

Turk sat up on the bed in her hotel suite smoking a blunt. Drugs were prohibited by law of the C.O.C. but Turk was into breaking all of the rules lately. She disconnected Killah and dialed Drea's number. Drea answered on the second ring after checking the caller I. D. "Hey girl."

"Chris said eight ah clock." Was all Turk said before hanging up. She was at odds with everyone who planned to follow her cousin and drop out of the family. She dialed Lady's number. "What's up girl? Where you at?"

"Over Toinette's house." Lady answered as she held Toinette's head between her legs with one hand and her cell phone in the other. "Why what's up?"

"I got some business we need to discuss. Meet me at your house in an hour."

"Is it important?"
"Very!"
"I'll be there." She answered and they both hung up. Lady leaned her head back on the bed, dropped her phone and placed her other hand on the back of Toinette's head and held it there until she climaxed. Toinette crawled up Lady's body until they were face to face.
She placed her tongue inside of Lady's mouth and the two women were stuck in a long passionate kiss. Lady palmed Toinette's ass and tickled her clit while their lips continued to lock.
"You about to leave?" Toinette asked as she pulled away long enough to look into Lady's eyes which were now a light blue.
"Yeah I gotta take care of some business. You need somethin' while I'm out?"
"Something to eat. And bring us a man back. I want some dick tonight."
Lady sat up, leaned over the side of the bed and picked up her Prada jeans. She reached in her pocket and handed Toinette two $20 bills. "Order somethin' to eat because I might take a minute and I don't feel like bein' bothered with no nigga tonight. But if you want one I'll bring one home for you." She said and began getting dressed.
"I want one for both of us. I like watchin' you wit' 'em too."
"Not tonight. Maybe tomorrow. I met this fine ass nigga at the club before I went out of town. I'll call him tomorrow."
"Well I guess I gotta wait 'till tomorrow." She responded with a puppy dog face.
"I'll bring somebody back tonight." She said knowing damn well that she had no intention on returning herself.
"You gone fuck 'em?"

"We'll see. I'm out." She said. Lady kissed Toinette on the lips and headed out of the door. She jumped in her black Lexus LX 470 and headed towards her house.

Lady walked inside of the house and found Turk sitting on the couch with a disturbed look on her face. "What's up girl?"

"What if I tell you that I might got a plan to keep our crew in tact? You gone be down wit' it?"

"What is it?" Lady questioned.

Turk smiled and began to explain her master plan.

"Chris what's up?"

"What's up? You sound like something is bothering you."

"Where are you?"

"Riding down Military Highway. What's wrong?"

"We need to talk about your cousin. Meet me some where."

"Meet me at the spot."

"Okay. I'm on my way." Drea said as she drove her SC 430 from her Burbage Grant neighborhood towards Norfolk. She pulled up to the spot a little more than an hour later. She opened the door and greeted Fu with a hug.

"What's up Drea?"

"Nothing much baby brah." She responded and took a seat next to Killah on the couch. Fu took a seat on the opposite end of the couch, picked up his Playstation controller and un paused the game.

"So what's on your mind?" Killah asked.

"Has Turkn been acting funny to you?"

"Every since she found out that I was retiring."

"Well she act like she has an attitude with me too. I'm ready to call it quits right now. I 'on't think that I can make it another year with her attitude."

"Shorty we gotta maintain. Osama is sending me two hundred and sixty three bricks. We got twelve left. After these two hundred and seventy five we can call it quits. We pumping out twenty five to thirty a month so if we can maintain at least twenty eight bricks a month we can be finished in a little less than ten months. Which means that you and your crew would only have to work four."

"I'm wit' it as long as Turk can remain focused. If she begin to affect the way we conduct business I'm out. I'm only doing this for you."

"Well I certainly do appreciate it. I'll talk to Turk." He ensured.

The three of them continued to sit on the couch playing the game and killing time until eight o' clock arrived.

Turk concluded her little private meeting with Lady around a quarter to eight. She arrived at the spot out Pinewood a little after eight thirty.

Killah was furious. "Shorty we need to talk."

"I don't know if you noticed or not but I haven't been in a talkin' mood lately. Now how much dope do ya'll need for tomorrow so we can hurry up and get this shit over." She said dismissing his conversation, she turned her back toward him and walked to the closet. Her actions enraged Killah. He followed her, grabbed her by the shoulder, spun her around causing her to face him then grabbed her by the collar. He could smell the good green all over her breath and clothes. "You high?" He questioned.

Turk grabbed Killah by the arm and pushed him. "Look, I let choo get away with throwin' me across the room when I was chokin' the shit out of your wife. We not about to make this puttin' yo' hands on me shit no habit. Next time I'mma leave yo' black ass stinkin'. I'm grown and if I wanna smoke weed I can. You wouldn't even have this connect if it wasn't for me. Ali would probably still be here spoon feedin' yo' dumb ass. The only reason Osama reached out to you was 'cause of me. I killed the people who killed Ali so he is forever in debt to ME! I put choo on remember? And it ain't like we ah family no more anyway."

"Listen cuz we are going to always be family. We still have to conduct ourselves like we've been doing the past four years. We don't have time for you to be on no new shit."

"Is we gone cut this shit or what. I ain't got time for no fuckin' lectures. I raised yo' punk ass not the other way around. Now how much dope ya'll need?"

"Yo Turk just get a brick out the closet. I ain't got time for you and Killah bullshit tonight. I'm trying to get this over with so I can get home." Fu said agitated.

"Fuck you nigga. You ain't apart of this original family in the first place you coward mu fucka."

"Listen Turk you chill the fuck out and Fu you're way out of line. Turk get the brick out of the closet and lets get this shit done so we can get back to business tomorrow. I don't know what the fuck you're on but you need to be off that shit before tomorrow. We got a lot of boy to move in the next year and I need you to be able to function properly. Plus you are going to have to lead the Organization by yourself once I retire and I'm going to be the first to tell you that with you, Tasha, Lady, and Blue's attitude you won't make it."

Turk reached inside of the closet and removed an individually wrapped kilo of heroin. "First of all Chris, who asked you what the fuck you think and if I don't make it, I'll die in these streets like a real gangsta' bitch. Remember if you ain't got nothin' to die for you ain't got nothin' to live for. Your mother taught us that."

"Turk I'll get with you when we're alone, right now we got work to do." He said as he removed four blenders, shifters, some Banita and some Quinine from the cabinet. Turk pulled out the playing cards and plates, then she and Drea joined Killah and Fu in the kitchen.

It took the four of them almost two hours to cut the entire brick. They cleaned up their mess and prepared to leave. Drea picked up her cell phone and called Lady while Fu called Blue to inform them that it was time to bag up and prepare for the day. The four of them grabbed their belongings and headed for their cars. Fu and Drea left to drop the work off to Blue, Tasha, Tika Bell and Lady while Killah and Turk stood in the parking lot conversing.
"Yo, cuz I talked to Osama and he wants you to call him. I told him about my retirement and that you will continue to run the Organization without me."
"I already spoke to Osama."
"Turk we can't go a whole year like this. I really don't see why you are so upset in the first place, but we have to work this shit out. I love you cuz and we got to continue getting this money together while we still can. The only two people my mother really taught me to love was myself and you. I will always be there for you even though you just threatened to kill me a few hours ago." He said with a smile. Turk smiled herself. "Well if you can't see why I'm upset then there's' no need for me to try to explain. But you don't have to worry about me causing any more problems. If you want to retire and walk away from all this tax free money then that's on you. More money for me. But let me ask you this. How big of a part did my sister play in your decision to retire?"
"A big part. But me and Tee-Tee are not seeing eye to eye at the moment. But I do believe that if it wasn't for her and Diamond then I wouldn't give a fuck."
"That's what I thought. There's no love lost fam'lay." Turk said and gave her cousin a hug. They both jumped in their vehicles and headed their separate ways.
Fu and Drea pulled up to a spot out Crown Point about twenty minutes later. (Crown Point was a quiet

neighborhood composed of nice apartments and town houses located about three blocks away from Military Circle Mall.) They walked inside of the town house and found Blue, Tasha, Tika Bell and Lady sitting at the kitchen table already in position. Little baggies, sandwich bags, and small capsules covered the table.

Fu sat the key of Boy on the table. "It's ah whole thing. Hit me when ya'll ready." Fu said. The four of them nodded that they understood and got down to business.

CHAPTER SEVEN Oh Boy
Heartless

Blue followed the same path that Tasha took in reverse. Instead of starting in Berkley and ending out Olde Huntersville, he would start out Old Huntersville and finish in Berkley. Tika Bell covered the North Side and West End in the same order that Lady did. After they both completed their drops they too met each other out The Park.
Blue parked his Royal Blue 2003 Lamborghini Murcie-lago, with red and white stitched leather seats on the corner of Holt St. He stepped out of the $230,000 dollar vehicle and adjusted his Cartier frames so that he could get a better look at the two males that were walking in his direction. It took only a brief second before he figured out who they were and called the tallest of the two. "Yo Worm." He yelled and took a seat on the hood of his car. He checked the time on his iced out Cartier wrist watch and waited for the two young men to join him.
"Blueburry! What's the deal daddy?" The shorter of the two asked. He held out his fist and Blue touched it with his fist.
"Ain't shit Popcorn. What's the business?" He asked and touched fists with Worm.
Worm and Popcorn were two of Blue's workers. They were both from Tidewater Park and had been nothing but loyal to Blue since day one.
Worm was sort of tall, dark skinned, with a rugged looking afro and bug eyes. He earned the nickname "Worm" from his ability to rebound a basketball like the great Dennis Rodman.
Popcorn was short, and dark with a head full of waves. Both men were paper chasers who strayed away from violence.

Worm was a year older than Popcorn but appeared to be at least ten years wiser.

"What's up Worm? I got five extra bundles. You think you can move it?" Blue asked.

"Yeah we can handle that." Worm answered.

Blue stood up from off his hood. He let the doors up, placed the key in the ignition and turned the radio station to 102.9. He turned the volume up to 15, then back down to 9, then up to 12. He quickly removed the key from the ignition and a small stash box opened up on the drivers side door close to the floor. He grabbed the five bundles from the box and closed it. He let the doors down and handed the five bundles to Worm. "Just give me a hundred and twenty five dollars off this."

"I got that for you now." Worm said and removed a knot from his pocket. He peeled of two fifties, a twenty and a five dollar bill and handed them to Blue.

Blue placed the money inside his pocket. "You know I'm 'bout to take over this empire, so ya'll niggas need to step up your game 'cause I'm lookin' for two young thorough breads to step up under me." Blue said as he sat back down on his hood like it was a throne.

"What's up wit' Killah?" Worm asked.

"Him and Fu got some other shit they tryin'na put together so they steppin' aside and puttin' me in charge while they go legit."

"It look like you in charge already. Brand new Lambo, given away bundles for twenty five. What's really good?" Popcorn added.

Blue smiled. "This ain't shit. In twelve months it's goin' down for real, so ya'll niggas better be ready. I'm doin' all my recruiting out Da Park. I ain't fuckin' wit' no outsiders." Blue said. His words astonished the two young hustlers.

They both contemplated before speaking. Simultaneously they both said, "I'll let choo know what's up tonight." touched fist again and walked into a house on the corner of Holt St. across the street from where Killah grew up.

Blue pulled out his cell phone and dialed Tika Bell's number. "Yo shorty, where you at?" I got some shit I need to take care of." He said discontentedly.

"I just got in The Park Blueburry. I'll be there in a second." "Well hurry up." He yelled and hung up.

Tika Bell drove up in her Benz truck less than one minute later. They discussed exactly who had what in case something happened to one of them, the other one would know what to collect and from whom. This was pretty much the crews' reason for meeting up out The Park every morning that they put work out on the streets. They both agreed upon a time to meet up to begin collecting the money before they parted ways.

Worm and Popcorn sat inside the house on the corner of Holt St. in complete silence. They were both thinking long and hard about Blue's offer while bagging up an ounce of boy to go on the block with the extra five bundles that Blue gave them.

Popcorn put the last of the boy in a small black baggie with a white God Father symbol on both sides of the bag and dropped it in a sandwich bag along with the rest of his half and placed it in his underwear. He looked up at Worm who had long been finished. "You ready fam'?" He questioned.

"I been ready." He answered. "A you think that nigga Blue serious?"

"I 'o'nt know. He act like it."

"You know that nigga joke and play so much you never can tell. Some'm just don't seem right to me though." Worm said and stood up to hit the block with the boy. Worm needed some knowledge and he would soon receive it. Popcorn rose to his feet and followed Worm out the door. As soon as they stepped outside an older modeled Pearl White on White Cadillac Coupe Deville with shiny white wall tires, drove up and parked. A tall clean cut older cat in his late fifties exited the vehicle.

He approached the two young men. "Let me get two bundles Shawdy." He spoke with his deep southern drawl. He fixed his glasses on his face, reached in his pocket, removed two hundred dollar bills and handed them to Worm. Popcorn gave the customer the two bundles and shook his hand.

"What's up Fast? We ain't seen you 'round here in ah few months. "Worm spoke."

"Yeah I know mann. I got this broad over Hampton and you know I got ah crib over there. I been sendin' her out to score all the dope lately, while I lay back in the house. It's nice over there too mann. It's a few ruff spots like Norfolk but as a whole it ain't nothing' like this raggedy mutha fucka mann." Fast said.

Fast was a true O. G. (Original Gangster). A true hustler from the old school, another one of Norfolk's many ex-Kingpins turned dope snifers. Fast moved major heroin from the early seventies through the mid eighties. He caught a 35 year fed beef (420 months), in 1986 and did 14 years 7 months under the old law which was sixty five percent with Parole. Fast was now considered a very wise man, with an old school game and plenty of knowledge. A lot of young hustlers turned to him for advice.

Worm was one of those young hustlers. He valued Fast's opinion like a poor man valued gold. Worm leaned on the front of his burgundy on burgundy Mazda MPV. "Fast what choo think about Killah and his crew?" Fast tilted his glasses. He leaned against the van next to Worm. "What exactly do you mean mann. I known them youngens a long time. I use to catch Blue cuttin' school, make him get in my car and drop him off in the front of Ruffner. Now I don't know if he went in the front door and came out the back but I made sure he got there." Fast laughed. "That's my nigga mann. When I came home last year he bought me the Deville and Killah gave me one of his houses."

"You ain't heard nothin' about them niggas?"
"Shawdy what exactly is you askin' me? Is these niggas snitchin'? Is that what you tryin'na find out?"
"Yeah. Blue said somethin' about takin' over Killah and Turk's business and he wants me and Popcorn to team up with him, but somethin' don't seem right about that."
"Honestly if I were you I wouldn't do it. The best way to stay is on the block. Them niggas movin' way too fast for two younges like ya'll. Now I'm not sayin' that they working with the police because I haven't heard that they were working but realistically it would be hard to believe that at least one of them isn't working because some shit you just can't get away with. These niggas ridin' around in half ah million dollar cars, killin' folks and shit and not one of them has been arrested since they started gettin' major paper. All these niggas in the city fallin' and they still standin' and they the real major playas. The heavy hitters. I just realistically don't see that as possible in a small city like Norfolk. When I was movin' all that boy in the seven'dees, I had the Norfolk police on pay roll, Portsmouth, Da Beach, Chesapeake and the Mayor of Norfolk were all on my team but when the feds came none of them could help me. You can buy your way out of the State but the feds don't want nothin' but they time mann and these niggas is definitely fed material. I shol' hope them niggas ain't police because I fuck wit' all of them, know their parents and everything mann, but I don't

fuck wit' no police so if they are I gotta cut'em off. I don't think they are though mann, but you never can be too sure. My partner's son set me and his father up so I don't put nothin' past nobody mann, but if I were ya'll I would keep doin' shit the way ya'll doin' it. If it ain't broke don't fix it because if they ain't workin' they buildin' one hell of ah case.

Look at this. Say you in a room wit' a bitch and the ho say that she a virgin. Would ju rather that bitch tell you no or take it slow?"

"Take it slow." Worm answered.

"There you go. Take it slow baby. Ah slow grind is better than no grind." Fast said and stood up to leave. "Well Shawdy I gotta roll. I'mma go hit this old broad off wit' this dope dick." He laughed and walked to his car. He held one of the bundles of heroin up to his nose. "Oh Boy!" He said with a smile, jumped in his car and pulled off. The two friends were cracking up in laughter at Fast's last comment. Popcorn looked at Worm. "Man, that old nigga Fast crazy Ace. If Blue for real we gotta get this paper wit' 'em." He said between laughter.

"Shitt! Fast got plenty of sense and he right. I ain't fuckin' wit' it. Ah slow grind is better than no grind. I'm not about to walk in on another nigga conspiracy or another nigga beef. I ain't no dummy shorty I was raised by old heads."

"Well if he serious I gots to roll wit' 'em. Them niggas gettin' way too much paper on they level for me to turn down."

"That's yo decision Ace. I can only decide my future." Worm said. The two friends continued to sit on the block, pumping the boy while talking shit.

Blue sped down Princess Anne Rd. past Booker T. Washington High School when he noticed a green Navigator behind him that had been following him since the moment he drove out of Tidewater Park. He hurried through the traffic light at the corner of Princess Anne Rd. and Ballentine Blvd., as it turned red causing the Navigator to speed through the red light. Blue swung a quick right turn into the Feather N Fin parking lot and watched the Navigator drive past through his rear view mirror. Blue hopped out of his car and walked into the small boxed shaped chicken restaurant. The place was completely empty so he was able to walk right up to the cash register and place his order.

Moments later the door swung open and a heavy set, dark skinned male with cornrows approached Blue. "Yo what's up Paul?"

The sound of his government startled him. He turned quickly to see who it was that was so familiar with him. The look on Blue's face was as if he had seen a ghost. He smiled. "Yo what's the deal Kurk. I thought you was dead. I must be loosing it." He said and turned his attention back towards the cashier.

"Naw I ain't dead yet. I been layin' low but ya'll got the majority of my lil' crew. Only me'n K.O. left Baby."

"You got one thing right. You ain't dead YET! We'll get cha. You and K.O." Blue handed the cashier the money for his food and received his order. He turned to leave but ended up face to face with Kurk's Desert Eagle .44.

"Run yo mutha fuckin' pockets nigga. You must be loosin' it. Loosin' your fuckin' mind to show yo face in my hood. Kurk barked and slapped Blue senseless with his pistol.

The cashier screamed and ducked behind the cash register. Blue was dazed. His vision was slightly blurred as he stumbled up off the counter. "You finished? 'Cause I ain't givin' you ah bitch ass thing." Blue's eyes got big and a slight grin appeared across his face. "Do what the fuck you gotta do." Blue spat.

The sound of a .44 echoed through the small restaurant. Blood splattered everywhere. The cashier's screams turned into cries as she now feared for her own life.
"I ain't gone always be around to save yo pretty red ass. Now lets get the fuck out of here." A female's voice said as she turned to exit the place.
Blue stepped across Kurk's lifeless body. He looked down at him, removed his 10mm from the small of his back and fired two rounds into the dead man's head. "That's for slappin' me nigga. One down, one more to go." He said and walked into the parking lot. "I love you too Lady." Blue said being sarcastic and blew her a kiss as he jumped inside of his Lamborghini and skidded out. He grabbed his cell phone that was vibrating and spoke into the receiver. "Yo."
"You owe me one nigga. You lucky I was ridin' through and seen yo car and decided to stop and fuck wit' choo. You do know that nigga would'ah killed ju don't cha?" Lady asked.
"I 'on't know what the fuck that pussy ass nigga would'ah done and don't care 'cause he dead now." He said as if he were invincible. "Sike! Naw for real I know that nigga would'ah killed me that's why I'm glad ju showed up, now why the fuck you didn't kill that nigga before he slapped the shit out of me. The left side of my face hurt like ah bitch." Blue said stretching his jaw muscles.
"What evah nigga." She said laughing and hung up.
"Man I need some pussy." Blue said to his self. He opened his food and bit into his boneless chicken breast sandwich. "Tsss! Now my mu fuckin' food cold fuckin' wit' this clown ass nigga." He said as he drove around in search of a score. Twelve hours and two scores later it was time for Blue to collect and meet up with Tika Bell. Shatoya, his steady girlfriend for the past three years tapped him to alert him that it was time for him to get up.

Shatoya resembled the super model Vanna Black. Long black hair, smooth flawless walnut skin, firm breast and curvaceous hips. Her mother must have been a quarter because her daughter was definitely a dime. "Blueburry wake up. It's ten o'clock." She cooed in her sexy southern accent.

Blue rolled over, wiped the coal out of his eyes and strained to see the time displayed on the digital clock that rested on top of the dresser. He sat up to get dressed as he noticed that it was 10:00pm on the dot.

Shatoya was so punctual. Although Blue never asked her for much, anything that he did ask her to do, she did it and without argument. "You coming back tonight?" She questioned.

"Yeah I'll be back." Blue answered as he continued getting dressed. He walked into the bathroom to get his personal hygiene in order and headed towards the front door.

"Blue you comin' back?" Lil D questioned as Blue walked through the living room.

"Yeah I'll be back lil' man."

"Bring me some'n back."

"What choo want?"

"I 'on't know. Jus' some'n." He answered shyly.

"Yeah ah'ight." Blue responded, kissed Shatoya on the lips and headed out of the door.

    Blue contacted all of his runners and was ensured that the money was ready to be picked up by all of them. He went about collecting the money in the same manner that he dropped the work off. As he approached Tidewater Park to collect from Worm and Popcorn, he called Tika Bell on her cell phone. "Yo, you ready?"

"Yeah. Well almost. I just gotta wait for Freeze fat ass." She sighed.

"This fat nigga slow er' night. We might have to cut his fat ass loose and get somebody else to run Park Place."
Tika Bell laughed. "I know that's right….. Hold on here he come now." She said as Freeze approached the passenger side of her truck and climbed in.
"Here shorty. My baby momma came out here wit' her bullshit and threw me off schedule for a minute but all the work is gone and all of your money is here. I'll catch you tomorrow." He said, handed her the money and exited the vehicle before Tika Bell could respond. "Blue I'm back. I'm on my way now. You ready?" She said as she placed her phone back to her ear.
"Yeah. I just gotta holla at Worm and Popcorn for a minute but I'm already out the hood."
"Okay. I'll be there shortly." She said and drove towards the park.

Worm and Popcorn patiently waited for Blue to arrive. The two young men grinded all day until the ounce, plus the five bundles were complete and they counted $20,100 dollars. Shortly after they counted their daily earnings for the fourth time Blue knocked on the door. Worm cleared the money from the table while Popcorn went to answer the door.
"Who is it?" Popcorn asked holding his Tech. 9 tightly.
"Blue!"
Popcorn cracked the blinds and peeked out the window to make sure that it was in fact Blue who was knocking. Once it was confirmed, he opened the door and let him in.
Blue gave Popcorn five as he entered the house. "What's the deal shorty?" He asked Popcorn as he approached Worm and slapped him five. Worm removed $7,000 dollars from the twenty grand and handed it to Blue. Blue flipped through the stack of seventy, hundred dollar bills without actually counting it. "It feels about right." He said and placed

the money inside his pocket. "So what's up? Did ya'll two think about my offer?" He asked changing the subject to what he was still there for. Worm and Popcorn both nodded in agreement. "So what it is?" He asked then started rappin.
"Shiitt! In these times we gotta hustle
cuz our pockets be hurtin'
lil' niggas wanna get fronted from who got work
Is you ready for dat
you wan' rock da bus
let ah nigga know where dey at so ain't no stoppin' us
If you handle yo bin'ness right I'mma promote cho ass
you bitch out and tryn' kite I'mma come smoke yo ass
the bricks dat I'm givin' you dey tryin' blood ta get
the fiends be comin' to because dey love dis shit
so don't come wit' dat
No one buyin'
da shit is proof
ah nigga tried to rob me
nobody wuz comin' through
Snitches
I can't hav' dat
Bitches
I can't hav' dat
Riches
you can have dat jus' bring me my cash back
Look it's all gravy wit' me go 'head 'n shine
Dat's how ya' play it wit' me ya big time
All I want is da gees
wit' ah trunk full ah keys
ah Lamborghini on twenties you got some'n you can giv' me
Huh!
Niggas ain't doin' nuttin' for me fo' free
Why I put trust in you niggas
cuz ya'll be tryin'na run gee

But I 'on't like ta dream about gettin' no cheese
in da future wanna see my fuckin' pockets O-Dee
Up until den
ya'll gone keep thuggin' behind ah project buildin'
smokin' dat fire weed wit' da ghetto children
plottin' on a way dat you can make ah million
Lord."
Blue rapped the entire first verse off of Juveniles' 400 Degrees album, changing words as he saw fit. Worm smiled as Blue rapped.
Popcorn bobbed his head to the words as if he could feel them. "I'm wit' cha dog." He said and reached out his fist for a pound.
"So what's up wit' choo Worm?" Blue questioned.
"I'mma pass Ace. Keep doin' shit the way I been doin' it." Worm answered calmly. Blue stared at Worm coldly. Worm embraced the stare and returned it without blinking.
"What's the ice grill fo' Ace?" He questioned trying to decipher his friends look.
"Shiitt ain't no ice grill play'ah. That's yo' decision. If youn't wanna step up in life I can't make ya." He said and stood up. "I'll holla at cha'll niggas
in the A. M." Blue said, slapped Popcorn five and headed across the street.
Tika Bell was sitting at the table counting money when Blue walked in. He removed the seven grand that Worm gave him from his pocket and laid it on the table. He reached inside of his black Nike back pack and removed a large amount of money. "What choo come up wit'?" He asked in reference to the money she collected.
"Ah hundred and twenty six." She answered.
"Add seven grand to that. So that's ah hundred and thirty three." He said and wrote the figure down on a piece of paper. They divided up the remainder of the money to be

counted and came up with $112,000. Blue removed the $125, that Worm gave him for the five bundles and another $300, for the loose three bundles that he got rid of his self. He wrote down the new figure and added it to the other one. "So we got two hundred forty five thousand and twenty five dollars." He said and picked up his phone to call and inform Fu that they were ready.

Fu responded by saying that he was on his way. Blue and Tika Bell recounted the money again to make sure that they had the total correct.

Fu arrived at the spot in less than ten minutes. The three of them counted the money one last time then Fu called Killah. "I'm ready." He said then hung up.

Shortly after Fu ended his conversation, Killah pulled up. He pulled out his phone and dialed Fu's number. "I'm outside." He said.

Moments later Fu appeared with a book bag in his hand. Killah popped the trunk and Fu placed the bag inside. "It's two hundred forty five thousand, four hundred and twenty five, in the bag."

"Okay Ace. Let's ride." He said and drove out Pinewood. Fu jumped in his whip and followed.

Three months later............
Killah, Turk, Fu and Drea headed towards the apartment where the heroin was stashed to get prepared for Fu, Blue and Tika Bell's last day of the quarter. Things were pretty much back to normal throughout the C. O. C. Family as well as inside of the Cameron household. Turk made amends with everyone that she had confrontations with, including her sister. She announced that she no longer had any ill

feelings towards those who chose to retire and surprised them all with gifts.

"How much boy do you want me to get out?" Turk asked Fu as she unlocked the door and turned on the light.

"Let's put out fourteen hundred. It's our last day on the grind for another three months. My-as-well try to get rid of fifty." He responded with a smile.

The crew had really stepped their game up tremendously, pumping out an average of forty two ounces or (1,176 grams) a day through eighty-nine days and for a finale they were going for the big five-0. Fu and his crew were responsible for getting rid of a hundred and three keys and eight ounces in eighty nine days. These fifty ounces would push the total to a hundred four keys and twenty two ounces.

The next day the crew literally flooded the streets with boy. Blue kept Popcorn by his side in an attempt to show him the ropes. He had been showing him the drop spots and collection points for the past two months. Blue even convinced Popcorn to upgrade his whip from his 1998 Mazda MPV to a beige 2003 Land Rover Range Rover. Popcorn glided his new machine down Holt St. like he owned the road. He parked on the corner, climbed out, looked around, took a deep breath and walked towards Worm. "Yo what's the deal Ace?" He asked with his neck, ears and wrist glowing.

"You got it." Worm answered as the two friends embraced. "Blue put us on wit' two o's today and only wants back eleven for' em."

"Okay we can swing that. I see you stepped up your game play'ah. Don't move too fast hustl'ah. That's all I can tell ya."

Popcorn smiled. "Shiit this ain't nothin' fam'lay. I just picked this joint up this mornin'. They got another one just like it if you wanna go down tomorrow."
"Naw I'm good. I'm tryin'na stay below the radar."
"Look fam, we like brothers. If I shine you shine. I respect your decision not to join the team and I'm'ma make sure that you get all the boy you want for the lowest number. I'm not one of those niggas that plan to blow and forget about the hood. I'm'ma keep this shit poppin' just like Killah." He said and reached out to embrace his partner again.
"I can respect that homey. Real niggas do real things."
"Believe that. Now let's cut this shit up so we can get this money." Popcorn said and they both walked into the house.

Killah was across town in Virginia Beach at Kelly's Tavern outside of Pembroke Mall in a meeting with Ty. After the one sided shoot out, the State of Virginia forced Ty to close down Shadows. Now the families of the slain victims were suing him for negligence and the ATF wanted to know how the guns made it past security.
"I'm telling you Chris, this is a fucked up situation for everybody. I'm not worried about the club. You gave me more than enough money to handle
that. It's these fuckin' feds. They questioning all of my security, my staff and they are not going to stop until they make an arrest. We might have to sacrifice somebody to get them off me."
"Listen Ty. There's no need to panic. We can always find some young nigga from the Park, give him a few hundred grand, promise to keep money on his books and hold him and his family down while he do his bid. Get Pamela to work on his case and we can probably get him a deal for no more than fifteen years. We just got to find somebody with no criminal history. But before all that, let's see what the feds

know first then we can put our plan in motion. I never been in no shit like this so I don't know how they might handle it, but trust me when I tell you: No one will testify against us and get away with it. If they thought they could, someone would have been come forward. They still don't have any leads and that shit happened three months ago. Now you will probably lose the negligence suit, but both of the dudes that got killed that night mothers get high so you can more than likely settle out of court for less than a half a mil'. Don't worry cuzo. Everything is going to be alright." Killah ensured. Ty soaked in every word that his good friend spoke. "I guess you're right homey. We'll just see what happens." He said. Killah finished off the remainder of his glass of grape juice and stood up from the table. "You good? Because I got to meet with my travel agent at twelve o'clock."
Ty nodded in agreement and stood up to leave. Both men left a hundred dollar bill on the table for the waitress and headed out of the restaurant.
Killah drove to meet with his travel agent to discuss The Family's vacation to St. Tropes in four days. After all of his travel arrangements were situated he drove home to spend some quality time with his wife.

Tehran was enjoying her beautiful mansion all by herself. She had already taken a swim in the pool, soaked in the Jacuzzi and was now reclined outside of her bedroom on the third floor balcony over looking the Atlantic Ocean through her Christian Roth aviators. Tehran was taking sips of her homemade Courvoisier Strawberry Lemonade that she made out of strawberries, lemon wedges, fine sugar, L' Esprit Courvoisier, Triple Sec and club soda when her husband graced her with his presence.

Killah pulled up a seat next to his wife. He sat quietly beside her momentarily admiring her beauty. Killah knew that he loved Tehran and was sure that she loved him but he couldn't honestly say that they were ever in love. He placed his hand on her shoulder making her aware of his being there.
"You scared me." She said with a light giggle. "How long have you been out here?"
"It doesn't matter. Where's everybody at?"
"Diamond went out and I gave Tawanna the day off so I could be alone."'
"So if you gave Tawanna the day off , who do you expect to cook and clean?"
"It'll be alright 'till tomorrow. I needed some Tee-Tee time. What choo doin' home?"
"I did pay for this palace, didn't I?" He asked.
"You did." She answered agreeing with him.
"Well the King should be allowed to Bless his palace with his presence when he get's ready to." He spoke of his self in third person." Besides I missed my wife."
"Is that so?"
"Yes it is so and I got plans for us so throw on some slippers and let's take a ride."
"Some slippers? I gotta put on some clothes." She said dressed in only her zebra patterned reversible tie bottom two-piece top and bottom bikini by Sunsets Separates and her extremely short Roberto Cavalli shorts.
"Just put some slippers on. We're going to travel by water. Meet me at the boat dock in ten minutes." He said as he stood to leave. Tehran finished her drink while Killah went to his Yacht to prepare a quick yet tasteful meal of pan fried catfish with stewed okra and cornbread.
Killah's Yacht was truly magnificent. The 110' Motor Yacht was fully loaded with five large staterooms, seven and a half

marble bathrooms, formal dining room fully furnished with the latest electronics, large hydraulic garage enclosing two wave runners, a Jacuzzi on the fly bridge, on-deck master suite with private office, spacious twenty eight and a half inch beam, twenty one plus knot cruise plus crew for six and a $7.5 million dollar price tag.

Tehran arrived at the boat's dock in approximately eight minutes. When she arrived Killah was dressed in a black wife beater, a pair of black Ralph Lauren Polo trunks and some black leather Bally slippers.

"Let's ride captain." Killah said to his cousin Ricky Jr. who was posing as the ship's captain.

Ricky Jr. was the son of Killah's mother's oldest brother Ricky Sr.. Ricky Jr. was a square who had absolutely no knowledge of the streets at all. "All Aboard!" He shouted as he cranked up the engine on the powerful sea mansion and took to the ocean.

Killah sat Tehran down at the dining room table and served lunch. A slight smirk appeared across her face.

"Something funny?" Killah questioned.

"I'm impressed. I never knew a kill'ah had this in him." She said sarcastically. "Is this the beginning of something new?" She asked.

"Who knows? Just enjoy your meal. I have ten hours to spare so let's enjoy each other's company. Tomorrow isn't promised so let's live for the moment." Killah said as he and his wife prepared to have a candle lit meal.

After they both finished eating they gassed up the two wave runners and sped through the ocean like two kids at Christmas time with new toys. The married couple played in the deep blue sea for hours, before heading back to the Yacht.

"Let's jump in the Jacuzzi." Tehran whispered in Killah's ear as she allowed her Cavalli shorts to hit the ground. She removed her bikini top and bottom and climbed in the hot tub, ready to get her grown woman on. Killah followed suit and joined his other half in the Jacuzzi. He turned the jets up on the tub and pulled Tehran close to him. Tehran smiled before kissing her husband passionately. She wrapped her legs around his waist, grabbed his penis and inserted it into her tunnel of love. The married couple made slow intense love for what seemed like hours although it was more like twenty five minutes.

Killah looked up at Tehran after releasing all of his warm semen inside of her. "Let's go to the bed so we can stretch out." He said. Tehran removed herself from the Jacuzzi, wrapped a towel around her waist and sashayed towards the master suite. Killah killed the jets connected to the Jacuzzi and walked to the captain's office. "Ricky J., let's turn this baby around and head home." Killah instructed and turned to go join his wife in bed.

"Eye-yie Captain." Ricky Jr. said and prepared to swing the ship around.

Killah entered the master suite and found Tehran stretched out on the king sized bed with her legs spread wide open and three of her fingers deep inside of her vagina.

"What took you so long?" She moaned.

Killah smiled at the sight of his lovely wife lying in front of him pleasing herself. "You couldn't wait huh? Well big daddy here now so you can bring your little warm up routine to an end." He said and literally dove between her legs face first. He allowed his tongue to take over where her fingers left off. Killah tongue sexed Tehran's clitoris for a while before he allowed her to return the favor. Tehran took her husband's thick, black muscle deep into her mouth. She worked her jaw muscles like a pit bull in the midst of a brutal encounter. Tehran used a tight grip on the penis with her mouth while giving head. Her oral was so good that you really melted in her mouth and not in her hand, but Tehran considered herself too pretty of a woman to allow even her husband to ejaculate in her mouth. For real it took Killah over ten years to convince her to give head at all but you know what they say, once you start it's hard to stop and now she was beyond pro status. Tehran sucked all of Killah's juices to it's head then used her hand to cause the ejaculation. Killah and Tehran sexed each other on and off for roughly two hours and fifteen minutes.

Tehran climbed out of bed, walked into the bathroom to freshen up then headed into the kitchen. Fifteen minutes later she returned with two jerk turkey burgers with tropical salsa, potato wedges and two lemonades. She popped in a DVD and fed her husband his potato wedges while eating her food at the same time.

Killah and Tehran were enjoying each other's company so much that neither one of them even realized that the Yacht had come to a complete stop and they were parked at the boat dock where the trip started.

"Yo cuz I'm gone." Ricky Jr. announced after knocking on the door to the master suite. Killah looked at the clock on the wall." Damn I didn't even realize that we were home." He said as he gazed at Tehran. "Listen I might as well go and collect this money early. If you want we can ride to the Bahamas tonight and stay for two days. Finish enjoying each other."

Turk promised to take me out tonight, but if the offer still stands in the morning you got a deal."

I'm really in the mood to go tonight but I guess we can wait." Killah said as he locked up the Yacht and they headed into their mansion. Killah got dressed and took to the streets while Tehran showered and began to get ready for her night out on the town.

Killah called Fu and told him to start the collection process. Fu, in turn, reached out and touched Blue and Tika Bell in that order. He was surprised to hear that they were both en route to collect and would be getting back with him shortly. Fu called Killah to let him know what the deal was.
"Anywhere between thirty minutes to an hour." He informed.
"Okay. I'm'ma be laying out Mission College until everything is in order." Killah said and disconnected their conversation. Forty five minutes later Killah pulled up to the spot on Holt St. "I'm outside." He said as Fu answered his phone. Moments later Fu arrived as usual with his nap sack in his possession. He placed the bag in the trunk and closed it. "It's three hundred forty seven grand, two hundred in the bag." He said, walked to his Seville, climbed in and followed Killah across town.
Turk was on the phone with Tehran when Killah and Fu walked through the door. "Tee-Tee, Chris and Fu just walked through the door, let me count this money real quick so we can get out of here. Finish getting ready and I should be there in about two hours or so. Okay?"
"Okay girl." Tehran responded and hung up the phone. Killah, Turk, Fu and Drea all pulled up a chair at the dining room table and took a portion of the money to count. They counted the money by hand then used the money machines to recount it. Each time they came up with $347,200. Killah and Turk both took out their thirty percent of the income giving them $104,160, for the day. That left $138,880 to be split six ways. Fu took sixty percent of the $138,880 which equaled $83,328 to divide with his crew. He put $41,664 aside for him and $20,832 a piece for Blue and Tika Bell. Drea took the other forty percent which totaled $55,552, pocketed $27,776 and $13,888 a piece for Tasha and Lady.

The four of them stashed their money on their persons and headed out of the door. Killah turned out the lights and locked the door. "Listen we are leaving for St. Tropes Sunday morning." He said and turned his attention to Turk. "I hear that you are taking Tee-Tee out. Be safe." He warned. "Don't I always?" She responded and they all filed out.

CHAPTER EIGHT   Is That Cho Chick Heartless

"Hey Tee-Tee what's up girl? I'm pulling up now. You ready?" Turk asked as she drove through the main gate of their estate.

Tehran was in her bedroom in front of the mirror putting the finishing touches on her outfit. She wore a fabulous denim and linen Dolce and Gabbana dress with a pair of rhinestone trim Manolo Blahnik sandals. She put on her kite-shaped diamond earrings that were hand crafted in platinum by Michael Beaudry, her Michael Beaudry fancy pink, yellow, orange, and white diamond bracelet and her three stone diamond necklace. She admired herself before answering her sister. "Yeah I'm ready. I'm on my way downstairs now." She answered. Tehran hung up the phone, boarded the elevator and rode it to the first floor. She placed the palm of her right hand inside of the automatic door's activation box and the door opened. *"Good day Tee-Tee."* The voice automated system said as the door closed and Tehran walked outside. She approached the passenger side of Turk's Cream colored, with peanut butter leather interior, 2003 Ferrari Modena 360 coupe.

"You drive? Turk instructed and moved over to the passenger's seat.

Tehran walked around to the driver's side and climbed in. "You kills me like you always gotta be chauffeured around." She joked as she drove around the circular drive way. She pulled up to the main gate and recited her name. After the voice activation box recorded the waves of her voice the gate opened up and she drove through.

Turk reclined in the passenger seat. She pulled out her phone and dialed
Lady's number. "Lady what's up. You made it to the club yet?"
"Hell no. I had to whip this bitch Toinette's ass. I'm on my way though."
"What choo and her fighting for?"
"The bitch just aggravates me. She wanna go out with us and I told her that she couldn't tonight so she decides that she wants to show off so I beat her ass."
Turk couldn't help laughing. "Stay on point girl. I need you."
"I got cha. I'll be up there in a minute. You already there?"
"Naw. I'm just leaving my house."
"Okay. I'll see you up there. You got Tee-Tee wit' cha?"
"Yeah."
"Well I'm on my way." Lady said and they both hung up. She looked over at Toinette who was sitting on the couch holding her eye. "Shorty come get the door and you better not leave this fuckin' house. I'll be back later." She said and headed out of the door. Lady jumped in her Suburban and headed towards the club.

Killah laid across the bed with his face beaming in excitement as he witnessed Tika Bell swaying her hips seductively to R. Kelly's "Sex Me." Tika Bell gyrated her entire body wearing nothing but a pair of black Prada boots. Killah massaged his rock hard penis as his eyes followed her hips as if they were being hypnotized. Tika Bell crawled onto the bed like a Cheetah in the jungle. She pinned him down on the bed and placed her tongue inside of his mouth. The two remained locked in a long passionate kiss for what seemed like an eternity. Their lips finally unlocked and she slithered down his body like a snake but before she could engulf his manhood with her mouth, he picked her up and turned her around so that her ass rested right above his face. Killah placed his tongue deep inside of her wet vagina. He controlled her hips moving them slowly, in a circular motion, up and down on his tongue. Tika Bell moaned in ecstasy. She placed her middle and index fingers in her mouth and began sucking on them. Killah sucked and played with her clitoris so good that she began squirming like a fish. Tika Bell couldn't take it any longer. She needed something harder in her mouth than her two fingers. She leaned forward and put her lips around the huge muscle that stood at attention before her. She began sucking like a wild woman in search of her ultimate goal. They both sucked and licked each other in a sixty nine position until they finally exploded in each other's mouth.

Lady pulled up to the front of the Broadway Night Club and parked directly in front of the entrance. She took notice that Turk wasn't parked in her usual spot out front but thought that she saw her Ferrari parked on the back street. She walked inside the club and searched for her girlfriend. (And I don't mean that literally.) Lady spotted Tehran at the bar so she knew that Turk couldn't be too far away. She continued to survey the scene when she noticed Turk standing at the other end of the bar wearing an all black Gucci dress, with a matching Gucci bag draped across her shoulder and a pair of black Gucci sneakers on her feet. Lady moved in the direction of her partner but was cut off by a tall, handsome, well dressed brown skin man.

"What's good Miss Lady? You forgot about me, because I never received my call that I was promised last December.?" Lady blushed. She had been meaning to call him but never got around to it. For some reason she really wanted to get

with this guy even if it was only for one night. She looked him directly in his beautiful brownish green eyes and smiled. "Believe it or not I really want to get with you. If you will allow me to I promise I'll make it up to you. Let me buy you a drink."
"I bet you don't even remember my name."
"You ah gambler?"
"You got damn right!"
"Well bet something."
"Bet that drink."
"Kwame. Kwame Lee, and I'll take a double shot of Patron." She answered with a smile. Kwame smiled from ear to ear as he walked to the bar to order Lady's drink. "I'll be over there with my girl." Lady said pointing in the direction of Turk. Kwame nodded that he understood and Lady walked off.
"Hey girl." She greeted Turk with a hug. "Is everything in order?"
Turk looked as if her mind was in another world, but she wasn't high or drunk. She was completely focused on something or someone. Lady remembered that same look the night Ali was killed. "Yeah everything is in order." She answered without once taking her eyes off the figure that she was focused on. Moments later Kwame came over to where Turk and Lady were standing with two drinks in his hand.
"I didn't know what your friend was drinking so I got two double shots of Patron." He said and handed one drink to Lady and the other drink to Turk.
"Thank you." Turk responded and sat her drink down on the bar.
"Thanks Kwame. Let me kick it with my girl for a few then I'll have time for you." Lady said. Kwame agreed and went to mingle with the rest of the party goers.

Broadway was the king of the Tidewater Wednesday night, twenty five and older crowd. The club located in Norfolk off of Virginia Beach Blvd. was full beyond capacity.

Tehran received her drink from the bartender and walked over to join Turk and Lady. The stare that she received from her sister sent chills through her entire body. Tehran attributed the dreadful look to a possibility of her sister being under the influence so she brushed it off. Tehran guzzled down her entire drink in one swallow and sat the empty glass on the counter. "I'm going to shake my ass. Where ya'll gone be?" She asked.

"We gone be right here." Turk answered.

"Okay. Well keep your eyes on me." She said with a smile. Tehran swayed her hips to Memphis Bleek's, "Is That Yo Chick." and vanished into the crowd.

"Don't worry. I will." Turk responded to no one in general with an evil grin on her face while Lady laughed and sung along to the music.

(A couple of hours later....)

Turk and Lady remained stationed at the end of the bar. Turk kept her eyes glued to Tehran while Lady focused her attention on the front entrance and it's surroundings.

"Oh shit!" Lady screamed loud enough for Turk to hear her over the music.

"What's up?"

"There go Blueburry."

"Where?" She asked without removing her eyes from her sister.

"He just came through the door. He on his way over here now. Damn this nigga might get in our way."

"That won't happen. Besides you know Blue probably came looking for somebody to fuck."

Blue walked over to the end of the bar where the two women were standing. "What the fuck ya'll doin' layin' in the cuts."
"Same thing you doing." Turk answered.
"I doubt it. I came to find me a jump off to take home wit' me so I can fuck." He said. Blue turned towards Lady and laughed. "Shiitt you might be doin' what I'm doin' but Turk up to somethin' else." He said and pinched Lady on her cheek.
"Fuck you nigga." Lady barked.
"Trust me, if I get enough liquor in me I just might fuck you." He said and hugged on Lady playfully.
"Nigga get cho retarded ass off me."
"Yeah you right. You holdin' me up anyway." He said as he adjusted the collar on his Armani Exchange, four button up, short sleeve shirt. He looked down at his blue five time zones Jacob and Co. watch. "You know I like to time myself to see if my game still up to par. I gave myself ten minutes to scoop ah bitch and be out of here and I wasted almost five over here wit' cha'll. It was one o'nine when I walked in now it's one twelve so I got seven minutes to score. Now I gotta say anything and hope it work." He said and walked away.
Blue scanned the crowd until he located a victim. With only five minutes to spare he attacked. He walked up on a short, fine, sister that resembled Nia Long. He tapped her on the shoulder as she danced with a guy who was dressed like he could be in the Navy or some other branch of the Military. She turned to face the rude individual and found Blue standing close enough to steal her breath if he wanted to. One look at Blue draped in all of those diamonds almost caused her heart to melt. She had seen him on several different occasions, driving a different car each time or somewhere dressed in the finest designer clothes or

covered in the finest jewels, with a different black or Spanish sister by his side. Blue flashed her a smile. The guy that she was dancing with attempted to say something but Blue held his hand up in his face to cut him off. "Hold Play'ah. I ain't come to talk to you." He said dismissing anything that the guy might have had to say then turned his attention back towards the beautiful female.
"Not to be rude but my time is money and believe it or not I got a whole lot more money than I do time. All I want to know is if I can leave here with you right now. Tonight! Before you say no and miss out on a platinum opportunity let's go." He said and held out his hand.
Without realizing it she took Blue by the hand and prepared to walk off with a perfect stranger. "Wait a minute. I gotta tell my girl that I'm leavin'."
"Call her and leave a message. He said as he escorted his latest prize past Turk and Lady. "I'll get up wit' cha'll later." He smiled and kept it moving.
"That boy ain't shit." Lady said as she shook her head and smiled. She watched Blue as he moved quickly out of the door.
Blue was so busy trying to beat his time that he walked right by the short, stocky, light skinned fellow with thick cornrows. Blue let the doors up on his Lamborghini so that him and his new found lady friend could enter and drove off with the doors opened.

K.O. was feeling himself. He was talking big boy shit, while holding out a fist full of money, fronting for the crowd that was standing out front waiting to get in. He had missed Blue fly by him because he had his attention on the fine young lady's rotund apple bottom that stood in line directly in front of him. By the time his stick man asked, "Yo ain't that that nigga Blue?" Blue had already jumped in his whip and pulled off.

"Man fuck that nigga Blue. I'm out tryn'na find some pussy. He can die another day." He said with a smile still eyeing the young lady in front of him. K.O. was being closely followed by two new members of his crew.
Pat and Wayne were both new to the robbery business, but they were seasoned vets to the streets and murder game. The three of them walked inside of the club grilling everyone who made eye contact with them.
Lady laughed as she watched the three stick up boys enter the club wearing all black Willie Esco jean sets, with an air brushed picture of Kurk and the letters R. I. P on that back.
"What choo laughing at girl?" Turk questioned.
"These three clowns that just walked in the door. K. O., Pat and that young ass nigga Wayne."
Turk chuckled. "Fuck them clowns. We here on a mission." She responded still focused on what she had been focusing on for the last two and a half hours.
"Well we need to do what the fuck we came here to do before these niggas start actin' stupid."
Turk finally removed her eyes from Tehran but only for a brief second. She turned to Lady and said, "Okay. Let's do this" then headed towards the dance floor. She approached her sister who was sandwiched between two men dancing. She leaned close to her and whispered. "Let me use your phone."
Tehran reached inside of her tiny beaded Gucci bag in search of her cell phone but decided to give her the entire bag and continued to dance.
Turk removed her car keys from the bag and handed them to her sister. "I got some business to handle. I'm'ma step

outside for a second." She said and headed towards the front exit. She stopped past the bouncer at the front desk to inform her that she would be standing out front and would be returning shortly. Lady moved to the opposite end of the club. She stepped to an extremely dark, vicious looking cat with dreads and a mouth full of gold teeth. She whispered something in his ear and pointed in the direction of K.O. and his crew. The guy with the dreads in turn, tapped his stick man and they along with two other cats approached the dance floor. Lady moved swiftly towards the exit to get Turk. "Yo go get Tee-Tee so we can get out of here. It's about to go down." She said and turned to walk back inside.

Turk abruptly ended her conversation. She killed the power on the phone she was using and headed back inside of the club. She maneuvered her way through the crowd until she reached Tehran. "A go get the car and meet me around the front and hurry up. Some shit is about to start and we need to get the fuck out of here. Turk demanded and snatched Tehran by the arm.

Lady led the way to the exit, but before they made it through the front door the cat with the dreads snuck K.O. with a sharp right hook flooring him and a huge fight escalated.

Lady and Turk turned to stand guard at the front door, both gripping their weapons while Tehran went to retrieve the Modena. Tehran dashed through the parking lot. As she hurried past Lady's Hummer she asked herself, *Why don't we just get the truck and drive to the car;* but she didn't waste any time pondering. She made it out of the parking lot and on to the back street where Turk's Ferrari was parked. With the Ferrari well in her

eye sight she put a little pep in her step. Tehran hit the alarm for the doors to unlock and for the engine to start. She approached the vehicle, reached to open the door and out of nowhere a medium sized figure with a black long sleeve shirt on, black jeans, black Timberland boots and a black bandana covering the face appeared. "Bitch if you swallow hard I'll blow yo mutha fuckin' head off." The person said through clenched teeth and placed the barrel of a gun to the side of her head. "Now get the fuck in." The person commanded. Another similarly dressed figure appeared from behind a Nissan Quest mini van. The figure held a gun to the back of Tehran's head long enough for the partner to get in the passenger seat. The second figure jumped inside of the Quest and followed Tehran as they drove off.

Turk and Lady stood impatiently in front of the club. "Come on Lady, let's get in your truck and see where this bitch is at." Turk said as if she was highly upset. Lady began to laugh out loud before she caught herself. "What the fuck is so funny?"

"Nothin'. I was just thinkin' about somethin'." Lady answered as she started up her Hummer. She drove around the block to where Turk's Modena was parked but it wasn't there and Tehran was nowhere in sight.

Turk pulled out here phone and dialed Tehran's number but no one answered. "I know how to find my fuckin' car." She said vividly displaying her anger.

Lady shook her head from side to side like it was a shame, as she listened to Turk's driving instructions.

Killah and Tika Bell laid nestled up in her king sized bed, watching DVD's in the nude.
The two had been sexing each other for hours and her engine was still revving. "Chris I'm horney." She whined pouting like a sad puppy.

Killah smiled. "Woman you stay horney. You need to go to sleep. Here suck on this until you fall asleep." He laughed and grabbed his penis.

Tika Bell smiled a devilish grin and rubbed her hands together. "Mmmm my favorite." She said and dove in. Tika Bell worked the head of his penis like it was an oversized pacifier for real. She began to suck and stroke the long muscle in its entirety.

Killah was just beginning to enjoy himself when his cell phone rang. He checked the caller I. D and noticed that the number was unlisted so he ignored it. The phone immediately began to ring again after it hung up. The number still showed unlisted but this time Killah answered. "Yo."

"What's up Killah Cam?" A male voice said excitedly.

"Who the fuck is this?

"Don't worry about all that Hustlah. We got cho bitch nigga."

"Man who the fuck is this?" Killah questioned again as he sat up on the bed and motioned for Tika Bell to discontinue her services.

"Listen nigga! While you askin' all these questions we got cho bitch tied up on the floor squirmin' like ah fish out of water. Now check this out. We want five million dollars dropped off at….

Killah cut the kidnapper off in mid sentence. "Hold the fuck up. You want five who? Nigga you must be out of your mother fucking mind." He said with a chuckle. "Ain't no bitch in the world worth five million dollars. What the fuck you think you dealing with a weak mother fucker. I'll tell you what Hustler, keep that bitch it's a part of the game. I appreciate the favor." He said laughing before hanging up the phone.

Tika Bell looked up at Killah. "Who was that?"

"Shiitt, I don't know. Some nigga talking about he got Tee-Tee and want me to drop off five mil' to get her back. The fuck is these niggas smoking out here today? Killah's phone rang again. "Yo."
"Ah'ight listen. Maybe five mil' was too much to ask for but we know you got the paper so you got to come off at least two and a half or your chick is dead." The kidnapper said now pleading.
"Well what the fuck is you waiting for? She should have been dead. The truth is she was dead when you snatched her. I'm not giving you niggas shit so stop calling me. Ya'll will just be some broke mother fuckers with a body and a hell of a price to pay if I ever catch ya'll pussy ass niggas. Ya'll kidnapped the wrong one. If you really want some paper, come and get me. I'll kill everyone of you scared bitch ass niggas." He said then hung up again. "Tika Bell strap up. I got a tracking device on Tehran's phone so these niggas are dead."
"Tee-Tee'll be dead by the time we find her."
"So what. As long as these niggas die too I'm content. Don't nobody take shit from me, threaten me and expect to live." Killah dialed Turk's number but no one answered. He dialed the number again, still no results. He dialed Fu's number then turned to Tika Bell. "Tika call Drea, Tasha and Lady and tell them what's up."
Fu was deep in a good night's sleep when his phone woke him. "Yo." He answered.
"A Fu. Somebody kidnapped Tee-Tee. Squad up and ride through Bad News (Newport News Va.) until I find out where they are at. Call Blue and tell him to get a crew and ride through Hampton."
"Okay fam'. I'm on that now. Call me back when you find her." Fu jumped up, got dressed and ran out of the door like a fire man. He dialed Blue's number as he raced to his car.

Blue had the Lamborghini on cruise control, gliding down interstate 64 through Hampton when his phone rang. "Yo." He answered in a weak tone. The female that he picked up from the club was giving him the meanest head in the whip that a sister could give.

"Blue where you at? Killah called and said that somebody kidnapped Tee-Tee and he need you to assemble a crew and patrol Hampton until he tracks her."

"Well I'm in Hampton now but I got this broad wit' me. I'm'ma drop shorty off some where but I ain't got time to go back to Norfolk and round up no niggas. I'll partrol this joint dolo."

"Okay. Well I'm'ma ride through Bad News, see what we come up wit'."

"Bet."

"Later."

"Later." Blue said and they both hung up. He looked down at his female friend who was earning her Maters' Degree in Brain Surgery and said. "Yo shorty I gotta drop you off somewhere. Either I can give you some cab money or drop you off at ah hotel and pick you up on my way back to Norfolk."

Nia Long's twin took a pause in her action. "Just get me on your way back." She responded without argument and went back to work on Blue's ten and a half inch man. Not too many women could say that they gave head in a Lamborghini on an open road before.

Blue got off on the Lasalle exit and pulled into a Super 8 about a block away. He handed her $1,000 and told her to rent the best room that she could find and to order herself something to eat if she got hungry. Blue wrote down his cell phone number and held it tightly in his hand. "Call me and let me know the room number. Oh before I give you my number, what's yo name?"

"Onika." She answered flashing a weak smile. The question made her feel like a cheap hooker. Here she was performing oral sex on a perfect stranger who didn't even take the time to ask her her name. *What the fuck! Men do it all the time. She thought, before exiting the raised passenger door.*

"Onika." Blue repeated out loud to his self locking the name into his mental Rolodex and drove off.

While Killah was on the line with Fu, Tika Bell was explaining everything to Drea.

"WHAT? WHO?" Drea yelled now fully awake. She spoke so loudly that she startled her husband that was asleep next to her.

"We don't know who yet but Chris has a GPS device connected to Tee-Tee's phone and he wants you to ride around Suffolk until he locates her. He got some people on their way out there to help." Tika Bell instructed.

"Okay. I'm on my way." Drea said. She hung up the phone and leaped out of bed to get dressed.

"On your way where?" Her husband questioned with a bit of an attitude.

"Somebody kidnapped Chris' wife and we have to go...." Was all she was able to say before she was interrupted.

"So because his wife got snatched my wife is supposed to risk her life to find her. Why don't he just call the police and report her missing?" "Reggie please don't ask stupid questions. You're from the streets and you know that Chris is not going to include the law in any of our affairs." Drea sighed as she grabbed a hand sized fully automatic weapon and a semi-automatic handgun. She secured her Mac .11, her sixteen shot P-95 Ruger and closed the vault that was

located in her walk-in closet. Drea returned to her bed side and attempted to give her husband a fare well kiss.
Reggie drew back his face and held up his hand in effort to avoid the kiss. He stared his gorgeous wife in her beautiful eyes and said; "Andrea if you leave this house, when you return I won't be here."
Drea sighed. She gazed at Reggie's handsome appearance. This brother was fine, dark chocolate. He had curly hair and was tall and slim. Drea looked deep into her husbands soul. "Baby if I return and you're no longer here remember that I will always love you but understand that this is something that you wanted to do for the longest so please don't use this as an excuse, because you know what my life is like and you understand what comes along with it. The things I do for Chris are the same things that he would do for me. The same way if something were to happen to you he'd be here for me. So if you want to leave Reggie then leave. It's your choice." Drea said. She strapped on her vest, put on her over sized black Tee-shirt, walked out of her bedroom and headed out of the door.
Tika Bell contacted Tasha next. She wasn't the least bit surprised to catch Tasha wide awake and in the presence of some nigga. She gave Tasha all of the details and told her that Killah needed her to patrol the City of Portsmouth." Be on the look out for his call." She instructed.
"Okay." Tasha agreed. Tasha was at the Holiday Inn in Chesapeake by Greenbrier Mall getting her freak on. She disconnected Tika Bell and began to put on her clothes.
"Hold on shorty, where you goin'?" The guy that she was with asked as she continued to get dressed.
"I got some shit I gotta do." She barked with her snotty attitude.
"Bitch you had me pay for this room, got me out here eatin' yo pussy and you gone bounce before I get mines off."

Tasha finished getting dressed. She retrieved her pistol off the night stand next to the bed. She removed the magazine to check the amount of bullets that were inside. She inserted the magazine back into the gun, walked up on her male friend and smacked the shit out of him with it. "Who the fuck is you callin' a bitch you punk ass, broke ass nigga." She balled up five $100 bills and threw them at him. "This for the room. Now hop in that old ass Lex' and go buy you some pussy. BITCH!" She barked, spat in his blood covered face and walked out of the room. As Tasha entered her Stronoway Silver with Charcoal leather interior 2002Aston Martin Vantage Coupe, her cell phone vibrated. "What's up?"

"Tasha do you know where Lady is?"

"Last I heard she was going to meet Turk up Broadway. You called her?"

"I'm about to. Turk isn't answering her phone. If you catch up with either one of them tell Lady to work Chesapeake and Turk to cover The Beach (Virginia Beach, Va.). Or, you can handle Chesapeake and tell Lady to cover P-Town." Tika Bell disconnected

Tasha and dialed Lady's number.

Lady sped through the Downtown Tunnel that led from Downtown Norfolk to Downtown Portsmouth and vice versa. She checked the I.D. on her cell phone as it vibrated violently. "This Tika Bell." Lady said as she turned to look at Turk who was giving her directions from the passenger seat. "What the fuck she want this time ah night?"

"What the fuck you think she want?" Turk asked. "She probably got word about Tee-Tee. Fuck that bitch. We on a mission." Turk said as Lady continued to drive the Hummer like it was a NASCAR down Effingham St. She made a right on Lincoln St. in Prentis Park where they spotted Turk's

Modena parked in front of an older modeled, run down house, next to a white Nissan Quest. Lady pulled her Hummer into a spot behind the mini van and killed her lights.

"Keep the engine running." Turk ordered.

The two women geared up for war. Besides their everyday hand guns that they had on them, Lady had an AK 47 and a .50 Caliber assault rifle in the back of the truck. Turk grabbed the two handguns, while Lady took hold of the AK and they both exited the vehicle.

Killah patrolled the city of Portsmouth like a mad man. He and Tika Bell had to split up because they never could get in touch with Turk or Lady so he decided to cover P-Town while Tika Bell held it down in Norfolk. The GPS signal that he had connected to his phone showed that Tehran or at least her phone was somewhere in Downtown Portsmouth. Killah contacted Tika Bell first since she was the closest to Portsmouth, being in Norfolk. "Tika they got Tee-Tee somewhere in Downtown Portsmouth. Hurry up and get this way. Call Drea and Tasha and by the time ya'll get here I'll know exactly where she's at." He called Fu next and told him to deliver the same message to Blue.

Killah checked the GPS map on his phone, and noticed that the red dot was still in the same location. He touched a few buttons on the Maybach's navigation system and realized that the dot was coming from the Prentis Park section. Killah made a right on Lincoln and drove the long street looking both ways until he spotted something that looked strange but familiar. He parked across the street but not directly in front of the house that Turk and Lady walked in a little more than a half an hour ago. He dialed Tika Bell's number back. "Ay Bay. I think I know why Turk and Lady haven't been answering their phones."

"Why not?" Tika Bell asked like she was afraid to hear the answer.

"I think them niggas snatched them up too. I'm out Prentis Park on Lincoln Street. Let everybody know and hurry up." Killah instructed. He dialed Fu's number and repeated the same speech word for word. He got out of his car, walked to the trunk and removed a twelve shot, sawed off, pistol grip pump shot gun that had been rigged to shoot like an automatic. He pulled his .50 Caliber, Deseret Eagle handgun from his waist, closed the trunk and sat on top of it.

Killah sat still on the edge of the trunk thinking about the situation at hand. It was very well a possibility that Turk, Tehran and Lady could all be inside of a house across the street from where he sat, dead. *But why didn't they say they had Turk?* He thought. Killah was confused. Suddenly a huge wave of hurt covered him instantly like the Tsunami. For the first time since his mother threatened to kill him, he felt like shedding a tear, but he hadn't cried in so long that it was almost like he forgot how. The possibility that the only person he truly loved could be laying dead in a house across the street from where he sat was beginning to eat away at his conscious. He began to tap his foot on the pavement as he sat impatiently waiting for the door of the house to open up, or for the members of his crew to arrive. " I guess when I told him that no bitch in the world was worth five million he decided not to tell me about Turk and Lady. I would've given them niggas a hundred million for Turk. But that's okay. These pussy niggas gone die and I put that on my mother's grave." He said to his self and nodded his head up and down to confirm that he understood. Killah began to think of who from Portsmouth could be responsible for this. Fat Shawn was the first name that came to mind. Big Lynn, Thin, Skinny Shaun from London Oaks and a few others raced through his mind. It didn't matter: He was prepared to run up in that

house and kill who ever was responsible. Less than a minute later Tika Bell drove up. A few minutes after that Tasha showed up, then Drea, then Fu, and then Blue. It took approximately twenty five minutes for the entire crew to form. Once they were all together, Killah began to go over his plan of attack. All of a sudden every light in the house that the kidnappers were in went off. This alarmed Killah and company causing each member of the crew to grip their weapons and aim them at the house. "Yo they must be on the way out. Get ready." Killah whispered as he waved his arm and pointed towards the house like a Sergent calling his troops to war. They all got low and began to creep in the direction of the house when out of nowhere the house became completely lit but Virginia Power had nothing to do with this electricity. It looked almost like fire as the heavy artillery from inside brought light to the dimmed house. A few moments later the shots ceased. Killah and his crew were now on their toes, with their weapons still aimed at the front door. Killah noticed that the engine of Lady's Hummer was still running. The front door to the house became ajar and the figure of a recognizable woman appeared in it's shadows.
"HOLD UP! DON'T SHOOT!" Killah yelled as Turk stood in the doorway. Turk strolled out of the house followed by Lady who was carrying Tehran's lifeless body across her shoulder. "What the fuck?" Was all that Killah could say.
"It's a long story. Take Tee-Tee so we can get the fuck out of here. Everybody inside is dead and we have to get the fuck out of Portsmouth." Turk said, jumped in her Ferrari and sped off. Lady handed Tehran to Killah, jumped in her Hummer and pulled off.
Killah stood in the middle of Lincoln St. clutching Tehran in his arms. He faced the rest of his crew and asked. "What the

fuck just happened here?" Everyone shook their heads from side to side as if to say they didn't understand.

"A Killah we gotta get out of here." Fu suggested and they all began to file out.

Blue remained staring at Tehran in Killah's arms. "Damn Ace. I just seen shorty in Broadway havin' a good time. This shit fucked up. I gotta ride back out Hampton man if you need me for anything hit me up." Blue said and hopped in his whip but didn't pull off.

Killah slowly walked over to his Maybach. He opened the trunk and placed Tehran's blood soaked body inside. He sat in the driver's seat looking towards the house that he just witnessed Turk and Lady come out of. He wondered who or if anybody was actually inside dead, but he would have to find out from either the news or the streets. He started his engine, blew the horn at Blue and drove off. "Damn Tee-Tee." He said out loud. He had tried on several different occasions to explain the dangers of the streets to his wife. "You just wouldn't listen." He said. *I'm glad Turk is alright.* He thought as he drove towards Norfolk in preparation to have Dr. Isaac pick up his wife's body and drop it off at the coroner's office.

Killah drove home still wondering if somebody was in fact dead inside of that house or not. If it was a whole lot more would follow and if not he was in a real fucked up predicament. Killah followed the proper procedures to enter his Estate. He opened the door to his mansion and walked inside.

"I thought you was my mother." Diamond said and turned to walk away without noticing the blood that covered her father's clothes.

Killah shook his head as he removed his shirt. "Damn. Diamond!" He whispered to his self and took a seat on the couch. He decided to wait until he woke up to tell his daughter about her mother's death. Throughout all of the events that took place he had somehow managed to forget about his precious Diamond being without a mother. Killah laid still across the couch staring at the ceiling until sleep finally held victorious in the battle. The next morning, Killah went to join Diamond in her bedroom. He took a seat on the edge of her bed and gazed into her eyes. He couldn't help but to think of Tehran. It was just like staring at a younger, darker version of the woman that he had Dr. Isaac drop off at the morgue less than twelve hours ago. Killah didn't waste any time. He grabbed his teen age daughter by her hand and got straight to the point. "Diamond your mother was kidnapped and killed last night."

Diamond stared at her father coldly as if he were responsible for her mother's death but she didn't respond. "Diamond that's the reason that I never take you and your mother out in public, that's why I bought you and her those guns and taught ya'll how to use them for fear that one day this might happen. Baby there's a lot of jealous mother fuckers in this world that will kill you because you drive a Benz or snatch your mother or any one that they feel is close to me in exchange for money or my life. That's why I tried to keep you two a secret to the streets until I retired and got us the fuck away from here. But I'll promise you this. Everyone that's responsible for your mother's death will die and this shit will never happen again. I'll kill their entire families if I have to." Killah said visibly angry.

"Well don't forget to kill yourself because you got to know that you are responsible too and if anything happens to me, be sure to blame yourself for that as well." Diamond said as she stood up and turned to exit her room. On her way out the door she bumped into her aunt Turk. She gave her aunt a strong hug and held her tightly. "I'm'ma take me a ride. I need some fresh air." Diamond explained to Turk and walked away. She walked outside jumped in her Brilliant Silver, with Charcoal leather interior 2003 SL 55, dropped the top and drove off.

Turk joined Killah in Diamond's room. "What's up cuz? You alright?" She questioned as she took a seat next to him on the edge of the bed and gently patted him on his back.

"Turquoise somebody kidnapped and killed my wife. How the fuck could I be alright. I mean me and Tee-Tee had our problems but she was still my problem. What the fuck happened last night?" Killah asked still confused.

"Me, Tee-Tee and Lady went to Broadway last night. Not once did I take my eyes off of my sister until Lady spotted K.O. and them two other boys that he be with walk into the club. I stepped outside for one second to call some of my peoples. I went back inside to get Tee-Tee and Lady and that's when Fat Shawn and some of his peoples got to fighting with K.O. and them. Me and Lady stood guard at the front door while I sent Tehran to get my car in case we had to shoot up the place. When she never returned we hopped in Lady's Hummer and drove around the corner to the back street where my car was parked but it wasn't there and neither was Tee-Tee so me and Lady went looking for my car, that's when we found it out Portsmouth but by the time we got there Tee-Tee was already dead."

"Why the fuck wasn't your car parked out front where we usually park and where was Tehran's gun?" Killah asked. Something in Turk's story didn't make sense to him.

"It wasn't no spaces open out front and Tehran wanted to go in so she parked around the corner and I had her pocket book with her gun inside."

"So basically both of ya'll were slipping."

"I'll take that." Turk responded accepting responsibility.

"So who was inside of the house?"

"Lady said that they were some young boys that fuck with Fat Shawn."

"I thought Fat Shawn was in the club."

"He was but evidently he had some people outside squattin' on my car."

fuck were you and Lady doing?"

"Torturing them moth fuckas that killed my sistah. The same shit we did to them niggas that shot me and killed Ali."

Killah breathed a huge sigh of relief. "Turk we got a hundred and seventy one keys of dope left before I was supposed to retire. Now I know that you finally accepted my retirement and was prepared to take over without me but I'm not going no where until everybody behind my wife's death suffers. I won't have it any other way. I gotta call Uzi and Tank because K.O. should have been dead a long time ago. I'll handle Fat Shawn myself. It's war time. No nuts no glory." He said as he searched his cousin's face for a response.

A slight grin appeared across her face. "That's your call cuz. I'm riding with you." She said and gave him a huge hug. "I love you cuz. No nuts no glory."

"I love you too."

CHAPTER NINE   No Nuts No Glory
Heartless

Killah decided to postpone the Family's vacation to St. Tropes until the day after Tehran's funeral. His initial plan was to cancel but Turk convinced him to reschedule, saying that it would be good for the healing process.

Tehran was murdered on April 25, a day before Killah's birthday and buried on April 30, which happened to be Turk's birthday. The Homegoing Service was held at Faith Deliverance Church on a lovely Monday afternoon. Bishop Amos was in charge of reading the Scripture and delivering the Eulogy.

"Tehran Tania Boone Cameron, fondest known to her family and friends as "Tee-Tee." Bishop Amos opened up by saying. She continued to give a vivid description of Tehran's up bringing before she opened up her Bible, turned to Psalms: 27: and read verses 1-6. *"The Lord is my light and my salvation;*
Whom shall I fear?
The Lord is the strength of my life;
Of whom shall I be afraid?
When the wicked came against me
To eat up my flesh,
My enemies and foes,
They stumbled and fell.
Though an army may encamp against me,
My heart shall not fear;
Though war may rise against me,
In this I will be confident.
One thing I have desired of the Lord.
That will I seek:
That I may dwell in the house of the Lord

*All the days of my life,
To behold the beauty of the Lord,
And to inquire in His temple.
For in the time of trouble
He shall hide me in His pavilion;
In the secret place of His tabernacle
He shall hide me;
He shall set me high upon a rock.
And now my head shall be lifted up above my enemies all around me;
Therefore I will offer sacrifices of joy in His tabernacle;
I will sing, yes, I will sing praises to the Lord."*

Killah listened intently. He soaked up each and every one of the Bishop's words and analyzed them. Killah had no belief but he did consider his self wise and able to understand. Killah was joined in the front row by his daughter and Turk. Tehran's sister Keisha and her mother were also in the front row. If someone on the outside were to look in, it would have been almost impossible for them to tell that the members of that row were the husband, daughter, sisters and mother of the person lying dead in the 14 karat gold trimmed casket surrounded by reefs and flowers. You would expect for such close relatives to be drowned in tears and sorrow but not one of them showed any emotion or shed one tear. In fact not many people throughout the large crowded population of over a thousand guest shed many tears. The church gave off a gloomy vibe. Don't get it twisted, you could tell that someone had died and the people were in mourning but it just wasn't your usual funeral atmosphere. It was like these people excepted death better. Sort of like they were use to it. Bishop Amos looked up from her pulpit. She too noticed the difference in the faces of this particular crowd of mourners. *It's sad how*

these young black people keep dying. This is probably just one of a long line of funerals to come behind this incident. She thought, before turning her Bible to 1 Corinthians: 13 and reading verses 1-8. *"Though I speak with the tongues of men and of angles, but have not love, I have become sounding brass or a clanging symbol.*
And though I have the gift of prophecy, and understand all mysteries and all knowledge, and though I have all faith, so that I could remove mountains, but have not love, I am nothing. And though I bestow all my goods to feed the poor, and though I give my body
to be burned, but have not love, it profits me nothing.
Love suffers long and is kind, love does not envy; love does not parade itself, is not
puffed up;
does not behave rudely, does not seek it's own, is not provoked, thinks no evil;
bears all things, believes all things, hopes all things, endures all things.
Love never fails. But whether there are prophecies, they will fail; whether there are tongues, they will cease; whether there is knowledge, it will vanish away...." Bishop Amos returned to her seat after completing her scriptures and allowed her words to marinate.
"Turk I'm out of here. I had enough of this shit, I'll be outside in the limo." Diamond whispered and began to make her way through the aisle.
Killah watched Diamond as she made her exit but he didn't attempt to stop her, he simply allowed her to have her space. Killah turned to Fu and said, "keep an eye on shorty for me." then focused his attention back on the pulpit where the Reverend was giving a prayer of comfort.
Fu walked outside to join Diamond. Federal agents swarmed the outside of the church's parking lot, taking pictures of the

fancy stretch limousines and the various other foreign cars. Fu smiled at the men in black jackets and suits before joining Diamond in the stretch Maybach. "You alright baby girl?" He questioned.

"I'm good. I just needed some time to myself." Diamond said as the limousine fell quiet for a second. "Fu I hate my father."

The words caught Fu off guard so much that he couldn't even conjure up a response. All he could do was hold out his arms and offer her a warm embrace. Diamond gladly accepted and held Fu tightly. The two of them continued to relax in the limousine until the service was complete.

Killah stood out front dressed in a Navy Blue cotton suit by Valentino and a pair of matching Ermenegildo Zegna shoes, surrounded by Turk, Drea, Blue, Tasha, Tika Bell and Lady as people began to file out of the church. Turk and Lady wore matching Cinzia Rocca, black pin stripe pant suits, with black Kate Spade flat shoes. Drea and Tika Bell

wore dresses and shoes by Prada. Drea's outfit was beige while Tika Bell wore grey. Blue sported a navy blue cotton suit by David Chu, a pair of brown Louis Vuitton shoes with a matching brown coach belt, and Tasha wore a black jacket, blouse, skirt and belt with matching black pumps all by Yves Saint Laurent. They all congregated in the parking lot for a few minutes, consoling Tehran's family and friends before heading out to the cemetery.

Tehran's body was transported in the back of a customized Bentley Arnage wagon, from Faith Deliverance to Roosevelt Memorial Cemetery where she was laid to rest. Killah rode in the stretch Maybach with Diamond, Tehran's mother, Keisha, Aunt Gina, Dr. Isaac, and Isaac Jr. Turk followed in a 100" Ferrari Testarossa Limousine with the rest of the C. O. C.

The repast was held at a little hole in the wall gathering spot called The Sons of Norfolk on 29th St. in Park Place. The atmosphere had switched from gloomy into almost a party scene as family and friends drank expensive bottles of liquor, ate fried chicken, pork chops, ham, macaroni and cheese, collard greens, sweet potatoes and home made rolls while listening to music and dancing. Everyone was having such a good time that none of them realized that it was after midnight and the party had no signs of quitting. Diamond even wore a light smile as she and Turk danced together in the corner.

Killah approached Fu. "Yo Fu tell Spade to play three more songs and announce that the party is coming to an end. We still have to travel across the country tomorrow." He whispered.

Fu walked towards the DJ's booth to inform Spade that it was about time to cut out. "Yo cuz, Killah said to spin three more joints then we can bounce."

"Okay fam." Spade responded. "Alright ladies and gentlemen. We are about to bring this party to a close so fix you a plate and wrap it up because after these three songs we gotta wrap it up." He announced and began to mix into his first song.

Usually at a black gathering folks would leave as soon as the food and drinks were gone but because Killah provided more than enough of both he was forced to bring the gathering to a close on his own. The majority of the crowd had left before Spade was halfway through his second song. Killah received a chirp on his Nextel two way radio. "Come in." He answered.

"Yo cuz, Pat and Wayne just circled the block twice. Hold fast for a second until we defuse the situation." Will, the head of Killah's security said. Will contacted the other two security guards and informed them to be on the look out for

a white older model Oldsmobile Cutlass Supreme. Killah had two security guards posted out front and one on each corner of 29th St. A few seconds later, Pat whipped the '88 Cutlass around the corner with Wayne hanging out of the passenger's window rapidly firing a fully automatic Tech 9. Will and the other security guard that was posted out front returned fire while the other two raced towards the action. Bullets were flying from everywhere. Wayne continued to unleash round after round until Pat successfully drove past all of the members of security and sped out of Park Place. Killah chirped Will. "Yo is everything good?"
"Killah it's time. Get everybody out."
"Tommy where's Will?"
"He dead!" Tommy the other guard that was posted out front with Will answered.
Killah led the way to escape with his gun drawn. Lady was the closest to him followed by Tasha, Blue, Fu, Drea and Tika Bell. Turk allowed the remainder of the guest to exit before she escorted Diamond out.
Diamond walked out of the club and looked over to where Will was being tended to by the other members of security. She could tell that he was dead and turned to look at her father. The look that she gave him was cold. It reminded him of the way his mother looked at him when she told him that she would kill him the next time he cried.
Killah helped Diamond into her car. "Drive straight home and I'll see you when I get there." He instructed and placed his hand on her back. "And if anybody get's behind you don't be afraid to use your gun."
"Get your hands off me. I know how to handle myself." She snapped as she snatched away from her father. Diamond jumped in her SL 55, slammed the door and drove off. Turk jumped in her Modena and followed Diamond without being directed, almost like she read her cousin's mind. Killah

informed Tommy to call Will an ambulance and for him to lay low before he hopped in his Maybach and drove off. Killah was furious with his self. He had neglected calling Tank and Uzi to handle K.O., Pat and Wayne because he was too wrapped up with Tehran's situation. Now he decided to leave them out of it until he returned from his trip to St. Tropes. He considered calling the trip off again to stay home with Diamond but decided to take her with them instead to keep her out of harms way.

K.O. laid in his bed, smoking his early morning breakfast blunt filled with Lobster, (A lime green mid to upper grade of marijuana) while watching LNC. (Local News on Cable.) He turned the volume up on the television as the news team brought in a live broadcast of the event that took place early in the A.M.

"A shoot out that led to a double homicide erupted on Twenty Ninth Street in the Park Place section of the city….."

"Double Homicide." K.O. said to his self. "Damn my niggas put in work." He said and laughed excitedly as he continued to listen.

"In what was described as a drive by shooting, two lives were claimed. Twenty nine year old William Smith and five year old Tyshaun Harris were both found dead in the seven hundred block of Twenty Ninth Street in Norfolk. They both were pronounced dead at the scene. Smith was found dead in front of The Sons of Norfolk while Harris was lying asleep in his own bed." The reporter said sadly before showing an interview of a sobbing young woman.

"I just laid Tyshaun in his bed and laid down myself when the shoot out happened. It sounded like machine guns and cannons going off." The young sobbing mother said calmly as she remained in a state of shock. "I walked into his room and blood……. Oh my God blood was all over his bed." She said as she broke down and her tears flowed uncontrollably.

A young woman who was standing close by held her tightly in her arms and allowed her to cry on her shoulder.
The news reporter once again began to speak. *"Police are on the look out for an older model, white, boxed shaped Oldsmobile Cutlass. Witnesses say that two black men drove by at least three times and the last time they drove by they started shooting at Smith and another black male who also fled the scene.*
If anyone has any information please call Norfolk Crime Line at One-Eight-Eight-Eight-Lock-U-Up..."
K.O. was now furious. Not only did Pat and Wayne mess around and kill an innocent little boy, they were stupid enough to allow witnesses to get a vivid description of the get away car. He picked up his phone and dialed Pat's number.
Pat was still half asleep when he answered. "Hell-O." He said in a groggy tone.
"Do you know that ya'll stupid motha fuckas killed an innocent five year old boy?" K.O. questioned through clenched teeth.
"What?" He asked without being aware of what his partner just said.
"You and Wayne killed a little boy last night and the police are going to be all over ya'll asses because ya'll let somebody spot the car. Ya'll niggas fucked up for real this time." K.O. said in almost a panic.
"What choo keep sayin' ya'll for? All I did was drive the car. I didn't shoot nobody. And stop talkin' reckless over this mutha fuckin' phone." Pat explained in his defense.
"Well get Wayne and meet me at the spot. Ya'll niggas gotta hide for a minute." He said and hung up.

Pat and Wayne showed up at an apartment off of Ballentine Blvd., across from Ballentine School about forty five minutes

later. (Ballentine was another one of Norfolk's predominantly black ghetto's composed of older model houses and a few apartments.) K.O. was already inside when Pat and Wayne walked through the door. He was positioned on an old beat up couch separating small stacks of money when the two men approached. "What's up Ace? What's this shit Pat talkin' about I supposed to kill some little boy?" Wayne asked.
"Well it ain't no secret. The shit been all over the news. You can't do shit right."
"So because some little boy got killed in the middle of a shoot out I can't do shit right. Nigga I' on't see you bussin' yo' gun, so youn't do shit right neither nigga." Wayne yelled getting defensive.
"Yeah what ever nigga."
"What ever den. All you good for is robbin' ah nigga, youn't got the nuts to kill ah mu fucka."
"Look I ain't for all this arguin' shit. Just take this and find some where to lay low for a while." K.O. said and handed Wayne $5,000. K.O. knew that Wayne was telling the truth and he also knew that Wayne could probably care less about how old Tyshaun was or how innocent he was. The last thing K. O. wanted was to be at odds with Wayne, or Pat for that matter.
Wayne took the money and turned to leave followed by Pat. Wayne quickly spun around scaring the shit out of K. O.. Wayne smiled. "Yo fam' we gone need some weed to smoke while we layin'. Break us off about ah pound of dat lob'o." He said.
K.O. shook his head from side to side, sort of in relief.
"Shorty you become'n more of a problem than you worth." He said. K.O. went to the bama, weighed out a half of pound on the scale and handed it to Wayne. "Yo this ah half ah

pound, take this and I'll catch up wit' cha'll in a week." He said and walked them to the front door.

Killah decided to return the Family home after only four days and five nights of vacation. He wanted to be able to move the remaining one hundred seventy keys and fourteen ounces and handle all of his beefs before the first of the year which was only eight months away. They arrived at the Clear Port, (A private airport used for private jets and small commercial flights.) in Suffolk early Sunday morning. Killah immediately got back to work on the business aspect. He gave Drea and company fifty ounces that same night to go on the block the following morning.
Turk immediately got to work on the beef. She called Lady early Monday morning. "Hey girl."
"What's up Turk?" Lady asked as she whipped her Suburban in and out of the early morning Ocean View traffic.
"How long you think you gone be out makin' drops?"
"I just started. Give me about two hours. What's up?"
"I'm 'ma meet choo out the Park in about two hours. We gone ride out and have some fun." Turk said.
"That's what's up. I'll see you then." Lady added and hung up.
Lady arrived out the Park in less than two hours. Tasha was still out making her runs and Turk hadn't shown up yet so she kicked it with Worm who was standing on the corner alone. "What's up lil' homey?"
"What's up Lady?" Worm said excitedly. Lady very rarely kicked it with any one outside of the immediate C.O.C. Family, so she caught him sort of by surprise.
"Ain't shit. Where Popcorn lil' ass?"
"Shorty been on some new shit since he started fuckin' wit' Blue real tough."

"Oh Lord! What the fuck Blue done started now?" Lady questioned ready to hear the drama.

"Nutt'n for real. He just got Popcorn psyched up about his new position in the clique, when Blue take over."

"Take over what?"

"The Fam'lay when Killah, Fu and them retire."

"Blue need to stop that bullshit. Blue ain't takin' over no mutha fuckin' Fam'lay" Lady said and shook her head before she began to laugh.

Turk drove up in her Caynne Truck while Lady was still laughing. "What's so funny?" She asked. "Hey Worm."

"Watch this." Lady whispered to Worm as he waved at Turk. "A, is Blueburry supposed to be takin' over for Killah when he retire?"

"Hell no! And who said that Chris was retiring?" Turk asked.

"Nobody girl." Lady said and turned back towards Worm. "See? You should know how Blue exaggerate." She said with a smile and went to join Turk. Lady leaned on the driver's side window. "So what we gettin' into?"

"We gone take a ride. I just passed Tasha on Virginia Beach Boulevard so she should be pulling up in a minute...." Before Turk got all of her words out Tasha pulled up behind her truck and parked. Tasha hopped out of her Vantage Coupe and approached Lady. "What's up bitch?" She asked Lady. "What's good Turk?" She asked then ran down everything to Lady. "I gotta give Worm these two and a half ounces that Blue told me to give 'em then I'm going home to lay down. What cha'll 'bout to do?"

"Shit. Ride around for a minute. We'll hook up a little later." Turk said and waved for Lady to get in. "We gone take my truck. We ain't gone be long."

"A WORM! Watch my truck." Lady hollered across Turk and caught a glimpse of Worm nodding his head as she and Turk drove off.

Turk and Lady coasted down Princess Anne Rd.. Turk made a left on Ballentine Blvd., drove about three blocks, made a left on Tait Terrace and pulled into a driveway out front of a two story, older modeled blue house.

"Who the fuck live here?" Lady asked. She didn't deal with anybody out Ballentine and was sure that Turk didn't neither.

"This K.O.'s mother's house." Turk said with an evil grin.

"We gone catch this nigga while he sleeping. For real!" She said excitedly. Turk tucked her gun into the waist ban of her BCBG Max Azria jeans and climbed out of the truck. Lady's pistol was already secured in the small of her back so she too exited the truck and followed Turk to the front door. Turk rung the door bell, but no one answered so she rang it again.

"Who is it." The voice of an elderly woman echoed through the front door.

"Nikki. Is Keith home?" Turk responded in her most innocent voice.

K.O.'s mother opened the door. Ms. Owens smiled as she witnessed how nicely dressed and well kept the two young women were that stood on her front porch. "Keith's not home. I haven't seen him in a few days actually. Does he have your number?" Ms. Owens asked.

"Nikki." Turk repeated the name that she first gave with a smile. "Can you please give him a message for me when you see him?"

"I sure can honey."

Turk sized the elderly, plus sized woman up. Ms. Owens was in her later fifties but looked as if she was in her late sixties. Who ever said that excessive stress could put years on a person's appearance, must have known Ms. Owens. Her hair was thin and completely gray and her face carried more than it's fair share of wrinkles.

Turk's smile disappeared and her face was now covered with hate. She shoved Ms. Owens back inside of the house causing her to stumble and fall. Lady entered the house behind them, closed the door and less than five minutes later they were out. Turk dropped Lady back off out The Park and they went their separate ways.

K.O. pulled up in front of the house that he shared with his mother at twelve minutes until nine accompanied by one of his female friends. The young lady couldn't keep her hands off of K.O. as she kissed and fondled him all the way through the front door. "Chill shorty. I'mma break you off. Let me see what my mama doin' first." He said to the hood rat as they entered the front room. The young lady was nothing to look at at all. On a scale from one to ten, she was a four and that was only because she had a large, nicely shaped behind. The entire downstairs was pitch black and nothing looked out of place. K.O. guided his female friend upstairs with his right hand while he carried two bags of food from Feather N Fin in his left. He showed her to his room which was the first bedroom at the top of the stairs on the left. He handed her one of the bags of food, removed a pink lemonade from the drink holder that the young lady held for his mother and headed to his mother's room.
The lights were off and Ms. Owens was asleep in her bed and wrapped tightly in her covers. K.O. flicked on the light switch. "Oh Shit! MOM-MA!" He screamed as he raced to his mother's side. Ms. Owens was badly beaten and her sheets were covered with blood. Turk and Lady had punched, stomped and pistol whipped Ms. Owens for all of three minutes. Lady threw Ms. Owens's brutally beaten body across her shoulder, carried her upstairs to what looked like her bedroom, placed her in bed and tucked her in.

K.O. placed his hand on his mother's wrist to see if she still had a pulse. Once he realized that she was still alive he shook her lightly but Ms. Owens had lost consciousness so she didn't respond. K.O. ran back to his room. He grabbed an empty gym bag that was under his bed, opened up his dresser, removed five handguns and placed them inside the bag. "Nikki take my car and keep these until I come and get 'em." He said out of breath as he handed Nikki his keys and the bag of guns.
"What's wrong?" She asked as she jumped up, moved the bag to her side and began getting dressed.
"Somebody broke in here and fucked my mother up. I gotta get 'er to a hospital." He said as he pressed the last one on the emergency number.
Nikki picked up the bag, grabbed K. O's keys and headed out of the door. K.O. went and sat by his mother's side until the paramedics arrived.
K.O. had robbed so many people that he honestly had no idea who was truly responsible for his mother's assault. All he knew was that whoever was responsible for such a horrible crime had to be heartless or had a heart of stone. The only people that he could think of that fit in that particular category were Killah, Turk, Lady, Blue, Tasha and Fat Shawn. K.O. vowed to touch every last one of those six people either directly or indirectly until he found the right one but he knew that he couldn't expose his self too quickly or he was a dead man.

Three months later......
Fat Shawn had literally been missing in action. The night that Tehran was killed, he drove past his spot and the house was surrounded by police cars and homicide detectives. Without

knowing what went down, he realized that something was terribly wrong and decided not to hang around searching for clues. He drove to his crib, gathered up his two keys of cocaine, twenty one grams of heroin and rode out to a little spot in Chester PA., that his cousin Big T. R. put him onto. Fat Shawn laid low and got his hustle on in Chester for the past three months. He had cooked the two bricks of powder into three bricks of crack and broke each brick down to twenty and fifty dollar rocks. Fat Shawn was down to his last twelve grams of hard. He figured that the twelve grams would be gone before the night was over and planned to return home in a few days. Word on the street was that Killah wanted him dead so he decided to call him to at least shed a little light on the situation before blood was shed for a misunderstanding. He dialed Killah's number….. "A, yo Killah I need to holla at choo and it's real important."
"Who is this?" Killah asked half asleep, not recognizing the number that appeared on the caller I. D.
"This Fat Shawn, Yo. We need to hook up so we can talk." Killah was now wide awake. For the entire four years that he had been a major player in the dope game Fat Shawn had not once called him directly. Killah looked at the clock on his dresser and noticed that it was almost time for him to wake up and collect the daily income. "Where the fuck you at?"
"I been outta town for the past three months. Shit was crazy back home, now word is that choo got goons after me for some shit I know nothin' about." Fat Shawn said through laughter. "But that's cool. If you wanna war, I'll give it to ya'. You know I 'on't give ah fuck. I ain't nev'ah ran from no man and nev'ah will, but I think you'll wanna hear what I gotta say first."
"When will you be back?"
"In ah few weeks." He lied not wanting to tell Killah exactly when he planned on returning.

"Well holler at me when you get back, and if your information is valuable, and you had nothing to do with my wife's murder; you might not get yourself killed."
"Or have to kill you." Fat Shawn shot back.
Killah laughed. "Just hit me when you get back."
"Bet." Fat Shawn said and disconnected their conversation.
Ms. Owens stayed in a coma for twelve weeks. K.O. was sitting by his mother's side holding her hand like he always did during visiting hours, when she opened her eyes for the first time in eighty four days. K.O. had his head down and his eyes closed when his mother came to. He didn't realize that she was awake until he felt her attempt to pull her hand away from his. K.O. opened his eyes and looked at Ms. Owens, who was staring at him as if she were frightened. He smiled. "'Bout time you woke up." He joked. Ms. Owens had suffered a fractured skull, broken jaw, broken arm, ribs, a fractured hip and needed over fifty stitches and staples for bruises to her face and head. Her memory was temporarily gone for the most part and she had been covered in a full body cast for the majority of the time she was hospitalized.
"You okay mom?"
Ms. Owens tried to scream but she couldn't. She yanked away from her son and reached for the panic button that rested by her side. The nurse came racing into the room in a hurry.
"Is everything okay Mr. Owens.?"
"I 'on't know. She keeps pullin' away from me like she's scared of me or something'."
"She's probably just traumatized. Let her get some rest and come back in the morning." The nurse said.
"I ain't goin' no fuckin' where until my mother acknowledges who I am." K.O. yelled.
"Your mother has been in a coma for three months. She probably doesn't remember you at the moment."

"Well she better remember 'cause I ain't goin' nowhere until she do." He said, now with tears in his eyes.
"Mr. Owens please allow your mother to get some rest. She's been through a lot at her age." The nurse said pleading with K.O.
"She been resting for eighty fuckin' four days. Now I said I'm not going nowhere." K.O. yelled as he got up into the nurse's face. The nurse stormed out of the room and a minute later K.O.'s sister walked through the door. "Where the fuck you been at?"
"Excuse me?"
"I said where the fuck have you been?"
"I was out." She answered. She looked over at her mother and ran to her side after she realized that she was conscious. Ms. Owens smiled at the sight of her daughter. K.O.'s sister was easy on the human eyes. She was absolutely beautiful. She almost looked as if she could be the actress Nia Long's twin.
"Onika, your mother is in the hospital and all you can come up with is you was out."
"Uhh, she's only been here for twelve weeks and I've been here everyday so I believe that I am aware that she's in the hospital." She said sarcastically. "How long has she been up?"
"A few minutes...." He answered as the nurse came crashing back into the room with three security guards.
"Mr. Owens, I'm going to ask you again. Could you please leave?" The nurse asked for the third time.
K.O. rose to his feet. "What the fuck they s'pose to do?" He asked with his fist balled up.
Onika stood up and stepped between her brother and the security guards. "Keith Owens you better not." She said through clenched teeth. "What are you trying to do, kill our mother? Just leave and come back in the morning."

"Bu….." K.O. tried to respond but was cut off.
"Ah'ttt! Just leave Keith, damn." Onika said holding her hand up in her baby brother's face.
K.O. swallowed his pride and carried it out of the door with him. He walked through the parking lot and hopped in his 1978 Champagne colored Lincoln Continental sitting on thirties and lows. He dialed Pat's number. "Yo Pat. I'll be through in a minute. Get the van and be ready." He said and hung up as he drove off.

Worm and Popcorn were putting the finishing touches on a glorious evening. Only one bundle remained from the two and a half ounces that they received at the beginning of the day and Popcorn was in the middle of getting rid of that. Worm went inside to add up their daily income and call Tasha. He counted $51,700 and Popcorn still had another buck ($100) in work. Worm told Tasha that they would be ready in thirty minutes, stashed the money and headed into the bathroom.
K.O. sat on the corner of Holt St. in a Conversion van with Pat, Wayne and another one of their stick man's. K.O. was positioned behind the steering wheel clocking Popcorn's every move. Pat was in the passenger seat, Wayne sat directly behind the driver's seat and their stick man sat next to the door clutching an AK.
"Ssss! You sure you ready for this?" Wayne asked K.O. as he pulled on the Lobster. K.O. nodded in agreement as he witnessed Popcorn serve a customer and walk over to his Range. Wayne laughed. "My nigga grew some nuts over night." He said cracking up as he pat K.O. on the back and handed him the blunt.

   "Well you know what choo always say. No Nuts! No Glory!" K.O. said and took a deep pull on the blunt.

CHAPTER TEN   It All Falls Down
Heartless

Children ran wild in the street as the sun began to disappear giving way to the night. Two boys tossed a football as the street lights came on, one youngen worked on his handles, dribbling a basketball between his legs and around his back like an eight year old version of A. I . One group of young men shot celo while smoking weed and drinking forty ounces of 211 Steel Reserve. A group of adolescent females played double dutch and told stories about boys while a few of them sized Popcorn up as he searched his truck and this was only on Holt St. Popcorn rummaged through his armrest in search of a phone number that he received from some Spanish chick two days earlier. After coming away empty, he realized that he placed the number inside of a drawer in the spot's kitchen. Popcorn knew that the following day would be the last day on the grind so he figured that he would have a little extra time to invest in a new flame. If only he could have foreseen the future, he clearly would have focused more of his attention on the burgundy Conversion Van that was parked on the corner than some girl's phone number.

 "Yeah that's that nigga that be wit' Blue bitch ass all the time." K.O. said as he put the van in drive and sped towards Popcorn. You could hear the van's tires screeching throughout the entire back of the park. Stick man swung the door open and with Wayne's assistance snatched Popcorn into the van while K.O. flew out of dodge.

Since the group of females were already focused on Popcorn, they were the first to witness the abduction. They dropped their jump ropes on the sidewalk, raced to the spot where Worm was and banged on the door.

Worm was still on the toilet when the thunderous knocking began. Worm jumped off the stool, wiped himself, pulled up his jeans, washed his hands and went to see what all of the ruckus was about. He snatched up the Tech on his way to the door then looked out of the window before he opened the door. He noticed that Popcorn's Range was still parked in the same spot and wondered why this group of young girls were beating on the door like they had lost their minds. Worm had heard what sounded like tires screeching while he was in the bathroom but that was nothing new in the Projects. You were liable to hear anything out The Park. Never in his twenty three years of living did he expect to hear what these young girls had in store for him. "Yo, Yo, Yo! What's all this bangin' about?" He asked, waving his hand while he talked.
"Somebody in a burgundy van snatched Popcorn." One of the girls said with tears in her eyes and fear written on her face.
"What?" Worm asked to be sure that he heard what he knew he heard.
"Somebody snatched Popcorn." The group sang in chorus this time looking at Worm like he was crazy.
Worm ran back inside the house and called Tasha.
"Hey. Ya'll ready?" Tasha questioned after reading the caller I. D.
Worm took a second to respond. "Somebody snatched Popcorn." He said overwrought.
"Who?"
"I 'on't know who. These young broads just damn near beat the door down and told me. They say some niggas in a burgundy van. I heard tires screechin' while I was takin' ah shit but I ain't pay that shit no mind."
"Shit. Damn near everybody who got ah van in Norfolk, shit burgundy. Or white…. Don't worry. We gone handle this.

You still got the money right?" Tasha asked the only question that she really cared to be answered.
"Yeah I got the money."
"Meet me at McDonalds by Mission College in twenty minutes. I pretty much know who the fuck got Popcorn already." Tasha said and hung up.
Worm gathered up all of the guns and money that was in the house, jumped in his MPV and rode out. Tasha called Lady to explain the situation. She told Lady to call Drea and for them both to meet her at the spot out Mission College. Drea called Turk as soon as she ended her conversation with Lady.
"Hey girl." Turk answered.
"Turk we got a small problem."
"And what might that be."
"K.O. and them snatched Popcorn from out The Park. Lady called and said for us to meet her and Tasha at the spot out Mission College in about forty five minutes." Drea explained.
"Okay. Round up all the cash and I'll be through." Turk said and hung up. Turk rolled over and checked the time on her phone. *Nine twelve.* She thought. "If it ain't one thing it's a mutha fuckin' 'nother." She said as she dialed Killah's number. No one answered so she left a message on his answering machine. "Hey Chris. Meet me at the spot around eleven." She said and hung up. Turk climbed out of bed, walked into the bathroom to freshen up, got dressed and checked out of her hotel suite.

Killah was in the shower when his phone went off. He noticed that he had two missed calls and one saved message on his way out of the door. He recognized Shatoya's number as one of the missed calls and Turk as the other. Killah climbed inside of his black with red leather interior Brabus edition SL 600 and checked his messages. *"One new*

message." The voice inside the phone said. Killah pressed the number "One" on his phone to review the message as he drove to the front gate. "Christopher." He said to the voice activation box and waited for his voice to register. *"Hey Chris. Meet me at the spot around eleven."* He heard Turk's voice say over the answering machine as the gate opened up and allowed him to drive through. Killah hung up on the answering machine and called Fu.
"What's the deal?" Fu answered.
"Eleven." Was all Killah said before his phone beeped. "Hold on Fu... Yo!"
"Yo what's up Ace? I hit choo up earlier but choo ain't answer."
"I was in the shower. What's good?"
"Ain't shit good! K.O. and dem niggas done kidnapped my man Popcorn and I swear I'mma do this nigga some'm bad when I catch'em."
"Where in the fuck did he snatch him from."
"Worm say from off Holt."
"Yeah this dude has gotten beside himself for real now."
"I told ju we should've killed this pussy nigga when he shot up Tee-Tee joint for the funeral." Blue said heatedly.
"It wasn't the right time then. You know I do shit when I feel like it. My wife had just been murdered and I felt like some how I would have been the number one suspect."
"Yeah well I'll tell you what. Let me see this nigga."
"Listen Ace. Let me get this money situated and I'll get with you a little later. Now if you happen to run across shorty, do what you got to do but don't go searching for him. Think before you act. Sometimes killing a dude just isn't good enough. Just think. There's always a better way." Killah instructed as if he were giving Blue a direct order.
"Yeah ah'ight." Blue responded as if he never heard Killah's last command and ended their conversation.

Worm waited patiently in McDonald's parking lot for Tasha to show up. He nervously observed every car that pulled into the parking lot and every customer that went in and came out of the restaurant. After hearing that his best friend had been kidnapped, here he was sitting with over fifty thousand dollars cash in his back seat. To say that he was scared would have been a complete understatement. Tasha drove up approximately twelve minutes after Worm. She pulled into an empty parking space next to him and parked. Worm climbed out of his mini van, walked around to the driver's side of Tasha's X5 and placed a small bag of money in her lap through the window. "I said twenty minutes boy, how long have you been here?" Tasha asked jokingly.
"Yo it's sixteen thousand five hundred in the bag." Worm said and walked away with his head down.
Tasha could see that Worm was disturbed. He always wore a smile and walked with his head held high. "Yo Worm you good?"
"How else can I be?" He asked and shrugged his shoulders. "Hit me later and let me know what's up for tomorrow." He said as he climbed back inside of his MPV.
"I'll let choo know." Tasha said and drove around the back of McDonalds
into Mission College while Worm took the front exit that led to Princess Anne Rd.
Tasha walked into the apartment on the fourth floor and found Drea sitting on the couch flicking through the channels on the television. Tasha placed the money on the coffee table, took a seat beside Drea on the couch and the two women counted the money while waiting for Lady. Lady came crashing through the door about thirty minutes later with Turk right on her heels. She walked over to the kitchen table, unzipped her knapsack and emptied it's contents.

Lady took a deep breath like she was exhausted. "Come on ya'll." She said and took a seat at the round glass table. "Yeah lets hurry up and do this so we can get out of here." Turk said and joined Lady at the table. Drea and Tasha followed Turk and the four women quickly added up their funds. Turk placed all of the cash in one bag and led everyone to the door. The four women walked out of the apartment building and headed into the parking lot. "We'll get back with ya'll in a few hours." Turk informed Tasha and Lady, as she jumped in her Modena. Drea entered her SC 430 and the two women took the drive across town.

Blue cruised the entire Ballentine neighborhood in search of the burgundy Conversion Van that rode away with Popcorn. Even though Killah insisted that Blue not go searching for K.O. he did the exact opposite. Not only did he cover every corner in Ballentine, he also rode through parts of Norview and Ocean View, before he finally got tired and called off his one man search. Blue browsed through the numbers stored in his Blackburry until he came across one with five stars behind the name and dialed the number. *I hope this bitch pick up.* He thought as the phone began to ring.
"Hell-O." A female voice answered in an evil tone.
Blue smiled. This was the type of reaction that he received on a regular basis. "You got ah attitude about somethin'?"
"Blue I haven't talked to you in almost three months."
"So you mad about that? I didn't know you wanted to talk to me. Last time I checked I gave you my number first, so why haven't you called me?" Blue questioned.
"Blue what is it that you want? I already made a fool of myself by sleeping with you so quickly and was dumb enough to believe that you would get back at me. Now what would you like me to do?"
"I need to see you. Meet me somewhere."

"Meet you where? Boy I'm tired, I just left the hospital and I'm not going anywhere."
"Who's there?"
"Nobody."
"Well where you live at? I'm comin' through there then."
Onika took a deep breath. She really didn't feel like being bothered but the thought of being with Blue had her mesmerized. "Listen. I don't have time for your little games. I'm not one of them trifling ass hoodrats you probably use to dealing with. Now we shared a night together, it was good, I had fun but it's not like I do shit like that on the regular, so if you wanna come kick it, spend a little time with me that's cool. If you wanna have sex don't waste your time."
I know this ain't the same bitch that gave me head in the Lam' on the first night callin' somebody triflin.' He thought.
"Is you gone give me the address or what?"

Onika paused for a second before giving Blue the address to her apartment in the Coleman Place section of Norfolk. She figured that if she didn't, she
probably would not have heard from him again and that was something that she just didn't want to chance.
"I'll call you when I'm out front." Blue said and hung up.
Onika walked into the front room where her brother was stretched out on the couch sleep. She shook him violently in attempt to wake him. "Keith wake up... Get up boy."
"Huh? Girl what's wrong wit' choo?" K.O. screamed and rolled over to finish sleeping.
"Keith get up and go home. You know we 'on't even do the sleep over thing."
K.O. sat up on the couch and gave his sister an evil stare through his sleepy eyes. He yawned then rubbed his face before he placed his feet into his all black quarter top DC's. (Air Force One Nikes.) "I'm gone man. Don't look like ah

nigga can get no sleep 'round this bitch." He said still upset about having his sleep interrupted.

"Yeah, well come on then." Onika said and hurried her brother to the front door.

K.O. shook his head from side to side. "Youn't gotta worry 'bout me comin' over here to spend no time wit' choo at night no more." He said as Onika opened the door to let him out. K.O. stepped through the opened door and Onika closed it behind him. She returned to her room to freshen up for Blue when she heard a knock at the door. "Why don't men ever do what they say they gone do?" She asked herself and shook her head like she didn't have an answer as she walked towards the door. Onika unlocked the door and opened it. "I thought you were gonna..."

"You thought I was gone what? I forgot my keys." K.O. brushed past his sister, walked to the dining room table that was positioned in front of the couch that he was sleeping on, grabbed his keys and turned to leave. "I'm out." K. O said and threw up two fingers to say peace as Onika's phone started ringing.

"Alright." Onika said to her brother as she raced to answer the phone.

Killah sat at the kitchen table calculating the amount of Boy that they had left while Fu played against the computer in Madden '04. "Damn Ace! You know we only have fifty seven bricks and twenty ounces left after we put these fourteen hundred grams on the block tomorrow." He said with a huge smile. Fu paused the game and walked over to the kitchen table to see what his partner was talking about. "All of the dumpsters are empty, correct?" Killah questioned as Fu pulled up a chair.

"Yeah. Everything should be stashed in the closet." Fu responded as he took a seat and glanced over the numbers that his partner had written down.

Turk and Drea walked through the door as Killah explained the events that were to take place over the next few weeks and joined them at the table. Turk dumped the bag of money on the table. "What's up?" She questioned as she divided the money out to be counted.

"Just going over some numbers. What's good?" Killah questioned.

"Shit. Just so much bull shit going on." Turk responded with a sigh. "Let's hurry up and get this out of the way so I can get some rest. I'm tired!" She said then started counting.

The four of them counted the cash then divided and issued out the proper amount for each individual. Killah rose to his feet and walked towards the front door with Turk, Fu and Drea in tow. He hit the light, locked the door and the four of them headed towards the apartment where the heroin was stashed. Killah walked to the closet, removed a package and weighed out 1,400 grams. "Drea how much has Tasha been giving Worm and Popcorn? Two and a half right?" He questioned to make sure that he was on the right page.

"Yeah. Two and a half." Drea confirmed.

"Well we are not going to put anything out The Park tomorrow. Tell Tasha to drop Worm off Ten grand and tell him to chill for a week until we come back from vacation, and tell her to divided the extra two and a half out however she see's fit." Killah explained.

"Okay." Drea agreed.

The crew took to the kitchen to cut another monster and in a little less than two hours, The God Father was once again alive. The four of them cleaned up their mess, then Fu and Drea called to get everyone in their proper position. Killah hit the lights and locked the door and they headed for their cars. He stopped Turk in the parking lot as Fu and Drea entered their vehicles.

"Yo holla at me when you get home Ace." Killah instructed.

"Yeah call me when you get home girl." Turk said.

"Alright." Fu and Drea said in unison. They both hit their horns lightly and drove off.

Killah peered into his cousin's eyes as the two stood in the parking lot alone. "You know the dude Fat Shawn called me earlier." He said and searched Turk's reaction for any movement that appeared out of the ordinary.

Turk caught herself before she flew off the deep end. The sound of Fat Shawn's name caused her blood to boil. If it was anybody that Turk wanted and needed dead it was Fat Shawn. "What the fuck he want?" She questioned.

"He claim he got some news I can use."

"Well he better hope I don't catch'em 'cause I ain't trynna hear shit he gotta say. He gone die for what he did." Turk explained heatedly. "Where the fuck he at anyway?"

"Look. I told him that if his information is valuable and that if he didn't have anything to do with Tee-Tee, that I would let him live."

"What the fuck you mean IF, he didn't have nothing to do with Tee-Tee?"

"Exactly what I said. IF! You never know. Them young cats could have acted on their own, they could have been sent by someone else, OR." He said catching Turk off guard.

"OR what? Look I 'on't give ah fuck if them young niggas acted on their own or not he gone die for knowing them. You know how the game go."

"Or?" Killah paused and a smile appeared on his face. "He could be guilty." He said and shrugged his shoulders like he didn't know for sure. "I said that I'll handle Fat Shawn myself so let me handle him." Killah said and climbed in his car. He let the top down. "I'll see you later." Turk stood in the parking lot with her mind racing. She had no intention on allowing Fat Shawn to have some private meeting with Killah. She stared at her cousin as he reclined behind the wheel of his 600 with the roof off. Turk shook her head up and down like she had just come up with a brilliant idea. She jumped in her Modena and hit the horn lightly as she pulled off.

Blue reclined in Shatoya's dark purple Lexus GS 430 across the street from Onika's apartment and waited for her to answer her phone. He quickly ended his call and sat up in his seat as he noticed K.O. leaving the apartment where Onika said she lived. Blue adjusted the silencer on his 10mm as he watched K.O. walk to his van and climb in. Blue started to get out of the car, walk up to K. O's van and dump on him right there but for some reason he didn't. For the first time in the midst of a potential hostile situation, Blue decided to listen to Killah and think. He reclined back in his seat and waited for K.O. to pull off.
K.O. reached in the ashtray and removed a half of a blunt that he had put out on his way to his sister's house. He sparked the blunt and turned towards the back of the van. "You ain't dead yet?" He asked Popcorn who was lying in the back, tied up, gagged and badly beaten. K.O. put the van in drive, took a deep pull on the lobster and drove off.
Blue's phone had been vibrating since the moment he hung it up when he spotted K.O..
He waited until K.O. reached Princess Anne Rd. and made a right turn before he answered. "Yeah." He said with an attitude.
"Why you hang up?"
"Why you lie and say that won't nobody here wit' choo? I started to pull off. You got niggas runnin' in an' out cho house this time of night." Blue yelled, more upset with

himself than he was with her. He still didn't understand what made him decide to let K.O. slip away. He figured that Onika had to be of some importance to K.O. and decided that she would be the key to getting him back. *There's always a better way.* He thought.

"Boy that was my brother. Are you coming in or are you going to sit outside and play the role of the upset jealous lover?"

"Your brother?" Blue questioned all of a sudden feeling like he made the right decision. "Man open the door." He said. He removed his black Nike gloves from the back seat, put them on and exited the car. *This nigga Killah must be a genius or* somethin.' He thought as he walked towards the door. Onika came to the door dressed in a pair of short Baby Phat shorts, a wife beater and a pair of footie socks. She smiled and extended her arms to greet Blue with a hug. Onika was just as fine now as she was the night Blue met her. Everything from her face to her body structure was tight. She undressed Blue with her eyes. *Damn this boy is fine.* She thought as Blue accepted her invitation to a hug and held her tightly. Onika inhaled his Armani code cologne. "You smell good." She said as she took a step back and eyed him again.

Blue was dressed in a black and yellow Plaxico Burress Pittsburgh Steelers jersey, a pair of dark blue Coogi jean shorts with a yellow stripe on the side and a pair of black and yellow Nike Gortex boots. Onika didn't usually date the jean and boot type but Blue had a sister seriously thinking about changing her choice of men. "What's up shawty?" Blue asked as he was now sizing Onika up.

Onika couldn't stop herself from blushing. "How have you been doing?" She questioned as she closed the door behind them. Onika led Blue to the couch and allowed him to take a seat. "You hungry?" She asked being polite.

"Shorty it's after eleven ah clock, I ain't come over her to get nothin' to eat." Blue responded with a smile.
Onika returned the smile. "Well excuse me for being hospitable. Would you like something to drink then?" She asked.

"Yeah. Bring me some water." He requested and made himself comfortable. Onika seductively waltzed into the kitchen. Blue studied her hips as they swayed enticingly. Her walk was definitely mean and she knew it. She returned with a glass of water and a bottle of apple juice and took a seat up under Blue. He eyed the bottle of apple juice as Onika popped the top and took a sip. "Let me get that." He asked gesturing to the bottle of juice.
"Uhn uhn! You asked for water and that's what you got." She said and pointed to the glass of water.
"Well that was before I knew you had apple juice."
"Well, you should've asked. Sorry!" She smiled.
"So you not gone give it to me?" He questioned.
"Here boy." Onika said faking like she didn't want to give it to him. She placed the bottle on the table and walked to the kitchen to get her another one. She returned with a fresh bottle of apple juice and repositioned herself on the couch. "Man let me get the new bottle, I 'on't know where your lips been." Blue joked seriously.
Onika exhaled loudly. Blue was beginning to get on her nerves. "I know you didn't come over her to worry me to death. Here." She said and grabbed Blue by his cheeks and pressed her lips against his. "Now they been the same place yours been." She laughed then opened the fresh bottle of juice and took a swig.
Blue didn't find any humor in Onika's last move. He leaned back hard against the couch and started thumbing through his Blackburry. Onika flipped through the channels on the

television while trying to create small talk. She made several attempts to open up to Blue in effort to get to know him better but all she received was the cold shoulder.

"What's wrong with you?"

"Ain't shit wrong wit' me."

"Well why you bein' so anti social and acting so stupid?"

"Cuz that nigga won't cho brother." He snapped in search of the truth.

"Who Keith?"

"Who the fuck is Keith? I'm talkin' 'bout K.O."

"Youn't even know the damn boy so how you gone say he ain't my brother. Keith is K.O." Onika said angrily and stood up.

"Where you goin'?" Blue asked but received no response as Onika stormed into her bedroom. Blue removed his 10mm from the small of his back and sat it on the table in arm's distance. At that moment all sorts of thoughts raced through his head. *What if this bitch knew about me and K.O.'s beef the whole time.* He thought. "Man this bitch might've set me up." He mumbled. *I knew I should've killed that nigga K.O. when I had the chance instead of listening to Killah's dumb ass.* His mind spoke again.

Onika came storming back into the living room with a photo album in her hand. "Boy put that gun up. You ain't on the block." She said and waved her hand towards the weapon. She sat the photo album on the table. "Got me goin' through all this bullshit like you my man or somethin'. Move over." She snapped and took a seat on the couch Indian Style. She opened the large book filled with pictures and showed flicks of her and K.O. when they were children. "Now this Keith or "K.O." when he was five…." She started and flipped through the entire book. Onika pretty much journeyed through their entire childhood then out of nowhere she broke down and started crying. "Now my mother is in the hospital because of Keith's bullshit. She stayed in a coma for eighty four days and just came out tonight."

"What the fuck happened to her?" Blue asked. Not that he cared but this was something that he was unaware of. Turk and Lady had not mentioned their handiwork to anyone. Keeping secrets was something that they were both good at.

"I don't really know because she really wasn't able to say much but I'mma ask her when I go see her tomorrow. Blue placed his arms around Onika and held her close to him. "Do your brother know I fuck wit' choo?"

"No 'cause I really can't say we mess with each other." She answered staring him dead in his beautiful bluish green eyes. All of that emotion built up and Blue's sudden show of concern made Onika extremely horney. She started placing kisses all over Blue's neck and face as she unzipped his pants.

Blue lifted her chin so that he could look into her eyes. "What choo doin'?"

"What it look like I'm doing?" It was hard for her to continuously look him in his eyes. Blue had a way of looking a women in her eyes, causing her body to become warm and wet all over.

"I 'on't know 'cause I remember you tellin' me that I couldn't fuck tonight."

Onika smiled and wiped away a few tears that remained in her eyes. She looked at the time on her DVD player. "It's after midnight. It's a new day." She said as it was actually a little after one o' clock in the morning. Onika unfastened Blue's button, removed his rock hard muscle and held it in her hand.

Blue's phone began vibrating and he checked the I. D. then answered. "Yo...... I'm on my way." He said and hung up. He removed her hand from his boxers and fixed his jeans." Yo

I'll call you later. I wanna go to the hospital wit' choo." He said and stood up to leave. "What time you goin'?"
"Probably around nine. Just call me before eight."
"At night right?"
"Yeah."
"Ah'ight." He said and headed out of the door. Blue had every intention on killing Onika when he first entered her apartment but throughout the course of the night he had changed his mind. He was intrigued to know what happened to her mother plus he wanted K.O. to run into him with his sister. "This nigga Killah got me feeling like a real sucker." He said to himself. He climbed into the car and drove to the spot to meet Tasha, Tika Bell, and Lady.

Blue and company took almost five hours to bag up. He didn't bother to mention K.O.'s mother's attack because he wanted to gather all of the details first. As soon as the last of the diseal was packaged for sell Blue headed for the door. "I'll catch ya'll later." He said and walked out of the townhouse. Blue picked up his phone and dialed Onika's number. After two attempts with no answer he tried again. The phone had to ring at least twelve times before she answered.
"Hell-O."
"You sleep?" He asked knowing damn well that she was.
"What it sound like?"
"Youn't answer a question wit' a question. I'm on my way to finish what choo started."
"Boy what time is it?"
"Six twelve. Ah new day."
Onika laughed. "Call when you get out front."
Blue instantly grew hard at the sound of Onika's last comment. He smiled briefly. "Ah'ight." He answered and ended their conversation.

Tasha completed all of her drops before she headed out The Park to meet Lady and holler at Worm. When she arrived she noticed Lady's Hummer parked in front of the spot but she didn't see Worm anywhere in sight. As she attempted to exit her smoke gray BMW 745i, a green Lincoln Navigator pulled up hard on her side of the car forcing her to close the door. "Nigga what the fuck is wrong with you?" Tasha barked.
"Yo Tash' what's up?" The tall brown skin male with a low hair cut asked.
"Nigga don't choo work for da feds? Nigga I 'on't fuck wit' no police. Now please get the fuck out my way before I do something to you." She said and grabbed a hold of the P-89 Ruger that rested in her lap.
"Where you hear some shit like that?" The driver of the Navigator asked like the fact that he was a government informant was supposed to be a secret.
Lady came to the door and noticed her stick girl boxed in as the driver of the truck continued to try and explain his situation. She walked over to the truck and placed her .44 to the back of the guys head. "Baldy if youn't get cho hot ass from out of here, I'mma blow the back of ya brains out and see if you can think wit' the front."
"Damn Lady what's that about?" Baldy asked.
"We know all about choo Stanley and the only reason I 'on't kill you is because I ain't fuck wit' that Brambleton nigga you set up. Now you lucky that nigga supposed to have changed and told niggas not to get at cho ass because I heard about that bitch shit you did. Left that girl and them kids in the house while yo' punk ass jumped out of the window. You lucky the same shit ain't happen to her that happened to Hubb girl when his fat scary ass jumped out the window. Now if I ever hear you mention my name or anybody I fuck wit' name you know what it is." Lady spat.

Baldy didn't say a word. He put the Navigator that the feds bought him in drive and pulled off.
"What the fuck that clown want?"
"Shit if I know. He probably lookin' for some body to set up."
"Well if I catch that nigga again I'mma kill his pussy ass. Soft ass nigga can't hold water. Coward mu fucka." Lady said with her blood boiling. She really despised a snitch. Tasha climbed out of her car, tucked her gun inside her waist band and leaned against the driver's side door. The two females exchanged information as Worm drove up and parked. He climbed out of his vehicle and approached the two women.
"What's up Worm?" Tasha asked as she reached inside of her window and removed a white envelope containing one hundred $100 bills. Worm nodded his head upwards to speak and Tasha handed him the envelope. "Here. This ten grand. Killah said chill until we come back from vacation." Worm received the money and placed the envelope in his right pocket. "Ya'll hear anything else about Popcorn?"
"Naw. Ain't nobody seen K.O. and them nowhere." Tasha explained but as far as she knew, none of them went looking for him.
"More than likely shorty dead." Lady said out of nowhere. "That's just keeping it real. It's part of the game Worm. We can't sweat that shit. Just know that them niggas'll ah never get away wit' that shit. It's fucked up but that's the way it is at the top. You kill my dog, I kill two or three of yours." Lady explained the best way she knew how. "Look I'm 'bout to roll. I'll get wit' cha'll later." She said and walked over to her Hummer. She jumped in the SUV that was customized by Becker Automotive Design to resemble a person's living room. She turned the alpine up to full blast and drove off cranking Mia X. *"You don't wanna…. Go to war wit' ah solider…. No Limit TRU nigga… I thought I told ja."* Master P.

yelled through the six 12 inch W3's while "Menace II Society"
played on the five LCD DVD monitors as Lady disappeared. Tasha climbed back into her quarter to eight. "Blue gone holla at choo when we get back." She said to Worm as he jumped back inside of his P.V. Tasha hit her horn and drove off.

Blue left Onika's apartment around 4pm en route to Shatoya's house to change clothes. The house was completely still which was unusual for a hot and sticky Tuesday afternoon on the last day of August. The weather man was calling for a high of one hundred degrees but it felt more like two hundred. Lil D and Chris were usually in front of the television or a video game, sucking up all of the air condition around this time but they were nowhere in sight. Blue yelled for Shatoya but he didn't receive a response so he walked into the bedroom.
Shatoya was balled up on her bed in a fetal position, moaning like she was in pain. Blue raced to her side and noticed that she had tears in her eyes. "Bay, what's wrong?" He asked as he took a seat on the bed beside her. Shatoya looked up at him though her teary eyes and rolled over without saying a word. "Shatoya what's wrong with you?" He asked as he grabbed her by the shoulders and forced her to look at him. Shatoya tried to resist but was over powered. She stared at Blue coldly but still remained silent.
"I see you wanna act stupid." He said and rose to his feet. Blue was beyond pissed off. He walked over to the closet and removed a green James Whitley Green Bay Packer's jersey, some black Ice burg shorts and a pair of black and green Air Max 90's.
Blue only wore NFL and NBA jerseys of players who were from the "757." He threw the clothes on the bed, walked to

the dresser, removed a pair of black Dolce and Gabbana briefs and a white wife beater tank top.

He removed all of his clothes that he had on and looked at Shatoya who was still in a knot crying. "Act stupid then, I 'on't give ah fuck." He said and walked into the bathroom that was connected to the room.

Blue had completed his shower and was almost finished getting dressed before Shatoya finally got up. She sprung off the bed suddenly and raced to the bathroom. Blue could hear the sounds of Shatoya throwing up and the toilet flushing repeatedly as he threw on his platinum TWP chain, a larger platinum chain with a C. O. C charm, his green five time zone Jacob and Co. watch and headed for the front door. Shatoya walked to the sink, rinsed her mouth and returned to her bed. She noticed that Blue was gone and began crying all over again.

Blue entered his white with red leather interior Jaguar XKR and sped off. He had a little over two hours to waste before he was scheduled to call Onika. He drove from Shatoya's house in Popular Halls (An upper class black neighborhood with beautiful yet affordable homes.) to Janaf Shopping Center which was located less than two miles away. Blue stopped at the ABC store, purchased a fifth of Patron and returned to his car. He checked his Blackburry for a young lady that he could waste time on as he drove towards Va. Beach. He scanned his top ten "Best Overall Sex" list before stopping on number six. Blue had his women categorized in seven different categories, (Financial Status, Best looking, Best Body, Best Vaginal, Best Anal, Best Oral and Best Overall.) and rated them from one star to five stars. He totaled the amount of stars earned in categories one through six to determine his Best Overall.

Blue noticed that number six had a total of twenty-eight stars out of a possible thirty. She earned five stars in every category except "Financial Status." "Angel." He said to himself before dialing her number. Blue opened the bottle of Patron and took a long hard swallow as the phone began to ring.

"Hello." A sexy female voice with an Asian accent answered. "What choo doin'?"

"Nothin'. Just chillen. Who is this?"

"I was headed that way so I figured I'll come through and play in that lil' tight wet pussy of yours."

Angel laughed as she was now able to distinguish Blue's voice and match it with his face. "Is that right?"

"If it's ah'ight wit' choo."

"I got company right now but he ain't talkin' 'bout shit. Let me get rid of him and I'll call you back." She whispered.

"That's what's up." Blue said and drove towards Lake Edwards. He stopped by a fast food restaurant off of Newtown Rd. and ordered a Spicy Chicken Combo with a Pink Lemonade. As he handed the cashier his money at the first window his phone rang. "Keep the change shorty." He said to the young teenaged boy that collected the money before answering his call. "That was quick." Blue spoke into the phone as he drove to the next window to pick up his food.

"I told ju he won't talkin' 'bout shit. Where you at?"

"Just leavin' Wendy's on Newtown. I'm on my way." He said and drove the block and a half.

Angel came to the door of her lovely three bedroom town house wearing only a three quarter length Trench Coat, belt and boots by Prada. Blue smiled as Angel unbuckled her belt and allowed her $4,000 jacket to hit the floor, revealing her nakedness. Angel was top of the line mean. She had a

perfect blend of Black and Filipino genes with 36 DD-24-43 measurements.
Blue wasted a little more than a hour and a half sexing Angel. He got off two strong orgasms and rolled out. He dialed Onika's number as he headed back towards Norfolk. "I'm on my way." He said as she answered the phone. Onika responded by saying that she was ready and they both hung up.

Turk, Tasha and Lady were enjoying a girl's night out at The Blue Hippo in Norfolk. (Located on Granby St, The Blue Hippo was a small and sophisticated restaurant where the meals began at twenty dollars an entrée.) The three women told jokes over plates of fresh Salmon and glasses of L' Aventure Zinfandel to kill time.

"A Tasha tell Turk what choo did to that nigga Dexter in the hotel." Lady said cracking up in laughter.
"What? When I slapped'em with the pistol?" Tasha questioned.
"Yeah!" Lady answered still laughing as she took a sip of her wine.
Tasha gave a play by play of the event that took place the night Tehran was killed. She explained from how Dexter performed oral sex on her, all the way up until her spitting in his face and calling him a bitch. "I had that nigga feeling like a two dollar hooker." She said causing an eruption of laughter among the three.
A group of diners that came out to enjoy the usually relaxed and quiet atmosphere, found Turk, Tasha, and Lady's outburst a bit rude. "Excuse me." An elderly white, professional looking male, with a head full of gray hair called to get their attention. "Could you people please keep it down? We are trying to enjoy our meal over here." He said

with an attitude. "Who the fuck is you talkin' to?" Lady questioned displaying an attitude of her own. "You need to turn around and enjoy your meal while you can still chew." She said and stood to her feet.

"Waiter. WAITER!" The white man yelled. The waiter appeared in no time and the white man explained the situation, while pointing towards Turk, Tasha and Lady. The waiter walked over to where the three of them were sitting and asked them to please keep it down.

Turk grabbed hold of the situation by nodding that they understood and waited for the waiter to leave. "Come on ya'll let's go before we fuck around and end up in jail tonight." Turk said loud enough for the white man and his family to hear. She stood up and grilled them all on her way out of the door.

The three ladies walked out of the restaurant. "It's about time for ya'll to pick up anyway." Turk said as her phone vibrated. A huge smile covered her face as she answered the phone. "Yeah….. Nothing. Just leaving Tasha and Lady… Nowhere really. Where you want me to go?... You eating?... Well I'm on my way." Turk said still smiling as she hung up.

"Who the fuck was that that got choo cheesin' and shit bitch?" Lady asked.

"Reggie."

"Reggie? Who the fuck is Reggie?" Lady questioned confused.

"Drea ex." Turk said nonchalant.

"Bitch you fuckin' Drea's ex husband?" Tasha asked with her hand covering her mouth in shock.

"Yeah. Why not? Bitch ain't one of us. Besides she ain't want him."

"You ain't got no heart for real. I'm glad I don't got ah man. You and Drea been best friends since I can remember." Tasha explained.

"Well the ho shouldn't've crossed me. Talkin' 'bout she retiring too. All for a nigga that done left her dumb ass."
"You ah dirty bitch. That's all I'mma say." Tasha said and shook her head laughing. "Ain't she Lady?"
Lady remained quiet. She had an entirely different feeling about the situation because she was emotionally attached. Lady shook her head and decided to keep her comments and her feeling to herself.
Turk read the look on Lady's face and smiled. "Look I'll catch ya'll out Da Park. By time ya'll finish collecting I should already be at the spot." Turk said. She hopped inside of her 360 Spider, Tasha jumped in her 745i and Lady climbed in her Hummer and they all drove off.

Blue and Onika walked into her mother's hospital room a little after nine. Ms. Owens was wide awake, staring at the ceiling when they entered. "Hey mom." Onika spoke as she grabbed her mother's hand and kissed her cheek. Ms. Owens smiled and rubbed her daughter's hand. Blue watched as Onika and her mother interacted with one another. He noticed how badly she was beaten as he took a seat beside Onika at her mother's bedside. Ms. Owens still had all sorts of tubes and machines connected to her body to assist her breathing and eating. Onika lightly touched her mother's face below one of her scars. "You okay mom? What happened?"

Ms. Owens continued to rub Onika's hand and smile. She attempted to talk but her voice was faint. She pointed to a pitcher of water that rested on the table. Onika removed the pitcher and poured her mother a cup. Ms. Owens took a painful swallow and cleared her throat. "Some of your brother's girl friends." Was all that she was able to say.

As soon as Ms. Owens said the word girlfriends, Blue had figured out who the guilty parties were. He leaned close to Onika's ear. "Ask her can she remember what they look like." He whispered. He wanted to be one hundred percent sure that he accused the correct people.

Onika repeated the question to her mother. Ms. Owens took a second to respond. All she could remember was that one was tall, the other one was real dark and they both had meat on their bones. "I forget what she said her name was." She spoke slowly.

Blue was furious. He immediately blamed Turk and Lady for Popcorn's abduction. He wondered why they never reported the situation to the rest of the family. *I'm bringin' them ho's up on charges as soon as I see Killah.* He thought. It was considered a crime against the Family to create a potentially violent situation and not report it. Blue leaned back in his seat and allowed his mind to roam while Onika continued to comfort her mother.

A few minutes later the door swung open. Ms. Owens looked towards the figure that appeared in the doorway and cringed, while Blue sat up in his chair.

"Hey mom." K.O. yelled with a huge smile on his face as he entered the room with a hand full of balloons and flowers. His smile quickly vanished at the sight of Blue. "What the fuck you doin' here?" He yelled as he dropped the flowers, released the balloons and charged Blue. Blue stood up just in time to duck the wild over hand right that K.O. delivered. He countered with a sharp right hook to K.O.'s body, followed by a quick left jab to his chin, a right jab to the chin, a right hook to the jaw and a powerful left upper cut. Blue was so quick and accurate with his punches that his teacher and old friend "Sweet Pea" would have been proud. Before K.O. realized it Blue had hit him five times and he was flat on his back scrambling to get up. Onika jumped in front of Blue as he walked towards K.O. to finish whipping him. She placed her hands against his chest to stop him.

"Please Blue! Don't disrespect my mother. Please, please just leave for me." Onika pleaded more for her mother than her brother. Blue stared at Onika and bit his bottom lip. He pushed her lightly out of his way and continued to approach K.O. who was now back on his feet searching for something to use as a weapon. Blue removed his pistol from the small of his back and placed it under K.O.'s chin. Ms. Owens pressed her emergency button repeatedly.

"You ah dead man." Blue said and kissed K.O. on his cheek. Blue kept his tool aimed at K.O. long enough for him to exit the room. He tucked his weapon away and passed a nurse and two security guards who were rushing in the direction of Ms. Owens's room as he headed out of the hospital. Blue hopped in his car, opened the bottle of Patron, took a huge gulp, pulled out his phone and dialed Lady's number.

"Yo."

"Where you at?"

"Just got out Da Park. Why what's up?"

"I'll be out there." Blue said and hung up. He started his Jaguar and drove towards The Park like a bat out of hell.

Turk, Tasha and Lady congregated in the middle of Holt St. talking trash with a group of people from the back of The Park while waiting for Drea. It was crazy how much respect the people in the local Parks and Ghetto's showed the members of the C.O.C for what they consider "Keeping It Real." Keeping It Real is an old hood cliché used for those who made it out of the hood but never forgot where they came from. No matter how successful a person may have become, or how he or she became successful, as long as they show love to the hood where they came from they were considered someone who "Keep It Real". Keeping It

Real also applies to those who handle their business, won't snitch, can carry their own weight, stands firm on their word, and those who are not afraid to fellowship in the slums with the less fortunate without looking down on them. Now as soon as a person stops showing love they will no longer be considered as one who Keeps it real and may be subject to a random act of violence if they ever decided to return to the hood. As long as you show love to the hood, the hood will show love to you and each and every member of The C.O.C Family showed love to the hood therefore they Kept It Real. Turk, Tasha, and Lady loved to be in the mix with real live street level criminals. All three women were worth millions and here they were laughing and joking with petty larcenist, grand larcenist, armed robbers, rapist, murderers and all level of drug dealers and users. Purple Haze, Hydro, Chocolate, Lobster and Regular weed filled the air of the Downtown Norfolk Project. People talked on their cell phones, either making drug deals or setting up late night jump offs while the system in Lady's Hummer gave Holt St. the vibe of a block party.

Blue pulled up in the midst of the crowded block and parked in the middle of the street. He hopped out of his car, leaving the door ajar and walked up on Tasha with his gun in hand. Blue was twisted. He had downed the entire bottle of Patron plus his adrenaline was still speeding from his incident with K.O. "Yo hold this." He said to Tasha and handed her his 10mm. He continued past her and walked up to Lady who was leaning against her SUV, running her mouth. Blue shoved Lady with all of his power catching her completely off guard. He pushed Lady with so much force that he lifted her off of her feet and caused her to fly a few feet backwards. "Why the fuck you ain't tell me about K.O.'s mother?" He asked in a drunken rage. Blue's actions shocked everyone in the crowd so much that they formed a tight circle around him and Lady to get a closer look. Some wanted to see a good rumble while others wanted to see them cut out all of their foolishness. Everyone that remained in the crowd wanted to know what was going on and what would happen next.

Lady hit the ground, pulled out her trusty .44 and stood to her feet with the gun pointed at Blue in what appeared to be one motion. Turk jumped between the two and pushed Lady's gun hand down. "Lady put that fuckin' gun up." She demanded and waited for Lady to oblige before she turned to face Blue. Turk pushed Blue and yoked him up by his collar. "Nigga what the fuck is wrong with you?" She questioned.

"Man get cho mu fuckin' hands off me." Blue said as he snatched away from Turk's grasp. "Why the fuck ya'll ain't report what cha'll did to K.O.'s mother? That's the reason he came out here and snatched Popcorn. Ya'll bitches got my nigga killed." He said pointing his index finger in her face and spit on the ground to relieve his cotton mouth.

Turk smacked Blue in the mouth and snatched him by his collar again. "Nigga fuck Popcorn. Look around. Me, Tasha, and Lady the only Family you got. When Kurk was ready to turn your brains into cool whip, who was there to save you? It won't Popcorn, it won't Chris and it won't Fu soft ass. It was Lady! And when everybody else said they wanted out of the game leaving you for dead who were the only three bitches that had your back? Think about that." She said through clenched teeth loud enough for only Blue to hear and released his jersey collar with a shove.

Blue snatched his gun from Tasha and jumped back in his car. "Fuck that. I'm bringin' both of you bitches up on charges." He said before closing his door and driving off. Lady shook her head. "Girl I swear I was gone kill that nigga. Puttin' 'is got damn hands on me."

"Bitch you know I ain't gone let nobody get away with putting their hands on you. But I ain't gone let you kill the only real thorough nigga we got left. Not for some bullshit like that anyway. Plus if Chris punk out and change his mind about retiring Blue will be a real asset to us." Turk said as the crowd began to thin out.

Drea drove up shortly after. "We already counted." Turk informed Drea. "Look ya'll go and get some rest. We gone probably leave early in the morning." She told Tasha and Lady and jumped into her 360 Spider. "Come on Drea." Drea followed Turk out Pinewood where they along with Killah and Fu counted and divided the money.

"Anything new we need to discuss?" Killah questioned the table while surveying the occupants.

"No. Everything is pretty much the same." Turk answered.

"In that case, let the rest of the Family know that we will be leaving from the Clear Port, for Morocco at nine in the morning."

"Will do." She responded and they all headed for the door.

Blue rode around in circles for a little longer than a hour. Fu called to inform him that they would be departing for Morocco in the morning as he headed to Shatoya's house to get some rest. Shatoya was asleep in a pair of Victoria Secret underwear and a cut off Tee-shirt when Blue entered the room. He looked over at Shatoya as she slept and headed straight for the shower. Blue ran the water as hot as he could bare it and allowed the soothing streams to massage him while he cleared his mind. He couldn't stop himself from thinking about Turk slapping him and the words that she spoke. Images of Popcorn continued to race through his mind as well. He realized that every word that Turk spoke was true. He understood who would be there for him when the guns went off. He was aware that it was Lady who saved his life and would have died for him. He also knew that Popcorn was non violent and completely harmless, but he was the one who raised Popcorn and introduced him to the dope game so he felt somewhat responsible. *Fuck it. Can't sweat the inevitable.* He thought as he turned the water off to the shower. The last two days created a multitude of things for Blue to think about. He was pleased to know that he was now in the company of someone who truly cared about him. He couldn't wait until the jet landed in Northern Africa in the morning but the reality was that the night was not over and he still didn't know what was wrong with his wifey.

Blue climbed out of the shower, dried off and slipped into a pair of boxers. He crawled in the bed and pulled at Shatoya's underwear as she slept on her stomach.

"Stop." She said half awake and slapped his hand away. He continued to remove her panties while she continued to resist. "Blue I said stop, damn." Shatoya yelled with attitude and rolled over.

"I see you still in yo shitty mood." He snapped. Blue rolled to the opposite end of the Ultra King size bad, which was the size of three regular King size beds combined. "Fuck you then. Keep that shit." He barked. "I'll get plenty of pussy in the mornin'." He mumbled.

"What?" Shatoya questioned. She couldn't hear exactly what he said but she knew that it had to be something inconsiderate. Blue didn't respond, he just continued to lay there looking stupid with his lips poked out until he dozed off.

Blue could hear what sounded like someone rumbling through the closet as the noise interrupted his sleep. He glanced over his shoulder and realized that Shatoya was no longer in the bed so he figured that she was responsible for making all of the noise. He closed his eyes to finish sleeping

as the sound became lighter. Suddenly he heard footsteps but they didn't sound like normal footsteps. These were the footsteps of someone who was not trying to be heard. Blue could tell that someone was sneaking up on him. He opened his eyes just in time to stare down the barrel of his own gun.
"What the fuck is wrong wit' choo?"
"I'm tired of your shit Blue." Shatoya yelled with tears in her eyes.
"Tired of what shit? Bitch you better put that gun down 'fore you fuck around and get killed." He said as he sat up on the bed.
"Go 'head kill me. That's what the fuck you doin' anyway. Fuckin' all these dirty ass bitches bringin' that shit home to me."
"What the fuck is you talkin' 'bout?" He questioned confused. He couldn't remember bringing home any STD's since he gave her gonorrhea twelve months after they got together.
"Nigga you gave me herpes. And I'm four months pregnant." Blue placed his hand over his eyes and rubbed his temples. "Damn." He said quietly. There was really nothing he could say at the moment so he just remained quiet for a minute. Shatoya began to reconsider. She loved Blue to death and she couldn't see herself without him, besides it wasn't like he couldn't afford the proper medication. As Shatoya's mind played tricks or her, Blue's inconsiderate tongue spoke again. "So what choo gone kill me because some stinkin' ass bitch gave me herpes?"
"Naw I'mma kill you because you gave the shit to me. Blue youn't give a fuck about me. Now I gotta sit around scared to death until the results of my H I V test come back."
"Man fuck all that. If you gone kill me kill me. If you think that shit gone make you feel better or help the shit go away go 'head. I ain't gone try to stop ya." He said and threw his

hands to his side then folded them behind his head. Blue was cocky like that. He knew that Shatoya wasn't capable of murder.
Shatoya eyed Blue for a minute with her tears flowing quickly down her face. She said a quick prayer in her head before she pulled the trigger and left Blue's brains all over the wall like graffiti. She stared at his lifeless body for a second. She knew that his friends would never understand why she took his life and the truth was she no longer wanted to live. Shatoya placed the gun in her mouth and pulled the trigger.
Less than one minute after Shatoya claimed her own life Blue's phone vibrated non stop. Onika finally got tired of calling and decided to leave a message. When she spoke she was in tears. "Blue. This is Onika. Call me back when you get this message. *My mother just passed.*"

Fu dialed Blue's number. He looked down at his Presidential Rolex. "Where the fuck is this nigga at?" He asked out loud as he noticed that it was twelve minutes until nine.

"He answer?" Killah asked.
"Naw." Fu responded. Turk, Tasha and Lady all looked expressionlessly at one another. "Call Shatoya's house while I keep trying his phone." Fu said to Killah.
Killah browsed through his Black Burry for Shatoya's number. He dialed but no one answered. He tried two more times and right before he was about to hang up someone answered.
"Hell-O." A sleepy voice answered.
"Lil' D is Blue there?"
"Hold on." Lil' D said. He jumped out of his bed, stretched and walked to his mother's room half asleep. Lil' D knocked on his mother's door but never received a response. He

cracked the door and tears instantly filled his eyes. He threw up all over the floor as he witnessed his mother and Blue stretched out with grape fruit size holes in both of their heads and blood everywhere. He raced back to the phone. "CHRIS! He dead. My momma an' Blue dead. My momma an' Blue dead." He yelled and dropped the phone. Lil' D raced out of his room and ran out of the front door with no shoes or shirt on. He ran down the street as fast as he could as if he could somehow escape what he had just witnessed. "Lil' D. Darius. Darius." Killah yelled into the phone. He turned to face the rest of the Family. "Yo Blue dead." Killah said. He ran to his GTR, jumped in and sped off.
The rest of the crew all stood motionless for a split second. They still didn't believe what they just heard but didn't waste any more time trying to let it sink in. Killah and Fu were the only ones who knew where Shatoya lived so the five females had to follow Fu since Killah was long gone.
Fu led the charge from Suffolk to Popular Hall. As he raced through traffic his phone vibrated. "Yo."
"A Fu. Freeze in jail. The feds came and got'em last night."
"WHAT? Yo I got some other shit to deal with right now. Let me call you back."
"So you not gone go get'em." Freeze's baby mother asked.
"Look. Let me call you back." Fu yelled and hung up. *Damn! When your up. It all falls down.* He thought.

CHAPTER ELEVEN
Heartless
The Truth

Lil' D managed to track down a couple of uniformed officers as he raced through Best Square Shopping Center, which was located directly behind his mother's house. He explained exactly what it was that he was running away from and led the law to the scene.

When Killah arrived on Shatoya's street, the block was swamped with detectives. All it took was one look at the amount of law enforcement officers that covered Popular Hall Drive before Killah realized that Lil' D had spoken the truth. He placed his car in reverse, turned around and drove to Best Square. Killah pulled out his phone and dialed Fu's number.

"I'm pulling up now." Fu answered.

"Yo meet me in front of Cox Cable." Killah instructed.

"What's the deal? I mean what's happening, what's the situation?"

"Yo just meet me in the parking lot. I'll be out front." Killah said before hanging up. He climbed out of his car and took a seat on the hood.

Fu arrived with the cavalry shortly after. Turk, Tasha, and Lady all exited their vehicles, eager to know what was going on. "What's up?" They questioned in unison.

"Man shorty crib surrounded by police. I don't know what the fuck happened." Killah said calmly.

"Well where the fuck Blue at?" Tasha yelled.

"He probably in the house or already in the ambulance. I don't know. I didn't hang around long enough to find out. I can't afford to be seen on no crime scenes. Especially not a murder scene." Killah explained. "The best I can come up

with is to keep our ears open and see what we come up with. Fu go pass Shatoya's sister house and have her check into the situation. Everybody else go home until we know what's going on." He said and stood off of the hood.
Turk, Fu, Drea, Tasha, Tika Bell, and Lady all stood staring at Killah as he entered his vehicle. Water began to fill the eyes of everyone who stood staring except Turk and Lady. Tasha nearly had a nervous breakdown as she ran to her car. Fu walked dejectedly to his car and climbed in, as everyone began to file out. The truth was beginning to set in and judging by their long faces it was hard for them to handle the truth.

Onika was having trouble dealing with her own realization of the truth. Her mother's death weighed on her like a ton of bricks. Onika couldn't eat or sleep. She made a few more attempts to reach Blue but continued to get the same results. She was hoping that she could convince him to come over and comfort her. Onika didn't hold Blue accountable for her mother's death. She placed one hundred percent of the blame on her brother and considered Blue's actions done in self defense. K. O. tried to explain his reason for attacking Blue to his sister before they left the hospital but Onika didn't care to hear a word her brother had to say. Her mind was made up and K. O.'s version of the truth was null and void.

Freeze sat in the day room dressed in his Norfolk City Jail black and white striped uniform, watching the twelve o'clock news on WAVY TV 10. The newscaster was about to go into an in depth description of their lead story when a deputy approached the cell block.

"William Daniels. Attorney visit. Get dressed. I'll be back in five minutes to get choo." The heavy set female deputy yelled.

Freeze walked into his cell for a second as the news team went to live coverage from the scene on Popular Hall Drive. He made sure that his box braids were in tact before he returned to the day room and walked over to the bars without looking at the television. "Dep-ah-dee." He yelled and adjusted his uniform shirt.

The deputy returned shortly after, opened the cell block and led Freeze to the visiting booth. As Freeze entered the tiny box shape booth he noticed a familiar looking, heavy set, dark skin cat with dread locks. He eyed the familiar looking face for a second before he turned his attention towards the short, brown hair, white man that sat next to the dread. Freeze took a seat as the deputy locked the door. He switched his attention back on the dread as he remembered where he recognized him from.

"Yo you da cat that use to be wit' Baldy all the time." Freeze said and pointed towards the dread.

"So you know what that means?" The dread questioned with a huge smile.

Freeze placed his head between his hands. *I knew I shouldn't've fucked wit that nigga Baldy.* He thought as he realized how badly he had screwed up. Freeze had heard all of the rumors about Stanley the informant before he did business with him. In fact Freeze was aware that Baldy had one of their suppose to be stick man's set up a couple of years earlier. See in the streets people hear what they want to hear and believe what they want to believe. Freeze was one of those people who believed that if a person didn't do anything to him directly and still wanted to spend money with him he would expect it. "You know a snitch don't care who he tells on. As long as he continues to be allowed to stay at home with his family." The dread said in a flat tone. "Look I'm detective Kay and this is agent Gavin with the DEA." He said as he looked Freeze eye to eye.

Freeze understood that he had made an attempt to avoid the truth by dealing with Baldy and the truth is; No matter what the case may be. "A rat will always be a rat." He shook his head from side to side and hung his head. "How can I help myself?" He spoke into the table.

"Excuse me? We couldn't hear you." Detective Kay said. "I said how can I help myself." Freeze said this time loud enough to be heard clearly. Both agents smiled. "That's what we wanted to hear." Agent Gavin said.

The two detectives showed Freeze several different photographs of Blue, Tasha, Tika Bell and Lady. Freeze acknowledged that he knew Tika Bell and Lady since they were the only two that he dealt with directly. He told them that he was aware of Blue's involvement in the drug game through their football days together and he also mentioned Fu since the two of them were like family.

"Now listen William, we have been eyeing these four, especially these three for almost a year but they always seem to disappear for months at a time." Agent Gavin said and singled out the pictures of Blue, Tasha and Lady. "Now we were informed that we would not be able to make any direct transactions so we were led to you. We need you to jot down all the information you can think of about these three in particular and have it ready for us in the morning. We'll be back to visit you then."

Freeze leaned back in his seat contemplating his next words. "Listen I'm not tryin' to do no time at all. If ya'll want a heavy weight I'm tellin' you that Antonio Smith is the man. These three ain't shit. Tony be movin' two to three hundred keys of heroin across the country at a time."

Both detective Kay and agent Gavin laughed hysterically. "Two to three hundred keys of heroin at a time? We look stupid right? Now if you want to help yourself you need to start by telling us the truth." Agent Gavin said sternly.
Freeze eyed the two detectives as if they were crazy. *These mutha fucka's don't'know shit.* He thought. "That is the truth. Me and Tony like family." "I would like to think that if someone was moving that kind of weight
across the country that we would know about it." Agent Gavin said proudly.
"Evidently ya'll don't know nothin' but what a mutha fucka tell you. If niggas would keep they ma' fuckin' mouf closed ya'll 'll be late as shit."
Detective Kay smiled. "Now isn't that the pot calling the kettle black?" He asked quite punningly. "Okay this Antonio Smith; How is he able to move this kind of heroin?"
"Through his dumpster company, B-F-I."
"So the maker of B-F-I is a major heroin distributor? Elaborate." Agent Gavin said.
"B-F-I stands for Big Fu Industries. Fu and Antonio Smith are the same people. The dumpster company was started with drug money and the dumpsters are used to ship drugs. Now where he get's it from and all that I don't know. We talk but not that much."
"Do you think we can set up a buy?" Detective Kay asked. "I doubt it. Not directly from him anyway. But...."
Agent Gavin cut Freeze in mid sentence. "But what? Like I thought. You're feeding me bullshit. Just do what we ask. Write down the information about the three subjects in question and we'll see you in the morning or continue to bullshit and I'll let you rot in prison." Agent Gavin commanded. He stood from his seat and pressed a button to alert the deputy that both parties were ready to leave.

K. O. popped ecstasy pills, inhaled deep pulls of Lobster and guzzled down big gulps of knotty head, (Seagram's Gin) while he cruised the city of Norfolk in search of Blue. He rode through every Ghetto and Park except for the three downtown. (Carrot, Young's and Tidewater.) K. O. was high but he wasn't out of his mind. He had too many death wishes in those three particular neighborhoods to risk riding through them even though he knew that Blue was from Downtown.

K. O. rode down 26th street in Park Place when he realized that it was the 1st of the month which meant that the C.O.C were somewhere in hiding for at least a week. As he continued down 26th he noticed a heavy set, light skin cat with a huge afro sitting on a porch. K. O. stopped in front of the house and hit the horn.

The man on the porch recognized K. O.'s Lincoln and stepped off in the direction of the car. "What's up K. O.?" He questioned as he reached through the passenger side window to give K. O. some dap.

K. O. stepped out of the car, walked around to the trunk and opened it. The light skin cat took a quick step back as he witnessed Popcorn's badly beaten, lifeless body. K. O. smiled a wicked grin. "This what the fuck happens when you fuck wit K. O." He said fronting. Popcorn had lost a lot of blood from the beating he suffered by Pat, Wayne and their stick man and eventually bled to death. K. O. didn't kill Popcorn intentionally, in fact he was scared to death himself when he first found out that Popcorn was dead.

"Who the fuck is that?" The man from the porch asked.

"You know that young nigga that use to be wit Blue all the time?"

"Yo Booy! You fuckin' wit some wild niggas. You got to get the fuck away from here wit that shit."

K. O. laughed. "Scared ass nigga." He joked and jumped back in his car. K. O. proceeded to ride around showing off Popcorn's body for a little over two hours before he rode out Coleman Place en route to his sisters house. He laid low over Onika's house until the wee hours of the morning. Onika stayed barricaded in her room the entire time her brother was there.
K. O. called Pat and Wayne to help him get rid of Popcorn's body. He drove out to Ballentine where the three of them stuffed the corpse inside of a duffle bag. K. O rode out to a secluded area in Virginia Beach barely beyond the Norfolk border and allowed Pat and Wayne to dump the body into the Chesapeake Bay.

Agent Gavin and detective Kay arrived at the Norfolk City Jail around nine o'clock in the morning. Freeze had stayed up all night preparing the information that the two officer's requested. He presented an adequate amount of information about Blue, Lady, and Fu. He wrote a few things about Tika Bell, nothing major and he didn't have anything on Tasha. He allowed the detectives a moment to glance over his work. "Okay so when can I get out of here?" He anxiously questioned.

"Oh, you're gonna spend some time in prison. How much depends on how useful this information is to the higher ups. We'll be in touch." Agent Gavin said and the two detectives rose to leave.
Agent Gavin and detective Kay made the short drive from the City Jail to the World Trade Center on West Main Street to visit The United States Attorney's Office.
"Good morning agent Gavin." The white, blond hair receptionist said as the two detectives entered the large glassy building.

"Good morning. We're here to see Mr. Tayman." Agent Gavin said in response.

The receptionist paged Mr. Tayman's office to inform him that he had company. "Okay sir…." She said and hung up the phone." He's in his office."

The two detectives headed towards the elevator, got on and rode it to the eighth floor. After greeting Mr. Tayman's secretary they were allowed access to his office. Mr. Tayman met the two officers at the door and showed them to their seats. Agent Gavin placed the information that he received from Freeze on the large desk in front of him. The elderly, white attorney, with grey hair glanced over the information. It took him over twenty minutes to read over everything that Freeze had jotted down. A huge smile appeared across Mr. Tayman's face. "This is good. I should have indictments prepared for Peterson and James within forty eight hours." He said referring to Blue and Lady. "I want James picked up as soon as possible." Mr. Tayman began rubbing his hands together and smiled as if he had a personal vendetta against Lady.

Exactly One Week Later….

Blue's funeral was fashioned pretty much the same way as Tehran's. The only difference was the fact that Blue's service contained hundreds of beautiful sobbing women and the entire atmosphere was full of sorrow.

Onika sat in a row located in the center of the church surrounded by a few of her girlfriends. She ran across Blue's picture in the obituary section of the newspaper while searching for her mother's and decided to pay him her last respect since the funerals were on two different days. Both services were overwhelming for a young woman but Onika stayed firm and remained strong.

Hale's Funeral Home did a great job on Blue's body so that he could have an open casket. Killah knew that Blue wouldn't have it any other way but for the world to see just how fly he was one last time before he returned to the earth. Draped in diamonds and dressed in one of the finest cotton suits that Valentino ever made ensured that Blue was still a show stopper even while deceased.

After the viewing of the body the C.O.C family congregated in the parking lot. Once again federal agents decorated the outside of the church but this time they had a different agenda.

Agent Gavin and detective Kay followed the congregation out to Roosevelt. The agents allowed the service to conclude before they made their move. As Lady turned to leave, the two agents approached her. "Natasha James." Agent Gavin said holding a white sheet of paper in his right hand. "We have an indictment for your arrest." He said as hundreds of agents swiftly arrived at the scene making a bad situation worse.

Lady decided against resisting and allowed the agents to take her into custody without argument. She placed her hands behind her back and turned to face the rest of the crew.

"Ya'll chill. I'll be alright. These bastards ain't got nothin' on me." She said.

Agent Gavin performed a pat search on Lady and ran across a handgun on her waist. "She's loaded." He said as he removed the Desert Eagle and handed it to his side kick. As he was about to place the handcuffs on Lady the family's lead defense attorney stepped in to see what the situation was.

"Excuse me. I'm Pamela Anderson. Miss James' attorney. Would one of you mind telling me what's going on?" The beautiful Black and Italian born stallion said.

"Miss Anderson." Agent Gavin spoke. "If you would like, you can meet us downtown at the federal building." He said and turned to lead Lady to the car.

Agent Gavin and detective Kay escorted Lady downtown to the federal building on Granby Street. Gavin pressed the white button connected to the intercom. "Charlie we got one for you." He said. Shortly after a short, stocky, dark skinned man with a bald head opened the door. Charlie placed Lady inside of a holding cell and waited until he received his cue to usher her into a room to meet with the United States attorney.

Mr. Tayman walked into the room on the opposite side of the glass and took a seat. The attorney smiled as he browsed through a list containing Lady's current and previous charges. "Well, well well. So we meet again Miss James. This time under better circumstances."

Lady stared coldly at the U. S. attorney but she couldn't place where or if she ever saw him. "Meet again? I never seen yo' white ass before."

"Maybe not but I definitely seen you." Mr. Tayman said and cut straight to the chase. He ran down the list of charges that were on her indictment, from distribution of heroin, to threatening a government informant. "Not to mention possession of a firearm by a convicted felon. These are very serious crimes. We know all about your little crime gang. We have indictments for all of them." He lied. "Now you are facing a minimum of ten years to life for the gun alone. But! If you give up your accomplice I'll guarantee that you don't spend a day over five years away from your family."

"Fuck you." Lady said firmly.

"Okay. Think about it. I have to go meet with your lawyer Miss Anderson. She's outside waiting." Mr. Tayman said. He gathered together all of his belongings, rose to his feet and headed for the exit.

Two Weeks Later...

Business was moving slow for the family since the death of Blue and the arrest of Lady.
Killah and Turk were extremely cautious about appointing anyone the two remaining positions, although they continued to hit the block as if their team was at full strength, hustling by the code that the game don't stop because somebody got knocked, popped or dropped off the face of the earth. They all understood that drugs were being sold long before they entered the game and would continue to be sold long after their exit.
Killah called a meeting to discuss the distribution of the remaining keys of heroin. He had contacted a few cats from Baltimore, D.C. and Richmond to see if they were interested in buying at least ten keys. He arranged the meeting to hear what the rest of the family had to say before he made any moves.
Killah sat at the head of the table at the spot out Mission College scribbling on a note pad while everyone else sat attentively. "I know things are hectic right now but we still have work to do. If ya'll want to throw in the towel and call it quits I understand. Me personally, I'm content. I got a few dudes that I deal with who are interested in buying weight. I figure we could wholesale the rest and decide what we want to do from there."
"What kind of weight they talking and for what price?" Turk asked. "My man Kenny in B-More said that he could round up enough people to buy twenty one, Fats up D.C. said that

he could scrape together fourteen and Lil Vell down Richmond want ten and a half." Killah said. "I was thinking that fifty five would be a reasonable price since they got to come and get it. That's two million, five hundred two thousand, five hundred divided by seven."

"Seven? Ain't but six people here." Turk mentioned.

"Lady is still alive and very much a part of this crew."

"Lady? Pamela said that she talked to Lady yesterday and said this bitch talking about cooperating and supposed to be out on bond by the end of next week." Turk said.

"You don't think that she will sell out the family and risk her own life do you?" Killah questioned looking at Tasha.

"I doubt it, but if she do I'mma kill that bitch myself." Tasha responded.

"We might need to kill her ass anyway. A snitch is a snitch and we don't need our family name affiliated with no snitches." Turk added.

"Let's see what's said before we go planning another funeral." Killah informed his troops. "So it's confirmed that we move the weight?" He questioned.

"Yeah... That's cool... Fine with me..." They all said simultaneously.

"Consider it done. That'll leave us twelve keys two ounces. With that said this meeting is adjourned." Killah said bringing the meeting to a close.

The following day Lady met with her lawyer Pamela and Mr. Tayman to work out a deal. The conversation became heated as Lady continuously denied having any information about BFI, Fu or any other major heroin or cocaine dealer. "I told you that I didn't come in here to talk about drugs or drug dealers. I got information about murderers." Lady yelled before Pamela grabbed hold of the conversation.

"Listen my client has some very valuable legit information about some of the City's more recent unsolved murders. Now what I need is a guarantee that all but one of her charges are dropped and that one charge being the least severe."
Mr. Tayman gave Pamela's words some consideration and even though he wanted Tasha and now Turk behind bars he was willing to hear ways to remove violent criminals from the street. "If the information is legit I'll consider it."
"Mr. Tayman I don't need your consideration, I need a guarantee signed by you and a fourth circuit judge before my client reveals any further information. And trust me Mr. Tayman. You need this information." Pamela said then began to gather her things.
Once again Mr. Tayman allowed his mind to wonder. "I'll get to work on it right away." He said as he stood to leave.
"Thank you Mr. Tayman. Please be in touch." Pamela said with her hand extended for a hand shake. "I'm going to talk with my client for a few moments."
Mr. Tayman granted Pamela her wish and removed himself from the booth with help from the deputy.
"Lady are you sure that you want to reveal this information and turn witness for the government. You know how the family feels about snitches."
"Are you sure that you can get me less that five years?"
"With this information? I'm positive!"
"Then you got damn right. Fuck what the family think, they not in here. I am!"
"Okay. But you know that it's Chris who has the word because it is his Law Firm and he is the boss."
"Talk to him. Better yet, tell him to come see me."
"I'll bring it to his attention." Pamela said bringing their visit to an end.

Killah arrived at the City jail the following day accompanied by Fu and Fat Shawn as soon as visitation hours began.
Fat Shawn had contacted Killah shortly after Blue's funeral and the two of them had a brief discussion in person. Fat Shawn explained that he didn't even know the young cats that were found dead in his spot. He also told Killah that Turk and Lady arranged for him and his crew to rumble with K. O. and his squad and that the two ladies were supposed to meet him at his spot but when he arrived, the place was surrounded by the law. And he mentioned the fact that he was unaware that Tehran was in the club and he still didn't know what she looked like.
Killah decided that with Fat Shawn's revelation it would be in their best interest to confront Lady before he made a decision to allow a member from his firm to represent her. Lady entered the visiting room and took a seat directly in front of Killah and Fu.
"Lady." Killah spoke.
"What's up Chris? Tony."
"What's up?" Fu spoke.
"What's up wit cha'll" I know ya'll ain't forgot about a bitch."
"Same shit going on with us. Just trying to weather the storm without you and Blue. And I could never forget a member of The Family." Killah responded.
"I should be home soon."
"We heard. We also heard about the method you're deciding to use in order to get home. Explain that."
"Explain what? I'm not going back to the penitentiary for no twenty, thirty years. I 'on't give ah fuck what nobody say."
"So you decided you want to be a snitch?" Killah questioned.
"I didn't decide shit, and I don't look at it as snitchin'. I look at it as killing two birds with one stone. As long as my family, which is ya'll are okay I'mma do what I gotta do. I'm not tellin' on the fam' or any other drug dealer. I know mu

fuckas always sayin' that they don't wish prison on they worse enemies. Well I do. This way I 'on't gotta spend the rest of my life in prison and we won't have to worry about K. O., Pat or Wayne again in life. Besides them niggas'll tell on us. This way you can get out of the game without worrying about going to prison for one of them niggas." Lady explained.

Killah stared at Lady for a minute. He really didn't agree with her get out of jail free excuse but to a man who was on the verge of retiring from the dope game it made a lot of sense. It would be a whole lot easier for him to get out without K. O. and his crew around. Killah checked his watch and realized that he and Lady had been talking for six minutes. "Somebody else came to visit." He said as he motioned with a nod of his head for Fu to get Fat Shawn. Lady watched in amazement as Fat Shawn approached the booth and grabbed a seat across from her.

"YO! What's up Lady? Youn't look happy to see me." Fat Shawn said with a smile on his face.

"Why should I be?" Lady shot back.

"Well since the both of you are here, what happened on the night my wife was killed?"

Lady paused for a minute while gathering her thoughts. "Turk said she told you what happened."

"I want to hear it from you." Killah demanded.

"I met Turk and Tee-Tee at Broad…"

"Skip all that. Who killed my wife and what role did He play?" Killah questioned, stopping Lady in mid-sentence.

"I don't know. When we got there she was already dead." Lady said staring Killah eye to eye. Once she finished speaking she removed her
eyes form Killah and placed them on Fat Shawn. "And I 'on't know what he had to do with it but we found Tee-Tee in his crib and I think they were his peoples."

"I ain't know none of them niggas and you know that." Fat Shawn said in his defense.

"I 'on't know who the fuck you know." Lady began to talk as the deputy opened the door to alert the inmates that their visits were over.

Killah grabbed the phone from Fat Shawn. "Pamela said that she spoke with the U. S. attorney. She'll be to get you tomorrow. We'll finish this on the outside." He said as the deputy turned off the phone and removed the inmates from the booth.

Lady grabbed a handful of the sheets that dressed her bed as she tried desperately to prevent herself from wriggling in bliss.

Pamela and Mr. Tayman had arranged a bond hearing for Lady in exchange for her cooperation, earlier in the day. The judge granted her a bond and assigned her to house arrest, where she now laid in her bed getting serviced.

 Lady couldn't control her body as the tongue of the only person she ever loved made love with her clitoris. It had been a few months since the two last made love and Lady was enjoying every bit of it. Tears of joy filled her eyes as she found herself caught in complete rapture. After being sexually active with a variety of women and men, Lady now realized what she had already known for years and that is the fact that this was the only person that could stimulate her both sexually and mentally. Lady's body started to tremble as she had orgasm after orgasm. Her lover's tongue pleased every part of her body from her belly button, to both of her breast. Lady moaned in ecstasy as her lover's tongue caressed her neck and stopped in front of her lips.

She found herself breathing uncontrollably as if she were hyperventilating while she stared her lover in the eyes.
"You love me?"
"Yeah." Lady cooed.
"Would you kill for me?"
"Anybody."
"Anybody?"
"Yeah. Anybody."
"Would you die for me?"
"In a heartbeat." Lady answered truthfully as her lover played in her hair.
Lady's lover returned her stare then grabbed Lady by her cheeks and squeezed them tightly. "Well what the fuck did you say to the feds to get out of jail? What the fuck did you tell them?" Turk asked tightening her grip. " Bitch you do know that I will kill you if you cross me?" She yelled and released Lady's face.
The truth is that Turk was the one who turned Lady on to women. It was Turk who suggested that the two of them please one another while they served their time in prison and Lady realized that she was in love the very first time they had relations.
Lady gazed up at Turk through her puppy dog eyes. "I would never cross you. I love you too much. I gave the feds K. O. and them. I know youn't give ah fuck about them." Lady said.
"I heard Chris and Fat Shawn snuck up there to see you in jail. What did you tell Chris?" "I didn't tell Killah nothin' except that I met you and Tee-Tee at the club and somebody snatched her and we tracked them down and killed them. I'll die before I share any one of our secrets." Lady said sincerely.
"You better hope that's all you said. I'mma go talk to Chris right now and if he start tripping or acting stupid, not only

am I going to kill him but I'mma come back and kill you too. You know! I'm just to the point where I'm tired. Tired of people thinking that because we are supposed to be family that I won't hurt 'em." Turk said calmly. She removed herself from the bed and got dressed. "I'mma go see what he talking about. I'll be back later." She said and headed towards the front door with Lady on her heels. Turk spun around quickly. "Don't make me come looking for you." She said and walked out the door.

Killah sat in the middle of his Ultra King size bed discussing his plan over the phone with Tika Bell. "Listen we're leaving tonight. Pack a few things and meet me at the clear port in two hours." He instructed. Killah went over the remainder of the details before ending their conversation. He placed two Louis Vuitton travel bags on the bed and filled them with all of his jewelry and a few clothing items. Once he was through with his packing he dialed Fu's number.
"What's the deal Ace?" Fu answered.
"Listen there's been a change of plans."
"What's up?"
"Tika and I are leaving for Morocco tonight."
"Tonight? When did you decide this?" Fu questioned.
"A couple of hours ago. I'm out shorty. Fuck the money. We only got twelve joints left, let Turk, Tasha and Lady have that shit. Osama's been paid so we don't owe nobody shit. Listen Ace. Leave that shit alone. You are the only one that I'm telling this. We're going to pull out around nine. Call Drea after nine and let her know what's up. Tell her that I will get in touch with her as soon as we touch down. I'm gone baby. Love ya Ace." Killah said gloomily. He really didn't want to leave but he knew that he couldn't stay. He knew that if he stayed he would eventually have to kill Turk or she would have to kill him. Killah couldn't stand to see his Aunt Gina

suffer behind the loss so he decided to walk away. He removed a pen and a note pad from his dresser, sat down and wrote Diamond a letter.

>Diamond,
>   Somehow throughout my quest for money to provide for you, I ended up missing you grow apart from me. I can understand how it's possible for you to hate me because growing up I hated my mother. Even though she had my best interest at heart. I couldn't stand her because of the methods that she used. Trust me when I tell you that I had your best interest at heart.
>   Your mother was a different story. The only reason I married her was because of you. Your mother and I became parents at a young age and love is blind when you're young. Believe it or not the streets is what kept us together. I loved making money and she loved spending it. After you were born my mother said that my only obligation was to provide for you. She never said anything about spending time and I have been a good provider. Anything that you ever needed or wanted you received. Not once did I deny you. No matter what the request was. Aunt Gina use to always say that if you spare the rod you'll ruin the child. That means that I should have been
>beating your ass instead of showering you with unnecessary gifts but it's too late to start now.
>   As far as your mother's death is concerned and you saying that I am responsible. The truth is you're right because I never should have married your mother. She was no good for me from the beginning and if I would have received the letter from my mother that your mother never sent me, I would have never come home to her in the first place. Not once did your mother write me while I was locked up and when Turk got locked up and Ali died she turned her

back on me as soon as the money stopped rolling in, so if you want to keep blaming me go ahead. I'll except that but if you want to know the truth, I'm glad she's dead and I'm leaving town.
I'm leaving you a half a million dollars in your account. That should hold you until you are eighteen. After that you're on your own.

Killah completed his letter and delivered it to Diamond's room. He placed the letter on his daughter's dresser when the automatic door alarmed him that Turk was entering the house. Killah hurried out of Diamond's room and headed back to his own.

Turk and Diamond both entered the mansion simultaneously. Diamond was sitting in her Mercedes Benz E 320 Wagon when Turk pulled up in the driveway behind her. "Where you coming from?" Turk asked then placed her right palm into the activation box.

"Hello Turquoise." The voice automated system said as the door closed behind the two females. "I went to take your son to the mall. He kept worrying me to death so I took him to Greenbrier, so he could get some Jordan's then we went to eat."

"Did his grandmother give him the money I sent?"

"Yeah he got it. You need to buy that boy a car because I'm not a taxi."

"The boy just turned thirteen. Besides, you're supposed to want to look after your little cousin anyway. I looked after your father when we were younger."

"Please! Don't even mention my father." Diamond said and paused for a moment. She was very hesitant with her next question. "Why don't you ever spend any time with Lil' Ali?" Diamond asked. It was a question that she always wanted to know the answer to but she had been warned by her parents to ever mention the situation to Turk.

Turk eyed Diamond with an evil stare. "As long as I'm in the streets I don't have time to be close to no one unless they are in the streets with me. Maybe when I get old and grey I'll have time. I think a thousand dollars a week is worth more than time to a thirteen year old boy, if you must know. Besides I ask the fucking questions around here." Turk said as she boarded the elevator. Diamond joined her aunt on the elevator and road it to the second floor while Turk stayed on until she reached the third and headed for Killah's room.

Killah was in the midst of making an escape when Turk stormed into the room.

"Where the fuck are you going?" Turk asked gesturing towards the bags with her hands.

"Yo I'm out."

"What the fuck you mean you out?"

"I'm out. I'm done. What part don't you understand? I'm sick of this shit so I'm leaving man. I can't take this shit no more so I'm leaving. I don't even want to know the truth anymore."

"The truth about what?"

"None of this shit. Teharn, You, Fat Shawn, Ali! Nothing! This is it for me. Me and Tika are leaving the country indefinitely."

"You and Tika?" Turk questioned confused. "Man I knew you was fucking that bitch the whole time."

"Yeah well now you know for sure."

"So you packing up with that bitch and leaving just like that ?"

"Just like that."

Turk smacked her lips like a young school girl. "So I killed the wrong bitch?"

"What the fuck you just say?" Killah asked wide eyed.

"You heard me. After all I've done to keep this family together. All this shit we been through." Turk said allowing her emotions to do all of the talking. "That's why the fuck I killed Tee-Tee. She didn't get kidnapped. I shot the bitch in the head myself. Fuck her! She ain't do a got damn thing for you while you were locked up and she didn't give a shit about you when you came home. The only reason she stayed with you was because of the money. And I never liked that bitch no way. I took care of you. I put you in the position you're in today. Made you the man you are today." Turk yelled. Killah tried to interrupt but Turk continued to talk over him. "If I wouldn't have killed Ali there never would have been a C.O.C, and you'd still be the same soft coward ass nigga that you have always been. Running around calling yourself a killer." Turk said with a light chuckle. "The only people you killed were your father, and your mother scared you into that, and your best friend and that was an accident."

Killah's eyes became enlarged and his heart began to race. As bad as he wanted to escape the truth, he no longer could. Killah lunged forward and wrapped his large hands around Turk's neck. He used all of his three hundred and fifteen pounds to drive her to the ground with brute force.

As hard as Turk tried she couldn't escape Killah's cobra clutch. Her eyes
rolled into the back of her head and her breaths became shorter. Turk's life was fading at a rapid pace and just as she was about to take her final breath, Diamond burst into the room.

Diamond was visibly angry about the letter she had just read. She had come to confront her father when she noticed her aunt wrestling with death. Diamond removed a small .380 caliber weapon from her Chanel Bag that contained the letter. "Get Off Her!" She yelled before firing a single hollow tip round into her father's right shoulder. Blood splattered from Killah's body but he managed to maintain his tight grip. His adrenaline was pumping at such a high level that he couldn't feel a thing. Diamond fired eight more rounds into her father's upper torso, causing him to fall backwards from the bullet's powerful impact. Killah rested completely still on his back with his eyes shut tight resembling a dead man. Turk began coughing and chocking uncontrollably as she stood to her feet.

"You okay?" Diamond asked with a concerned look on her face. Turk nodded her head up and down to confirm that she was fine. "You think he dead?" Diamond questioned.

"I doubt it." Turk answered knowing that Killah always wore his vest. Diamond made an attempt to walk up on her father and fire her last bullet into his head but Turk prevented her from doing so. "Let him live. If he wanna leave let him leave. You don't have to worry about him doing anything to you. He not heartless for real." Turk said as she regained her composure. "Let's go. I gotta catch this bitch Tika." She said headed for the elevator en route to the front door followed closely by Diamond.

As Diamond reached the door seal, she glanced over her shoulder at her father. Killah remained motionless on his back with his canary yellow Polo top covered in blood. *He look dead to me.* She thought, then turned to catch Turk. "Go to my mother's house but do not tell her what's going on." Turk instructed as they both reached outside. Turk hopped in her Vanquish and exceeded the speed limit all the way to Tika Bell's house. When she arrived she noticed that all but one light was turned off. The house was completely empty and Tika Bell was long gone.

Tika Bell waited impatiently for Killah to arrive. She was eager to get out of the country and put everything behind them. The later it got the more she became worried as Killah showed no signs of his arrival. It was unlike him to be late. Thoughts of the day they found out that Blue was dead raced through her head. After numerous attempts to contact him with no answer, she decided to go search for him when finally her phone rang.

CHAPTER TWELVE   We Made It
Heartless

TWELVE MONTHS LATER………
Agadir Morocoo:
"Man fix your tie, you look terrible Ace." Fu said as he fixed his partner's Ermenegildo Zegna bow tie and adjusted his custom fit Etro Tuxedo Jacket. "Look at yourself in the mirror Ace. This is the biggest day of your life. Get yourself together." Fu added as he stood next to his partner dressed in a matching tuxedo. He placed his arm around his friend and smiled as they both looked each other over in the mirror. "You made it Ace."
"Naw. We made it!" Killah said with a smile. He took a seat as Fu continued to admire himself in the mirror. "So what's good Ace? It's been a year since we last saw each other. How is everything going with you? We haven't been able to sit down and kick it for a while, tell me something good."
"Ain't really shit good to tell you." Fu responded.
"Shiitt! You're alive, you made it here safely. Not to mention you're rich." Killah said with a smile. "And you're free. Physically and mentally."
"Yeah, well that's the obvious."
"That's enough. What more could you ask for?"
"I don't know for real." Fu said as he grabbed a seat next to Killah. He smiled for a brief second. "I missed you Ace. Shit so crazy back home. It ain't even safe out Suffolk no more for real."
"Yeah? What's been going on?"

"Niggas got gangs around the way now. That's crazy aint it? I'm talking about bloods and crips. These young niggas don't have no regard for human life. Half the time I think they be shooting with their eyes closed because they don't ever seem to hit their man. It's almost always some young boy or girl getting hit. It's just crazy. Then the nigga Freeze bring my name up to the feds so they been harassing my employees, now they got the IRS investigating me, trying to bring me up on tax evasion charges, money laundering and all types of bullshit."

"All your paperwork is in order right?"

"Yeah, everything is legit. Lady kind of keeping them off of my back anyway but that's a whole 'nother story."

"Oh yeah? What ever happened with her situation anyway?"

"Shit. She turned herself in shortly before you left. Said she didn't want to be on house arrest. She go to the half way house in six months. She locked up in Philly. She write from time to time."

"Six months? She only been locked up a year."

"Yeah well you know how that go. Wayne got life plus sixty five years for killing Will and that five year old boy. Pat copped out to just being the driver, testified on Wayne and he agreed to testify against K. O. for killing Popcorn and a whole bunch of other shit. I think he got like seven. K. O. been acting like he going to take these people to trial but his sister said that he might plea because his case is in the feds and they trying to put him to sleep."

"Who is his sister?"

"Oh shit man, this broad name Onika. And guess what? Shorty got a baby by Blue. Look just like that nigga. Same complexion, same color eyes and everything. Blue was fucking K. O. sister the whole time and ain't none of us know. You knew that shit?"

"Hell naw. That's news to me. You seen the baby?"

"Seen him" I keep shorty all the time like he mine. And his name Lil' Paul."
"That's alright." Killah said with a smile. "Ole Blue! I miss shorty. I know K. O. messed up behind that."
"You know he is." Fu laughed.
"You keep in touch with any of the girls? I mailed two wedding invitations and plane tickets to Drea for her and Tasha."
"I talk to Drea everyday. She in love with my nigga Dogg but he don't come home for another nine years. Him and your man June locked up together in Memphis." Fu said then got quiet. He put his head down and shook it from side to side. "Tasha got killed about six months ago. Some nigga name Dexter killed her. They found her body inside of her X5 by the airport. I don't even know the nigga but they caught him and charged him with her murder. We tried to get in touch with you but no one knew how to find you."
"Damn. I'm sorry to hear that. Did you plan her a nice funeral?"
"Yeah. Me and Drea paid for everything. It was a nice home going. We sent her home in style just like we did Blue."
"That's wonderful Ace. That's what family's for. Was Turk there?"
"Ain't nobody seen or heard from Turk since you left. Last I hear she supposed to had killed Baldy and the feds were looking for her for questioning. Now niggas say they seen Baldy but I haven't seen neither one of them. Diamond was there though."
"So word is that Baldy's dead?"
"That's what the word is but I don't know how true it is. What's good with you?"
"Everything." Killah smiled. "You said Diamond was there?" He asked finally registering what his friend just said.

"Yeah she stopped through. I guess she thought that she would run into you or Turk. What happened the night you and Tika were supposed to leave anyway? Tika called me crying, talking about she couldn't find you, then she called back and said that you got shot, then I didn't hear anything else until you called and told me you made it."

Killah chuckled. "You talking about crazy. That was the craziest night of my life. First Turk tells me that not only did she kill Tehran herself but she killed Ali too."

"What?"

"Same thing I said, then I grabbed her by the neck and tried to choke her to death. She was almost out to Ace. At first I could never see myself killing Turk but when I saw her life fading away it felt good, then Diamond came in my room and shot me nine times."

"Diamond shot you nine times cuz?"

"Yeah but only one of them really hit me."

"That shit is crazy."

"Ain't it though. But that ain't it. When they were about to leave I heard Turk say that she was going to look for Tika so I got up, called Tika, told her what happened, then I drove myself to Aunt Gina's crib to let Doc Isaac fix my shoulder. When I got there Diamond was in the living room. When she saw me she pulled out her little gun and pointed it at me. Fu on everything, I didn't want to but I punched her little ass with everything I had in the left and knocked her little ass out cold."

"She asked for that homes. She lucky you didn't kill her."

"For rear for real. But that shit is over now, I've moved on with my life, I'm happy and completely over Turk and Diamond. We made it cousin." Killah said and smiled at his friend.

"That's good homey. Although I don't ever think that you could be completely over Turk and Diamond, I'm glad to see you happy." Fu said and rose to his feet. Killah stood up as well and the two friends embraced one another. Killah and Fu were so far gone in the moment that neither one of them heard the knock at the door.

"Mister Cameron are you ready Sir?" A short pudgy man asked in his Moroccan accent.

The voice startled the two men.

"Oh. Oh yes! Yes I'm ready." Killah answered.

"Alright Sir. We will get started in five minutes Sir."

"Okay. Thank you."

"You ready to do this?" Fu questioned.

"I'm Ready!" Killah answered excitedly like he was about to play a sport or something.

"You don't feel funny getting married to your best friend twelve months after your wife got killed? You don't think that you're moving too fast?"

Killah thought for a second then smiled. "Not at all." He answered with confidence. "I got rid of all my cars, all of Tehran's cars, the Yacht, every business I owned except for the law firm, sold all of Tika Bell's things, left the mansion to Diamond and Turk. I'm completely free of the life I lived with Tehran."

"Well let's do this then."

The set up for the wedding was beautiful. Giant pieces of crystal, human statues, a waterfall and a range of gold sculptures filled the large, jam packed Convocation Center. Fu escorted Killah down the aisle. Killah was pleased to see seven of the ten people that he invited from America sitting in the front row.

Aunt Gina, Dr. Isaac, Lil' Isacc, Lil' Ali, Pamela, Ty and Tika Bell's mother all smiled as they laid eyes on Killah for the first time in over a year. Killah

smiled and winked at the row full of family and friends just as the sound of "Here Comes The Bride" filled the air.
Tika Bell was led by a group of young Moroccan girls age five to nine. Each girl had a basket full of $100 U. S. bills that they tossed at the bride's feet.
Tika Bell wore a lovely white Roberto Cavalli gown that extended about fifty yards long. Drea brought up the rear wearing an egg shell colored Roberto Cavalli dress.
The music ceased as the minister began to speak. "Dearly beloved. We are gathered here today to witness this man Christopher Cameron and this woman Shatika Walden be joined in Holy Matrimony." He said as the room fell completely silent. Killah could feel someone staring at him. It was almost as if their eyes were burning a hole in the back of his head. "Is there anyone here who feels that these two should not be married. Speak now or forever hold your peace."
Killah turned to face the crowd in search of the guilty pair of eyes when he noticed a slim, beautiful, dark skin sister, with gorgeous, long, light brown dread locks standing in the entrance. She wore a white Prada dress with a matching pair of Prada shades. She didn't resemble anyone that he knew but for some reason he felt a strong connection to this woman, then she smiled and tilted down her glasses. Her eyes were a dead give away. They were as cold as he last remembered. Killah tapped Fu on the arm so that he too could get a glimpse at the mystery woman, but when he turned around she was gone.
 "The ring please." The minister asked for the second time. Killah was stuck. He wondered how this woman knew where he was and how she managed to make it inside pass security. Now he wondered where she went and what was her motive. Fu removed the ring from his inside jacket

pocket and focused his friends attention back on the ceremony. "Repeat after me. With this ring I thee wed." "With this ring I thee wed." Killah repeated. "I now pronounce you husband and wife. You may kiss your bride."
Killah hesitated for a minute, completely nervous.
"What's wrong?" Tika Bell whispered as Drea looked on.
Killah turned back towards the entrance and there she was. This time she laughed loudly and pointed her index finger at him with her thumb raised like she was pulling a trigger. The distraction caught the attention of everyone in the building. Drea's eyes met with the woman's and the two ladies held a stare for a moment. *Damn this bitch Heartless.* She thought as the woman placed her shades back over her eyes and turned to leave. Only four people in the entire building knew exactly who the strange woman was by looking into her eyes.
"Who was that woman?" Tika Bell questioned.
"You don't want to know." Drea answered, then smiled as Killah finally kissed the bride.

The Beginning………….

Heartless is dedicated

In Loving Memory of..........

Melissa A. W. "Aunt Cookie" Ricks
Rahsaan I. "Fat Shawn" Greenidge Sr.
Margaret Budd "Aunt Margaret" Mcdowell
Elizabeth "Grandma" Malloy

When production began on this project we had each one of you here with us. I can't put into words how much I miss each and everyone of you and wish you were still here to experience the great things that The Creator has in store for The Trotman Family. And when the day arrives I promise to hold the ones down that held me down and you can put that on Mines. I love you Aunt Cookie, I love you Fat Boy, I love you Aunt Margaret and Grandma you are my heart and always will be. You always believed in me and I won't let you down. With that said Rest In Peace. God knows best and He obviously had use for the four of you or He would have left ya'll here with us. Life goes on, and so do we so lets get this money together.

Love Always

The Entire Family

Acknowledgements

I acknowledge all those who supported me whether it was for playing spots, hustling drugs or toting guns and busting heads or just doing what it was I was doing when I was doing it. This one is for ya'll.

To all the people from Norfolk, VA, Tidewater or anywhere else in The V. getting money legally I acknowledge and support you. To the ones from Norfolk or Tidewater getting major paper illegally by all means do you. Now if that day rolls around and the F.E.D.S come knocking (And I don't wish that on anyone), but if it comes and you accept your lick the way I accepted mines, the way you accepted all of the goods that came from the game and never Snitch, I support you.

For the ones who turned their backs on The Dogg, you know who you are. Please understand that there is nothing on Earth that can hold me down and the decisions each of you made, please live with them. I live with mine.

To my Fam and all of my peoples on the inside looking out. What up? Lets Get Money!

Last but not least I want to thank the three people who played very important roles in this project getting off the ground. If it weren't for ya'll three taking the stand and testifying on the behalf of the United States of America none of this would be possible. Shit! I might've been in the NFL making millions right now but thanks to ya'll I was able to tap into my mental. Thank you for taking 15 plus years out of the lives of the people who love me, four of which I will never see again. Please never forget that the streets take care of their own so when the Reaper comes knocking; Remember me and know that I'm probably somewhere smiling. And since ya'll already know who you are, and more than likely try to sue or some other Bitch shit like that I won't mention your names but I will say that Tidewater Park, Park Terrace and Brambleton are homes to a RAT! And I know this may sound twisted because we were all tight once upon a time; But Fuck all of ya'll. And every other Hot motherfucker in the World!

    Rest In Peace
Marque "Que" Coffey and Kevin Andrew Francis Trotman
                   Peace!

Made in the USA
Columbia, SC
03 July 2017